There was pink coloring Hattie's cheeks as she took a deep breath. "Are you sure about this?"

"Me and you?" Forrest asked. "I'm sure. One hundred percent sure."

She blew out a slow breath. "And you don't think it's...wrong?"

Maybe. Sort of. He wouldn't be pretending. "No." He was doing this in the hopes that Hattie would come to the same conclusion he had—that pretending they were happy and in love would make her see how happy they would be together, in love. Sure, it might be faster for him just to come right out with it, right here and now, but words weren't his strong suit. Besides, it could backfire and she could end things before he ever had a chance to win her heart.

"Okay," she said, breathless. "I mean, I don't know if anyone will buy it—"

"They will." Forrest was a man of action—so he took action. He bent and pressed a kiss to her cheek. "Trust me."

Dear Reader,

Welcome back to one of my favorite fictional towns: Garrison, Texas! As always, things are happening in the small Hill Country town. A wedding, to be exact. And while most weddings should be joyful occasions, this wedding has our heroine in knots. Game warden Hattie Carmichael loves her brother dearly and wants to be happy about his engagement, but she and the bride have history. And not the good kind. She's doing her best to forget the past and hope for the best—but she needs backup.

Lucky for Hattie, her true-blue best friend, Forrest Briscoe, has decided to stick to her side until the wedding is over and done with. He may not be the warm-and-fuzzy type, but he's never let her down before.

Pretending to be her boyfriend might be outside his comfort zone, but there is no way Forrest is going to let someone tear Hattie down. Sure, he's rattled seeing Hattie in a bridesmaid dress—she never wears dresses—and how pretty she is, but Forrest doesn't budge. Even when things get complicated and all their pretending starts to feel real, Forrest does his best to protect and care for Hattie. When the wedding is over and everything is back to normal, will he and Hattie still be the best of friends? Or something more?

Happy reading,

Sasha Summers

HEARTWARMING

To Trust a Cowboy

Sasha Summers

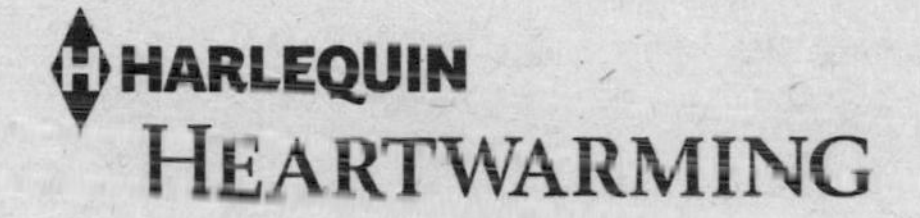

HARLEQUIN®
HEARTWARMING™

ISBN-13: 978-1-335-42664-2

To Trust a Cowboy

This edition published by arrangement with Harlequin Books S.A.

For questions and comments about the quality of this book, please contact us at CustomerService@Harlequin.com.

Harlequin Enterprises ULC
22 Adelaide St. West, 41st Floor
Toronto, Ontario M5H 4E3, Canada
www.Harlequin.com

Printed in U.S.A.

Sasha Summers grew up surrounded by books. Her passions have always been storytelling, romance and travel—passions she's used to write more than twenty romance novels and novellas. Now a bestselling and award-winning author, Sasha continues to fall a little in love with each hero she writes. From easy-on-the-eyes cowboys and sexy alpha-male werewolves to heroes of truly mythic proportions, she believes that everyone should have their happily-ever-after—in fiction and real life.

Sasha lives in the suburbs of the Texas Hill Country with her amazing family. She looks forward to hearing from fans and hopes you'll visit her online: on Facebook at sashasummersauthor, on Twitter @sashawrites or email her at sashasummersauthor@gmail.com.

Books by Sasha Summers

Harlequin Heartwarming

The Cowboys of Garrison, Texas

The Rebel Cowboy's Baby
The Wrong Cowboy

Harlequin Special Edition

Texas Cowboys & K-9s

The Rancher's Forever Family
Their Rancher Protector
The Rancher's Baby Surprise

Visit the Author Profile page
at Harlequin.com for more titles.

Dedicated to Dorris and Milton. Their real-life friends-to-lovers romance is the stuff of movies—or a good book. There is peace in knowing you're together again, likely playing Skip-Bo and dominoes and making each other laugh. We miss you!

CHAPTER ONE

"WHAT DID YOU SAY, Billy?" Hattie couldn't have heard correctly. The salon was busy, ladies chatting and laughing and carrying on like the world hadn't just come to a sudden screeching halt. *It's a mistake.* It has to be. *Please. Please, please, let it be a mistake.* "You're marrying who?"

"You always said I talk too fast when I get excited." There was no denying her brother, Billy, sounded excited.

Hattie wanted to be excited too, she did, but… She swallowed against the anxiety she hadn't felt in years, cold dread sliding down her spine. It happened every time she thought about Courtney, even today. It couldn't be her. Not *that* Courtney. *What are the odds?*

"Well, you do." Hattie tried to sound chipper, but she wound up squeaking.

Brooke Young, who'd been carefully running a hair iron over Hattie's strawberry blonde curls, stopped and stared at Hattie in the large illuminated mirror at Brooke's workstation. Mabel Briscoe, who was sitting on the counter inspecting her manicure, stopped blowing her nails to shoot Hattie a questioning look. Unlike Billy, they could see her—hear her—and know she was upset.

"Courtney Hall." Even through the phone, she could hear the smile in her brother's voice. "Can you believe it? Falling for a girl from Garrison—and not knowing she is *from* Garrison. How is that possible?"

How, indeed? "That's...funny." It wasn't the least bit funny. *It's my worst nightmare.* No, even her nightmares had never taken such a bleak and inescapable turn like this. *Billy, how do you not know who Courtney Hall is?* Had he just sat there all those years, pretending to listen, while she poured her heart out about the latest horrible, evil, mortifying thing the Queen of Mean had served up to Hattie that day? "Imagine that." It was getting very hard to stay calm. If she wasn't careful, Billy would pick up on her mood and that'd lead to questions and she didn't want to ruin this for him. He was happy, she could tell. Billy happy made her happy. She ignored the trickle of sweat down her spine. *It would all be fine.* Maybe it wasn't the *same* Courtney Hall…

How many Courtney Halls were there in Garrison?

She knew the answer and, for a second, she thought she was going to be sick right here in Brooke's salon chair in front of everyone. She cleared her throat and spoke quickly. "Billy, I got a call coming in." She sat forward, pulling free of Brooke's hold and the iron and concentrating on not throwing up or causing a scene. *Deep breaths.*

"An emergency?" Billy asked.

"Yeah. Looks like an orphaned fawn. Running down the road." Which *had* been a call last week. That fawn was now safe and sound at the local wildlife refuge. "I'll call you later?" There was no way she could listen anymore to Billy gush about Courtney Hall—his fiancée.

"Of course. Don't mention it to the folks—I want it to be a surprise. Go save the world, li'l sis." He chuckled. "Love you."

"Love you, big brother." She swallowed and hung up, resting her elbows on her knees to cover her face with her hands.

"Hattie?" Mabel's voice was soft, cautious. "Is everything okay?"

"I almost burned off your hair," Brooke said. "That bad?"

"Tell me something," she said, through her hands. "Tell me there was more than one Courtney Hall, about our age, that went to Garrison High School."

Silence.

Hattie's stomach rolled and flipped. "Feel free to lie to me. There has to be a different Courtney. A nice one." Hattie's gut was so tight it hurt. Something fierce. "There has to be."

Hands took hers. "Hey, now, Hattie." It was Mabel. "Talk to us."

"What's going on?" Brooke asked, dragging a stool over to sit at her side.

Hattie took a deep breath and sat straight and tall. That girl, the anxiety-ridden, nervous vomiter, didn't exist anymore. She was a tough game warden. One of two women in her class—with honors. She didn't get rattled anymore. And even if she did, her time at the academy had taught her to mask it. Yes, for the most part, her job was taking care of animals. But in Texas, a game warden was also a law enforcement officer. There'd been a few times she'd had to answer a call that involved domestic disputes, traffic accidents and the like. But she'd never thought she'd need that skill, that poker face, amongst family and friends.

Mabel, who was crouching in front of her, was looking more and more worried by the second. "Spill."

"Well..." She nodded, cleared her throat again, but the words stuck and her stomach did another flip.

Seconds later, Brooke pressed a glass of water into her hand.

"Thanks." Hattie held the glass in both hands, carefully taking a sip. "Billy is engaged to Courtney Hall. Remember Courtney?" She took another sip. "Apparently Billy didn't remember his fiancée from our high school days."

"Oh, no." Brooke sat back. "Courtney?" She shuddered.

"*That* Courtney?" Mabel asked, frowning. "She had a nickname, though, didn't she?"

"Most of them were *not* okay, Mabel," Brooke whispered, casting a quick glance around the shop.

"No, not *those* nicknames." Mabel winced. "The other one."

"The Queen of Mean." Hattie pressed the glass against her temple. Courtney Hall had pretty much ruined Hattie's high school years. Mabel and Hattie knew that. How could Billy *not* know? She gulped down the rest of the water.

"Are you sure?" Mabel, ever the optimist, asked. "I mean, *sure*-sure that it's her?"

Hattie nodded. "Courtney Hall. From Garrison. The one and only."

"What are you going to do?" Brooke took her empty glass, refilled it and handed it back to her. "You have to tell him, Hattie. Billy is a good guy—"

"He's so happy." Hattie cut her off. "If I tell him his fiancée was the one that…well, that puts him in an awkward position, doesn't it? Almost like he has to choose." Just thinking about it made her consider running for the bathroom—or grabbing Brooke's trash can. "He might not choose me."

Brooke was rubbing her back. "You're turning green, Hattie."

She nodded.

"Hattie…" Mabel took her hands. "Breathe. It'll be okay." She smiled weakly. "Hey, you never know…maybe Courtney is different now. People can change."

Hattie glared at her.

"They can." Mabel didn't sound the least

bit confident. In fact, she was chewing the inside of her lip, looking to Brooke for help. "Right?"

"R-right." Brooke blinked furiously, scrambling. "Look at Audy." She actually perked up then. "He's a wonderful father to Joy and a wonderful husband. More than I ever could have imagined." She wore that dreamy expression—her Audy Face, as Hattie called it. "If anyone had tried to convince me the two of us would be newlyweds a year ago, I'd have thought they'd been kicked in the head by a mule."

Mabel and Brooke laughed.

Hattie couldn't. Could someone like Courtney change? She remembered, with terrible clarity, a dozen incidences of Courtney doling out insults and snide comments until Hattie was in tears. Then a dozen more, leaving Hattie humiliated by a gleeful Queen of Mean. She stared into her water glass.

Mabel was nibbling on the inside of her lip again. "What can we do?"

"Whatever we can do, we will." Brooke was rubbing her back again.

"Not say a word about this to anyone. Period. Billy didn't want me telling anyone."

Hattie winced at the realization she'd done just that.

"Not a word." Brooke nodded.

"Me, too. Anything else?" Mabel waited, plainly concerned.

Hattie shrugged, the water sloshing in her glass. "What is there to do?" She stood and set the glass on the counter. "If he… If he is in love with her, then…" She broke off, watching as her two best friends tried, desperately, to come up with something comforting to say or do.

"No." Mabel shook her head. "No. I don't agree." She reached for Hattie's hand. "Even if he is in love with her, Hattie, he has to know what that girl did to you." She gave Hattie a long, searching look. "She wasn't exactly all sunshine-and-butterflies with me or Brooke, but she always went out of her way to pick on you."

Hattie remembered all too well.

"Mabel's right." Brooke crossed her arms over her chest, her eyes narrowing. "Billy was older. It's possible he didn't know her. If I recall correctly, she was pretty involved with R. J. Malone—once Audy made it clear he wasn't interested." She shook her head.

R. J. Malone had been mentioned more

than a few times over the police radio mounted in her black-and-white game warden truck. His name, then the code for public intoxication—plus a few calls of minor vandalism and theft over the years. While he'd never served hard time, he was familiar with all the judges and officers, bailiffs and county clerks in most of the county. He'd boasted about it to her the night she'd been forced to collect him from a rodeo two towns over. *Like that was something to brag about.* Hattie was all about following the rules and keeping order.

To go from the likes of R. J. Malone to her brother? Hattie's stomach was all knots and nausea now.

Her brother had gone off to law school, finished in the top of his class and was already being courted for a junior partnership. He was all hard work and discipline, never forgetting how their parents had scrimped and saved to make sure he could have the education he wanted and deserved. He was a humble man with a huge heart. *And now she's got her claws into it.*

Courtney Hall was beautiful. At least, she had been in school. Perfect figure, perfect smile, perfect hair. She was as close to a real-life Barbie doll as Hattie had ever seen. But mean as a snake. Not to everyone, of course. Adults loved her. Most of them, anyway. With them, Courtney was all smiles and feigned interest—until they walked away, that is.

Hattie remembered one time, in the high school library, Courtney had been listening to their librarian go on about her sick cat. Miss Roberts, the librarian, had lost her husband years before and her cats were her family. Courtney patted Miss Roberts's hand and made sympathetic sounds. Later, while Hattie was hiding from Courtney and her entourage in a bathroom stall, she'd heard Courtney tell her friends that Miss Roberts smelled like mothballs and had bad breath and was so sad and pathetic she didn't know why the school board didn't make her retire.

After that, Hattie had gone out of her way to be extra nice to Miss Roberts. Who'd never smelled like mothballs, had always carried breath mints and had a quirky sense of humor Hattie had found delightful.

"Are we going for some new look?" Forrest Briscoe's voice was laced with laughter.

Hattie had been so lost in her thoughts,

she hadn't heard his arrival. "What?" she asked, taking in his teasing smile.

"The hair?" He pointed at her reflection in the mirror. "What is that? Edge-y? Or emo?"

"Half-finished," Mabel, Forrest's younger sister, jumped in. "Be nice."

"I'm always nice." Forrest paused, looking at each one of them. "Someone die or something? You're all three looking a little long in the face."

Hattie glanced at her reflection and winced. Half of her strawberry blonde curls had been tamed into a sleek mass with a flip-up at the ends. The other half was au natural. All curls, a little frizz and absolutely no style to it. She reached up and ran a hand over her curls. *Courtney Hall would never, ever look like this.*

"Come on, Hattie, let's finish up." Brooke patted her chair. "After this, I say we go get a bottle of wine, sit on my porch swing and forget about our worries."

"Who's worrying over what?" Forrest asked, his brow furrowing.

"I like the sound of that. Let's do it," Mabel agreed, offering Hattie a blinding smile while completely ignoring her brother.

"I thought I was supposed to pick you

up." Forrest scratched the stubble on his jaw. "What's going on?"

"Nothing." Hattie waved away his question, sitting still while Brooke ran a long strand of curls through her magic iron. In seconds, the curls were gone. "Just...girl talk." She gave Mabel and Brooke a quick look, hoping to remind them that—like it or not—this whole mess was a secret for now.

"Yeah, *girl* talk." Mabel nodded. "You don't want to know."

"Oh." Forrest swallowed. "Okay, then." He sounded wary—like he was entering into unfamiliar waters.

"You don't have to look so scared, Forrest." Mabel frowned at him. "Hattie needs her friends right now. To...work through some *things*, is all."

"I'm Hattie's friend." Forrest was outright frowning now, his dark blue eyes shifting to Hattie's reflection. "So, talk."

Hattie had to smile at his expression. "Just like that, huh?"

He nodded, impatient.

"Forrest." Mabel's long-suffering sigh was teasing. "It's more of a...girl's night sort of thing."

He went back to looking wary, but stood

his ground. "Make up your mind." He crossed his arms over his chest. "Are we talking? Or am I leaving?"

Hattie considered Forrest one of her best friends, but their conversations tended to center around things they both valued: animal welfare, *Farmers' Almanac* predictions, rodeo, anything to do with vehicles, word-around-town, and, occasionally, their families. Forrest was the perfect example of what-you-see-is-what-you-get. If he said it, he meant it. Because of that, they'd never had a misunderstanding or disagreement. Hattie liked that she always knew where she stood with Forrest—that he was easy to read. And, right now, she could tell, more than anything, he wanted to leave. "You can go." Hattie waved. "But I appreciate the offer, Forrest. And I'm sorry you had to come all the way in town for nothing."

It was his turn to sigh. "You sure?" But he was already heading to the door.

"I'll bring Mabel home after," Hattie offered, laughing when the door closed behind him. "He looked like a deer in the headlights." She watched him walk in front of the salon's large picture window and disappear out of view. "But he had good intentions."

"As soon as I finish your hair, we'll go get some wine," Brooke said. "What about dinner?"

"I can make pasta?" Mabel offered. "I make a mean scampi."

"Sounds delicious." Brooke kept working, smoothing all signs of frizz or curl from her hair. "And it'll just be us. Audy's taking Tess and Joy to see all the horses and stuff at the fairgrounds. You know, he's helping with the setup for the Junior Rodeo this weekend. Beau's participating, of course."

"As long as you're sure I'm not throwing a hitch in anyone's plans," Hattie interrupted. There were a lot of Briscoes and they were a close-knit family. From oldest to youngest, there was Forrest, Audy, Mabel, Webb and, lastly, Beau. As such, Beau was also Brooke's brother-in-law. The Briscoe siblings were each other's biggest supporters. *Like me and Billy.* Thinking of Billy made her heart hurt all over again. She took a deep breath. "If y'all are supposed to go watch tonight, don't change that on my account."

"Watch Beau practice? No." Brooke laughed. "But Audy's offered to give him some pointers. I think he's missing rodeo-ing himself, so poor Beau is likely to get an earful."

Hattie grinned.

"He should coach," Mabel suggested. "I know my brother. He's surprisingly patient, when he wants to be. And rodeo is near and dear to his heart."

"That's a great idea, Mabel." Brooke tapped the end of her comb to her lips. "I'll have to figure a way to slip it into conversation—so it doesn't sound like we were talking about him." She rolled her eyes. "He likes to think that's all I do all day. Think or talk about him."

Mabel and Hattie exchanged a quick smile.

"I saw that. Not *all* day." Brooke giggled, setting her comb side. "So, girls' night? Yes?"

Hattie nodded. They were trying to cheer her up and, honestly, that's just what she needed. Enjoying wine and conversation sure beat sitting at home, with her insides stuck in a blender, waiting for Billy's call. Or worse, having her folks call for a chat. She'd promised she not to mention a word of Billy's news to them, and Hattie never kept a thing from her parents. *From anyone, for that matter.* This was something she'd definitely talk over with her folks to work through. They always had some piece of sage advice to help her calm her nerves and settle her mind. *Before*. But now? "Okay." She did her best to inject some enthusiasm into her voice.

"Oh, Hattie." Mabel hugged her. "We will figure this out."

Brooke moved in, hugging them both. "We will."

Hattie closed her eyes and willed herself to believe them. "Maybe you're right," Hattie said as their hug ended. "Billy wouldn't have asked someone like Courtney Hall to marry him—not the version of her I knew, anyway. He's too smart for that. Maybe she really has changed." Not that she'd ever be good enough for Billy, but still… "We're not in high school anymore. The reign of the Queen of Mean ended years ago."

And if I keep telling myself that, I might eventually believe it.

"WHAT WERE YOU THINKING?" Forrest stared at his younger brother Webb in total shock. "Webb… We should have talked about this." He'd only read the first few lines of the papers Webb had shoved his way before they'd all gone blurry and his heart had gone cold.

"You'd have tried to talk me out of it." Webb shrugged. "But this is what I want."

And that's that. His brother had every right to go and have his own life but… "Enlisting is a long-term commitment. A long time away from home—your family and friends." His throat was so tight, it hurt to talk.

"I know that, Forrest." Webb's face was redder by the second. "I didn't just rush into this. I know you think I'm not the sharpest tool in the shed, but I know what I'm doing."

Forrest stared down at the dirt at their feet, his hand resting on the side of the Briscoe Ranch truck he'd barely stepped out of before Webb greeted him, enlistment papers and all. "I never said that."

"You have," Webb argued, laughing. "You might have been teasing, but you said it. Uncle Felix, too."

Shame kicked him in the chest, while regret delivered a strong punch to the throat. No matter how hard he tried to refute what Webb was saying, he couldn't. Teasing was what they did. They always had. Knowing

Webb took their ribbing to heart? Well, Forrest wasn't sure how to fix this.

"You're gonna stay mad?" Webb's tone was a mix of frustration and resignation. "I figured as much—"

"No." Forrest cut him off. "I'm proud of you." He met his brother's gaze. "I… If this is what you want, then I want you to do it." He forced his eyes to focus on the paper, scanning for a date, the thud of his pulse echoing in his ears. *I'm scared for you. I won't sleep a night until you're home.* But Forrest wouldn't put that on Webb. That wasn't right. "What do you need to do before you leave?"

"Nothing." Webb rolled up onto the balls of his feet. "Nothing, really."

Once Forrest spied the date, he was hard-pressed not to hug his little brother close. "A week, huh?" He cleared his throat, handing him back the paperwork and forcing himself to smile. "You know you're not getting out of here without a send-off. Mabel will make sure of that." Now that the shock was wearing off, his heart was thawing out. He preferred the numbness and cold to the sharp twist in his chest.

"I figured." Webb was grinning from ear to ear, more boy than man.

Too young to enlist. Being twenty-two years old might make Webb a man on paper, but Forrest knew his brother had a lot of growing up to do. Maybe the military would help with that. Either way, it didn't matter now. It was done. There was no undoing it. And, if this was really what Webb wanted, Forrest would support his brother. No matter how hard that was going to be. "She know yet? Mabel, I mean?" But Forrest knew better. If she had, she'd have let on when he'd seen her at Brooke's salon. The one thing about his sister, she wore her heart on her sleeve—rather, her face.

"No." Webb shook his head. "I figured you needed to know first. You can keep everyone else calm."

Forrest shot his brother a disbelieving look. As far as he knew, he was the bossy older brother who "got in everyone's business" whether they liked it or not. Keeping everyone calm? That was news to him.

"Maybe not calm." Webb shrugged. "But they'll follow your lead."

Meaning Forrest needed to keep it together so the rest of the family did, too. It was a tall order, considering their past. Their eldest brother, Gene, had been gone a long time, but the hole he'd left in their family had never been filled. And now Webb was following in his footsteps… No. Gene had enlisted and never come home. Webb *would*. Webb, and his goofy grin, would be fine. *He has to*. "I'll do my best," he muttered.

Webb nodded, unable to maintain eye contact for long. "Well… I'll… I got stuff to do." He turned on his heel and headed down the hill to the horse barn.

Forrest stood there for a long time, staring off into space. His thoughts were jumbled, bouncing around so he wouldn't linger too long on something he couldn't quite process yet. Through it all, the only consistencies were worry, grief and Webb.

He scratched the stubble along his jaw, took a deep breath, and crossed the yard to the wide wrap-around porch of his family home, taking the stairs two at a time. He paused then, forcing all the worry and fear into the back of his mind, before opening the front door and walking inside.

"Forrest." Beau waved. "You coming tonight? If you don't, Audy'll be in my ear the whole time. Telling me what I'm doing wrong or how to do it better or—" He broke off. "You okay?"

"Fine, fine." Forrest hung his hat on one of the hooks lining the wall by the front door. At any given evening, there was a dozen or more hats on display. Audy had a few for show and one for work, the rest he'd taken with him after his and Brooke's no-frills wedding a few months back. Uncle Felix had four and each one was more beat-up than the last. Forrest had one for being social and one for work—both made to fit like a glove. Beau, being the youngest, kept his rodeo hat in a box in his closet, wanting to keep it dust-free and safe from any mischief his brothers might cause him. And Webb… Forrest's gaze hung on the tan Stetson Webb had been so proud to bring home. Just like the one Robert Duvall had worn in *Lonesome Dove*, or so he'd thought. Webb had scrimped and saved to pay way too much money for the hat, a fact they'd all given him a fair amount of teasing over, but he swore he never regretted it.

"Will you come?" Beau asked, slipping on a newly ironed shirt. "To practice."

A newly ironed shirt? For rodeo practice? Forrest gave his brother a more thorough inspection. Pressed jeans. Polished boots. "Tess going to be there?" he asked. His little brother's crush was a point of concern for Forrest—Beau only being seventeen and all.

Beau went red.

After the conversation Forrest had just had with Webb, it was clear he needed to be careful with his words. And, no matter his reservations with Beau's crush, he was still too raw from Webb's enlistment announcement to do more than say, "I'm sure that will be...*nice*."

Beau stared at him, suspicious.

"What?" Forrest asked, scratching at his jaw again. He was trying here. Wasn't he? At least he'd caught himself this time. Sort of.

"I'm waiting for the punch line." Beau stood, eyes narrowed and trained on Forrest's face. "Anytime."

That cinched it. No more teasing or poking or any of that. "Nope." He stuck his hands in his pockets. "The more to cheer you on, the better."

It took a full five minutes before Beau's posture eased and he smiled—albeit a small smile. "I think so."

Forrest nodded, definitely in unknown territory here.

"So you'll come?" Beau asked, tucking in his shirt and adjusting the mammoth Youth State All-Around Champion belt buckle he'd won the year before. "Keep Audy in line?"

"I'll do my best." He chuckled. "You know how he gets about rodeo."

"I do." Beau looked at him with a serious expression. "But you've been rodeo-ing just as long as he has."

He was pretty sure team roping didn't count for much, as far as Audy was concerned. Where Audy liked the individual events, Forrest had always worked best as part of a team. He'd been riding with Rusty Woodard since high school. Rusty was the header, Forrest took the foot. They'd won enough buckles and prizes over the years to have bragging rights—if Forrest had been the bragging type. "You driving?"

Red was sneaking up Beau's neck and into his cheeks again. "I was thinking of taking Tess for an ice cream after."

Forrest had a hard time not pointing out what a waste of gas it was for them to take two trucks—not to mention it was a school night. *But* Beau was earning his own money working at the grocery store and already had a full scholarship to the college of his choice, so unless Forrest came up with something quick-like, there was nothing he could do. "I guess I'll drive myself."

"Thanks." Beau smiled, looking closer to a little boy than a seventeen-year-old.

Forrest shook his head, feeling about a hundred.

Audy'd moved into town since he and Brooke got married. Mabel would be marrying Jensen Crawley next spring. While he was still getting over his long-standing aversion to the Crawley family, he was trying to be civil, if not friendly, with the man who had won his sister's heart. Now, Webb had enlisted, and Beau would be off to college in no time. Considering his home had always been loud, full of people and on the chaotic side, he couldn't picture it quiet and empty. So many changes. *Too many.*

In no time, it would be him and Uncle Felix alone on the ranch, trading insults, talking about the weather, the ranch and livestock, and eating canned chili every night. Two men—opinionated, set in their ways, with a competitive streak a mile wide? It wasn't exactly a pretty picture or the way he'd envisioned his future.

"I guess I'll meet you there?" Forrest

waited for Beau to nod before he headed into the kitchen. If he was going to make it through this evening without the usual verbal warfare with his brothers, he was going to need a lot of coffee. “Evenin’, Uncle Felix.”

“Forrest,” his uncle said, not bothering to set aside his newspaper to make actual eye contact. “What’s the plan for dinner?”

“No idea.” He poured himself a cup of day-old coffee and put it in the microwave. “Beau asked me to go along to practice—run interference between he and Audy.”

Uncle Felix’s dismissive snort was almost a laugh. “Well, good luck with that.” He folded his paper and set it on the table. “Maybe I’ll head into town, too. I heard something about a planning meeting for that whole Founders Festival thing. Might offer to lend a hand.”

Forrest pulled the piping hot coffee mug from the microwave, the ceramic singeing his fingers. He set the mug on the counter and shot his uncle a knowing look. “The planning meeting the Garrison Ladies Guild is putting on?”

Uncle Felix scowled at him an answer.

“It was just a question.” Forrest chuckled.

All of Garrison was talking about his uncle, Barbara Eldridge *and* Dwight Crawley. It seemed both men had set their caps for the lady and she wasn't making it easy on either one of them.

"And I know exactly *why* you asked that question." Uncle Felix stood and wagged his finger at him. "Maybe I just feel like lending a hand? Ever thought of that?" But he was headed out the door before Forrest could stop laughing long enough to answer him.

The *click*, *click* of Harvey's claws on the wide plank floor signaled the arrival of Audy's massive dog. A mix of Great Pyrenees and Great Dane, the giant dog would be downright intimidating if he wasn't so sweet tempered.

"Who knows, Harvey? You're welcome to stay out here, you know? With two lifelong confirmed bachelors and no babies around." Forrest scratched the dog behind the ear. "Then again, I get the feeling you're just as fond of baby Joy as Audy is. I guess she needs you around to protect her." He'd never been all that fond of babies, but he had to admit, Joy was a sweet little thing. All smiles and laughs—she had a new word every time he visited. She kept Brooke and

Audy on their toes, too. "I guess Brooke and Audy could use all the backup they can get, huh?" Harvey nodded his tail in answer. "I figured." Forrest picked up his coffee cup and drained it, the piping hot drink scalding the back of his throat. "That'll wake you up." He gave Harvey another scratch behind the ear. "I'll see you later, boy."

As he was driving through town, headed for the fairgrounds, his mind drifted back to the conversation he'd had with Webb. Then Beau. If his teasing had ever gotten out of hand, it had been unintentional. To him, it was just part of being brothers. But now that he knew his teasing had hurt, it made him second-guess himself.

He pressed a button on his dashboard, connecting his phone to Bluetooth. "Call Hattie," he said, the ringing echoing in the cab of his truck. Hattie was good at being his sounding board. If he had been too hard on his siblings and fooling himself all these years, she wouldn't hesitate to point it out to him. Plus, he could use an ear right now. This whole thing with Webb enlisting was weighing on him something fierce. So, when the phone went straight to voice mail, Forrest's mood plummeted. Being Hattie, she'd know just the right thing to say to make him feel better. And right now, he'd really like to hear what she had to say. Plus, Hattie always took his call—always—even if it was to tell him she'd call him right back. So her not answering wasn't right. Most of the time, he didn't let himself think about the dangerous scenarios or emergencies that were part of her job. Now, he couldn't stop thinking about them or ignore the trickle of unease slipping down his spine. He frowned, hit redial, and held his breath. *Come on, Hattie, answer.*

CHAPTER TWO

HATTIE WAS UNLOCKING her front door when a large shadow at the far end of her porch suddenly moved. "Who's there?"

"It's just me, Hattie." Forrest walked forward, his hands held up. "I've been calling you all evening."

"You have?" Hattie frowned, unlocked the front door and stood aside so Forrest could come inside. "I left my phone in the truck." It had been a choice. If she didn't have her phone with her, she wouldn't have to answer Billy's call. Or her parents'. Besides, she'd had a good time with Mabel and Brooke. Instead of worrying over the whole Courtney and Billy situation, she'd asked that they *not* talk about it... Instead, they'd had a few hours of laughing and talking and blocking out the rest. Laughter was always a better option than worry. But there was something about Forrest's posture that made her think his evening hadn't been as enjoyable as hers.

"I just dropped Mabel off at home. I could have seen you then, spared you the time and gas coming all the way out here." She and Forrest were like-minded when it came to being practical and frugal.

"I didn't know that." There was a gruffness to Forrest that she rarely heard.

"What's eating you?" She hung her keys and purse on the hook by her door and waved him into the kitchen. "You want some tea? Or lemonade? Or I can make some coffee?"

"I'm good." He leaned against the kitchen counter.

"Go on. Out with it," she said, his thundercloud expression making her pause.

He took a minute before he asked, "Am I a bad brother?"

Hattie was so surprised, all she could do was stare.

"I'm serious now, Hattie." He scratched at the dark stubble on his jaw. "Today… It's been something."

Tell me about it. But she didn't say that out loud. Forrest looked like he was carrying the weight of the world on his shoulders. There was no way she was going to add to that. This whole thing with Billy and Courtney was out of her hands anyway. It was better to direct her focus on something useful—like figuring out why Forrest would ask such a ridiculous question. Forrest? A *bad* brother? Where would he come up with such a notion. She took another look at him. *Coffee, it is.* She poured fresh grounds into a coffee liner, filled up the water and put the pot in place.

"Am I sarcastic?"

She nodded. "Of course you are."

It was the long silence and tightening of his jaw that told her that wasn't the answer he was looking for.

"What's this all about, Forrest?" Once the coffee was brewing, she put several oatmeal raisin and snickerdoodle cookies on a plate and carried them to her small kitchen table. "Sit." She pointed at the chair. "Talk." She waited for him to sit before getting two clean coffee mugs from the cabinet. "I didn't mean it as a bad thing. Yeah, you're sarcastic, but *I* think you're funny. You are funny." She glanced at him, noting the deep furrow of his brow. "Please, tell me what's going on."

"Well, to hear Webb and Beau talk..." He glanced at her then. Those big blue eyes of his were full of hurt. "I'm not very careful with my words."

Hattie forgot about coffee and the mugs

and crossed back, pulled the other chair close to his and sat. In all the years she had known Forrest Briscoe, she'd never known him to be anything but bighearted. Well, unless you were a Crawley. That whole feud thing had been going on for years, and he and Jensen had had more than one tussle. But that was years back, when he was young.

Even then, when he'd been about Beau's age, he'd cared for his younger siblings. That was when Forrest's parents had died and Forrest had become more father than brother to his younger siblings. She'd always thought that would be an awfully heavy burden for a young man to bear alone. Uncle Felix was a decent enough fellow, but he had no experience with kids or family or taking care of anyone other than himself. Forrest had had to pick up that slack.

It riled her up good to think any of the Briscoe siblings wouldn't see Forrest for the hardworking, devoted, protective and funny man he was. "You're their older brother. Sometimes, you might say things they may not want to hear. But that's what being an older brother means. I know this—I have an older brother, too."

Forrest's smile was fleeting. "Webb said

something that stuck out. I don't know when Uncle Felix or I said it, but I believed him—I'm sure we did say it." He shook his head. "And he held on to it. It bothered him."

"What was it?" She pushed the plate of cookies closer to him. "And eat one of those." She always kept oatmeal raisin and snickerdoodle cookies on hand just for Forrest. They were his favorites.

Forrest reached for an oatmeal raisin cookie, slowly turning the cookie round and round in his fingers. "Something along the lines of Webb not being the sharpest tool in the shed."

Hattie winced in spite of herself. "That one had to sting. But surely he knew you were teasing—that you don't *really* feel that way?" Even as she said the words, she knew better. Her brother teased plenty. But he, and their parents, had always been aware of the power of their words. None of them would ever have thought to say such a thing to the other. Even teasing.

"The thing is, teasing or not, it's not right. Or funny. If I was Webb?" He broke the cookie in half. "I'd be bent out of shape, too." He ate one half of the cookie and leaned back in the chair. "Why didn't I see that before?"

"I think it's easy to say things, sometimes, without thinking them through." The beep of the coffeepot had her standing and heading back across the room. "Or thinking about how it might make the other person feel." She filled both mugs and carried them, slowly, back to the table. "It wasn't intentional."

"I know that." Forrest nodded his thanks. "But, intentional or not, it stuck in his mind." He placed the other half of the cookie on the plate. "And I can't help but wonder if that's why he's enlisted."

Hattie's heart twisted. That, right there, was why Forrest Briscoe was here and struggling so. Once upon a time, Forrest hadn't been the eldest Briscoe sibling. It had been Gene Briscoe. Everyone had known and loved Gene. Hattie only had the faintest memories of the young man—but they were all positive. A smiling, fit, outgoing youth who left an impression. Gene had been Forrest's idol *and* his beloved big brother. Gene's tragic death, in the first year of his deployment and on the heels of their parents' deaths, had torn Forrest up.

And now this. Webb had put himself in a position where his life could also be in danger. Hattie had no right to feel angry with Webb, but she couldn't help it. Webb had to know how this would make the rest of his family feel? What sort of wounds it would open?

She stared into her coffee, forcing her anger aside. Forrest didn't need her in a temper; he needed her support.

And yet, as much as she didn't want to see Webb's side of things, his decision wasn't all that different than what she'd been through. Her family hadn't exactly been thrilled over her going into law enforcement. Over and over again, they'd encouraged her to try something else or consider all her options before she made up her mind. But Hattie's mind had been made up and she couldn't imagine doing anything else. If Webb felt that way about the military, then she couldn't fault him for his decision. It'd taken time but, after a period of adjustment, her family had accepted her decision. Knowing the Briscoes, they'd rally around Webb and do the same.

To this day, though, she was careful about which stories she told her family. When she'd been faced with a highly precarious situation, one where she might have been in danger, her parents or brother never learned of it—not from her, anyway.

She studied Forrest, trying to find just the right words. It pained her to think he felt responsible for Webb's decision. "Did he outright say that was why he's enlisted?" She crossed her fingers and toes and waited.

"No." Forrest shook his head, his gaze meeting hers. "But having that come out in the same conversation... Well, it's not a huge leap to connect the two."

Hattie couldn't argue his logic. "You're worried about him." It wasn't a question—she knew Forrest was worried about Webb. Everyone worried about Webb. If there was a hole to fall into, a rock to trip over or a swarm of wasps or fire ants to get into, Webb was the one to do it. The boy had broken more bones than anyone else in town. "And I understand why."

"I knew you would." Forrest shifted in his chair and leaned forward to rest his elbows on the table. "I know he's an adult and has every right to make his own decisions... I know I have *no* right to question his decisions. But, Hattie, I am."

It was the sheer rawness of his tone that had her reaching for his hand. Neither one of them were touchy-feely people, but this… She couldn't stop herself. "Of course you are. I mean, he *is* Webb. He's not *my* brother, but I'm questioning his decisions right now, too." She smiled, squeezing his hand.

Forrest remained silent, his blue eyes on her face, letting her hold his hand.

"I'll grant you the timing of that bit about your comment was…unfortunate but, Forrest, it could be that Webb simply decided now was the time for him to make a choice. It might have had nothing to do with the other." She suspected there was no convincing him of that, so she kept going. "As much as you don't want to hear this, there is nothing you can do." She held her hand up to stop his argument before it started. "You did a good job raising him. And don't argue with me because we both know you *did* raise him." The corner of his mouth curled up slightly. "Now all you can do is stand beside him and support him. Because if you don't, you'll regret it. Don't do that to yourself or to him. Or the rest of your family, for that matter. It's done."

Forrest squeezed her hand, then let it go.

He took a slow sip of coffee, ate the other half of his cookie and took another sip of coffee before he said, "I know. You're right. I just needed you to set me straight, is all."

That was the thing about Forrest—he had a good head on his shoulders. He had every right to get mad, stomp around and yell a little, or go drink too much. But that wasn't his way. Even though the idea of his brother enlisting stirred up all sorts of painful memories and ghosts, he'd managed to talk through it and make sense of it all. It didn't mean he was right with it, only that he'd come to terms with it.

If only I could take a lesson from Forrest. As far as their situations went, they were night and day. And yet, there was nothing either one of them could do to stop what was happening. They both knew their brothers were making the wrong choice. They both had plenty of factual reasons to prove they were making the wrong choice. But neither one of them was willing to lose their brother by putting their foot down and insisting those brothers listen and accept that they were wrong.

"What's with the hair?" Forrest reached

for another cookie, but his gaze was fixed on her hair.

Hattie reached up to run a hand over the silky-smooth locks Brooke had created. "Brooke." She shrugged. "She got some newfangled hair iron and knew the best way to test it was on my mop of curls."

"But it's not stuck like that, is it?" Forrest ate another cookie.

"Stuck like that? She's done it before, Forrest." And he'd commented then, too, she remembered. She frowned, stood and stepped into the hallway to look at her reflection in the mirror that hung on the wall. "It's not… bad?" She frowned. "Is it?"

"I guess not."

She spun to face him. "You guess not?" She had half a mind to put on her old John Deere baseball cap but… "If it bothers you, then don't look at it." Whether or not Forrest liked it, Hattie did. It was different. Tame. Almost…pretty. Not that she put much stock in that word or that she'd ever spend that kind of time on herself. But it was nice when Brooke did it.

"It's not that bad." Forrest rolled his eyes. "These cookies. They're good."

Hattie ran her hand over her hair again and sat.

Forrest seemed to realize something was wrong. “I did it again.” He shook his head and dropped the cookie he was holding. “That was mean. It’s your hair. If you like it, what does it matter what I think?”

“Forrest Briscoe, if that is your idea of an apology, I have news for you. What you just did there? That was not an apology.” She crossed her arms over her chest. “If anything, it was the exact opposite.”

“I said I was sorry.” He was frowning now.

“No, you didn’t.” She frowned right back. “You admitted it was mean. But that’s not the same thing as saying *I’m sorry, Hattie.*” She made her voice deeper, doing her best to imitate him. “Try something like, ‘While I’m used to your outrageously curly hair, this looks mighty fine, too.’ Or ‘It’s a change, but it’s nice.’ Or something.” She batted her eyes for extra effect.

Forrest was grinning now. “I’d never say ‘outrageously curly.’”

“No?” She shrugged, pushing back. “Apparently, you’re not saying ‘I’m sorry,’ either.”

"I *am* sorry, Hattie." He overenunciated each word.

"Now, see, you just managed to make your apology sound sarcastic." She threw her hands up in defeat. "I didn't even know a person could do that."

Forrest chuckled. "I guess I do need to work on the whole sarcasm thing, don't I?"

"Maybe." Now that her coffee was cool enough to drink, she took a sip.

"You've done more work in here." Forrest stared around the tiny kitchen with an assessing eye. "New cupboards?"

She nodded, proud of the progress she'd made. Her home, the Crooked Little House as it was known around town, sat on the very edge of the city limits.

"I'm still not convinced this didn't start out as a storage shed." Forrest shook his head, but he winked at her.

Hattie didn't let it get to her. Calling her home small was generous. But the place had a thirty-acre parcel of land behind it so, if she ever brought work home with her, she had room for any wildlife that might need rehabilitating before being returned to the wild. *She* didn't need much room anyway—it was just her. Sure, the whole structure sort of listed to one side, had squeaky floorboards, a water heater that made noises straight from a horror movie, and there wasn't an inch to spare, but she didn't mind. She was rarely home, anyway. And when she was, she did little odd jobs to try to make her crooked house a little more pleasing.

"I installed new cabinets *and* a new sink and hardware." She couldn't help but sing her own praises, just a little.

"You did?" Forrest was up. In two long steps, he was across the room, inspecting the sink, then kneeling to peer underneath at her handiwork. "Color me impressed."

"What color is that? Impressed, I mean?" Hattie reached for a snickerdoodle. Maybe it was making them for Forrest for so long but, over the years, she'd decided snickerdoodles were her favorite—followed by oatmeal raisin, then every other kind of cookie. Snickerdoodles and coffee with a splash of cream? *Heaven*. She nibbled on her cookie.

"You did the work yourself?" he asked, knocking on the sides of her new cabinets.

"Yes, sir." She turned, using the cookie in her hand as a pointer. "I went in, measurements in hand, to place my order at Old Towne Hardware and Appliance, but Rusty wouldn't do it. He insisted on coming out here himself when I'd finished." She rolled her eyes. "He wanted to see how it came together—since he'd ordered everything and we'd talked about it all for so long."

Forrest glanced her way. "He came out here?"

"I think the end result impressed him..." She shrugged, remembering how thorough Rusty had been. She paused, cookie midway to her mouth. "He said my measurements were perfect. As if there was any doubt."

"Nope." Forrest scratched his jaw.

Hattie shook her head. That jaw scratch was a Forrest thing. He was one of those men who could shave twice a day, if he wanted, his beard grew in so fast. By afternoon, his razor-sharp jaw had an impressive five-o'clock shadow. "Interesting."

Hattie wasn't sure what he was referring to. "That my measurements were correct?" Like there was any question about that.

"No. Rusty's not one for making house calls. Usually." Forrest was no longer inspecting her cabinetwork, he was inspecting her. "Rusty Woodard, huh?"

"What about him?" Hattie frowned at him. What did that look mean? What was he was thinking? "Is there another Rusty in Garrison?"

"No… No…" He shrugged, returned to his seat and picked up the last oatmeal raisin cookie. "Nice guy. Rusty, I mean."

"I guess." Hattie had never really given it much thought. "You know him much better than I do. Him being your roping partner and all."

Forrest nodded but didn't say anything else.

"Is there anything else I can do? About Webb, I mean. I know… I'm sure it makes you think about Gene." She hurried on. "But you can't let yourself get worked up that way. What happened to Gene was a horrible tragedy. Webb is going to be okay."

"Or, he'll get sent home during basic training with a broken leg from tripping over a footlocker or he'll catch some rare disease or something along those lines." She could tell it was taking an effort for him to joke about it.

"That does sound like Webb." If he needed to keep things light, she could do that. "Speaking of roping, are you and Rusty competing on Friday? After the youth rodeo, that is?"

"We were talking about my roping?" Forrest shrugged. "I don't know. According to the paperwork Webb showed me, he ships out Monday morning."

That quick? No wonder Forrest was panicking. It was one thing to know something like that was coming. But having it sprung on him this way? *Poor Forrest.* Not only was he dealing with the shock of Webb's enlistment, he was also facing the fact that Webb had just seven more days left at home. For all his brusque and sarcastic ways, Forrest was a family man. He loved his brothers and sister more than anything.

"I figure Mabel will want to pull some sort of goodbye party together." He cleared his throat, tugging at the collar of his button-down shirt. "Not that she knows." He was back at scratching his jaw again. "So far, he's only told me."

And now you've told me. "I'm happy to help, Forrest. You know that." She reached for another snickerdoodle. "I mean, I'll do what Mabel tells me to do. You know I'm useless at things like parties. Or people. Or being social." She giggled and a snort slipped out.

Forrest chuckled. "You always say that,

Hattie Carmichael, but I don't know a single person that doesn't think well of you."

Hattie felt a telltale warmth in her cheeks. "Look at you, giving me a compliment. And here I thought you didn't like my hair."

Forrest stared at her, long and hard. It started out familiar, the way Forrest always looked at her. But something about the tightening of his mouth and the slightest narrowing of his eyes set her back up.

"I get it, I get it. You don't like it." She sighed, setting her cookie down beside her coffee. "Getting back to your roping. Are you? This weekend? You and Rusty?"

Forrest's eyes narrowed a little more. "Probably." He shrugged. "I can get used to it." His gaze fell from hers, fixed on his almost-empty coffee.

"Forrest Briscoe, you're giving me whiplash. You could get used to what?" Hattie stood and retrieved the coffeepot, then refilled Forrest's mug.

"The hair," he mumbled.

"We're back to that?" She paused, frowning at him. "What I'd like to know is why it seems to bother you so much."

"I'm a man of habit. You've said as much a time or two, I think. I don't like change."

He stared up at her. "That—" he flicked a strand of her hair "—is change."

Hattie put two and two together then. Audy was married, Webb was leaving and Mabel was engaged to his once archenemy. Her hair wasn't the problem—it was just one more thing that had changed. "Well, don't get used to it. It won't last long." If letting her hair go curly eased some of his stress, she'd let it go curly. Besides, it was way too much work to do this on a regular basis. Hattie had never been one of those high-maintenance types, and she wasn't about to start being one now.

WEBB'S TUESDAY MORNING announcement went over better than Forrest had anticipated. Forrest immediately jumped up and offered Webb his support, hoping Webb was right and the others would follow his lead. Uncle Felix did offer his congratulations, but he also left the room almost immediately after. Beau and Audy were all handshakes and smiles, and Mabel, as predicted, let everyone know that there would be an all-hands-on-deck, every resident of Garrison invited, goodbye party on Saturday night.

Mabel pulled out a large yellow legal tablet and started making lists, while Audy, Beau and Webb sneaked out of the kitchen as fast as they could.

"This is going to take some planning." Mabel glanced up, did a double take, then stared around the room. "Where did everybody go?"

"Well… You do have out a tablet." Forrest pointed at the ever-growing list taking shape on her legal pad. "We've all learned, when you start making lists, we all get extra work to do."

"I'm not going to apologize for being organized." Mabel's chin tilted with just a hint of defiance. "You got home awful late last night."

"I had a lot to think about."

"Webb told you?" Mabel stopped writing and started tapping the end of her pen against the tablet. "I figured as much. Your eyes didn't bug out of your head. Your head didn't spin all the way around. And you didn't breathe any fire."

"All that?" Forrest had to chuckle. "That's some imagination you've got there, Mabel."

Mabel chewed on the inside of her lower lip. "Were you with Hattie?"

Forrest nodded.

"Did she..." Mabel shook her head. "Never mind."

That was when his sister's lack of a poker face told Forrest there was a whole lot Mabel was trying not to say. "Did she, what?"

"Nope." Mabel kept shaking her head. "I promised not to say a thing."

That didn't sound like Hattie. Secrets? From him? Forrest frowned. He'd been there for a couple hours last night. *What didn't she tell me?* And why was Rusty Woodard and his visit to her house the first thing that sprang to mind? *Maybe because he'd come all the way out to Hattie's place—just to measure for her new cabinets.* Anyone who knew Hattie would know she'd have measured at least twice before she was satisfied enough to write down the numbers.

"She can't really talk about it." Mabel shrugged. "Not yet."

Well, that didn't sound good. Not at all. "You can't say something like that and expect me to just bide my time." Forrest spun his coffee cup in his hands, his concern mounting.

"I'm sorry, Forrest. It's just..." Mabel's pen moved faster and faster. "She can't...she promised not to tell her parents yet."

Hattie told her folks just about everything.

"Mabel." Forrest's concern had turned into full-blown worry. "She's..." He didn't like pushing, usually, but nothing about this was usual. "She's my friend, too."

"I know. It's just...complicated." She fluttered her hand at him. "There's a lot to it. And I don't think she wants to have to go through everything because that would be too much like reliving it all. You know how there are things in your past that you don't want to revisit if you don't have to? Well, this is definitely one of those things."

Absolutely nothing his sister said made him feel the slightest bit better. If anything, he was feeling agitated.

"You can go on and scowl at me if it makes you feel better, Forrest. But I gave my word." Mabel went back to making her list.

I was better off not knowing a thing. He sighed and pushed himself up from his chair, carrying his empty mug to the sink and rinsing it out. "You expect me to sit and wait for her to tell me what's going on?" *And not worry?* "You know how I am about waiting." He turned to find Mabel staring at him, a smile on her face.

"She's fine, Forrest. I mean, she will be.

It's just…" She shook her head. "Stop. I can't. Don't make me feel bad about this. Just…be her friend. That's what she needs."

I am *her friend.* At least he thought he was. How could Hattie be going through something and not mention a word of it to him last night? Come to think of it, there *had* been that awkward exchange at Brooke's salon. Until now, it completely slipped his mind. But he remembered her face now—the shock and strain on it. His insides knotted up tight, regretting that the whole "girl talk" thing always had him heading for the hills. If he'd stayed, he might know what's going on, been able to help. As it was…

Something she was keeping a secret that was also "girl talk"? He had no idea. And it irritated him, something fierce. Forrest prided himself on knowing what needed knowing. Clearly, this was one of those times. To not know and have his little sister, sitting here, *not* telling him? It went all over him the wrong way. "I've got work to do." He pushed through the kitchen door, crossed the Great Room and out the back door—where he nearly tripped over something.

Harvey whimpered.

"You're the one laying in the middle of the door," Forrest snapped, bending to rub the dog's back. "I didn't mean to hurt you. You know that." He sighed, beyond frustrated.

Harvey sat up, his thick plume of a tail thumping against the wooden planks of the wraparound deck.

"I'll take it you forgive me?" He gave Harvey's chin a good scratching. "Good." Giving the dog a final pat on the head, Forrest walked across the porch, then headed down the steps to the gravel walkway. He followed the path winding through the cedars and oak trees, down the high hill where his home sat, to the massive operation that was Briscoe Ranch.

From up high, it resembled a wagon wheel—the main barn and offices at the center with various chutes and pens, corrals and exercise tracks leading to the livestock barns. One for cattle, one for horses, one for the bulls, even one for Mabel's goats. Before long, she'd have part of the place staked out for some of the wild mustangs she'd been working with that now needed a home. She'd tried to slip it into conversation over breakfast, but Uncle Felix caught on real quick and that was the end of that.

For now. One thing about Mabel, she was persistent. Knowing that was the only reason he'd left the whole Hattie thing alone. Mabel wouldn't tell. She'd given her word and she always honored it.

Most of the time, Forrest applauded her conviction. Today...he'd have been okay with her making an exception, this one time.

Audy glanced up from polishing his saddle. "Who got your tail feathers in a twist?"

"No one," Forrest mumbled.

"Right." Audy chuckled. "Fine by me if you wanna stay all puffed up like that."

Forrest glanced at his brother. "I'm not... nothing's puffed up."

Audy stopped polishing. "It was easier to say that. What I mean is you look wound tight and ready to tear the head off the next person that looks at you the wrong way." He tipped his hat back.

Forrest didn't bite.

"Whatever." Audy started whistling as he went back to polishing his saddle. Like he didn't have a care in the world.

Forrest made for his office, but paused. Audy had been with Brooke this morning—that's what married folk did. Audy had only been on the ranch so early this morning because Forrest told him it was important. Shockingly, he'd listened to Forrest and was standing with the rest of the family when Webb shared his news. But, *before* all that, Audy had been with Brooke.

"Audy." Forrest made a show of checking the saddle blankets stacked against the side wall.

"Yessir?" He stepped back to admire the saddle.

"Did Brooke say anything?" But he stopped. Was he really going to ask Audy if Brooke had said anything about Hattie? *What am I now, back in high school? Or worse, one of the Ladies Guild?* He'd never felt more like a fool. "Never mind." He grumbled, even more out of sorts by the time he pushed his office door closed behind him.

About an hour later, a text rolled in. Forrest pushed aside the livestock registry he'd been updating to see his phone.

Hattie.

He opened the text.

There Hattie was, her game warden cap lopsided on her wily curls, holding on to one of the biggest snapping turtles he'd ever seen. She was red-faced and sweaty, straining under the animal's weight. Forrest suspected it weighed a good forty pounds. *At least.*

This fella almost ended up pancaked beneath an eighteen-wheeler. He put up a tussle when I tried to get him off the highway.

He grinned.

Looks like you showed him.

He hit Send.

Came close to losing a finger though. Talk about ungrateful.

Forrest chuckled. He could just imagine her giving that turtle a real talking-to. If Hattie was going to do something, she committed. *Like saving a big, mean, ungrateful turtle from getting hit on the highway.*

Seconds later his phone rang. "Hey." Hattie sounded out of breath. The unmistakable sound of traffic so loud he barely heard her.

"Hey, yourself," he answered, leaning back in his office chair.

"How'd it go?" she asked, followed by a grunt and more heavy breathing.

"What *are* you doing?" he asked, smiling in spite of himself.

"Turning Mr. Snappy-Shell loose down at Shale Creek." She took a deep breath, the rumble and echo of cars fainter now. "Not that he seemed all that happy about it." She sounded winded as she asked, "Anyway, how did this morning go? With Webb? Your family. I've been thinking about it most of the morning."

He frowned. Here, he'd gone over and poured his heart out in her kitchen while she was keeping some big secret from him.

"Forrest?" There was a jarring slam, then silence. "Whew. It's hot out there. Blasting my AC now." She sighed. "I can't imagine living without AC, can you?"

He made a noncommittal noise.

"Someone wake up on the wrong side of the bed? Or did Webb's announcement not go so well?"

"It was fine. Mabel was already making a list for Saturday's party when I headed out this morning." *After she wouldn't tell me what's going on with you.*

"Sounds like Mabel, all right." There was

a smile in her voice. "I'm glad it went well. Not that I expected anything different. Saturday, huh? Sounds like it's going to be a busy weekend."

"Oh?" he asked.

"Billy is coming home." She paused. "He didn't say when, exactly, but he'll be here."

Forrest had known Hattie for…well, forever. She adored her brother and she wasn't shy about it. Normally, Billy's visits had Hattie on cloud nine. She'd talk fast, laugh and get excited over doing all the little things they did whenever Billy was in town. She'd never, ever, sounded *disappointed*. But that's exactly how she sounded. "That's not a good thing?"

She made a grunt-groan in response.

"And that means?" He was smiling again.

"Oh…nothing." Another weird sound. "Only… Forrest. There's something I want to tell you, but I promised I wouldn't tell anyone and I already told Brooke and Mabel, which I shouldn't have done."

No, you should have told me. But he stayed quiet.

"But it's…it's eating at me. All of it." She sounded all worked up. "I don't know what to do."

The hint of desperation was like a little tiny dart, hitting him square in the chest. Something *was* wrong. “Hattie.” He cleared his throat, wishing he had Audy’s way with words. “It’ll be all right. Whatever it is.”

And then another first happened—a horrible thing that had Forrest pushing out of his chair and scrambling for his truck keys. Hattie was crying. Not just crying, sobbing.

“Hattie. Come on, now, it can’t be that bad.” He wanted to believe that, but she was crying. Hattie Carmichael. *Crying*. It had to be real bad. And once he found out what it was, he’d help her figure out how to fix it. That’s what he did. Fixed problems. He wasn’t a talker—he was a doer.

“I… I… But it is,” she wailed.

“All right now.” He ignored Audy’s questioning look and kept moving. Out of the barn, up the hill, hurrying toward his truck. “Where are you?”

“I’m on 281.” She sniffed, then blew her nose. There was nothing feminine about the way she blew her nose. Hattie wasn’t that sort of woman. Half the time, Forrest didn’t think of her as a woman. She was just… Well, she was Hattie. “On the side of the road.” Her voice broke.

He didn't like the pressure building in his chest or the helplessness he felt. "That's an awful long highway, Hattie." He climbed into his truck and turned on the engine. "Where, exactly?"

She stared crying again. "Are you—you coming? Because I'm—I'm crying?" She sobbed again. "I'm f-fine."

"Hattie." He inhaled deeply, trying to stay calm. "Where are you?" He flew down the dirt road and peeled out onto the country road that led to Highway 281.

There was a long silence.

"Hattie." He took another deep breath. "I'm sorry. I didn't mean to snap at you."

"No, Forrest, I'm sorry." Her words wobbled. "Carrying on like a baby."

"I'm in my truck so tell me where I'm going." Whether she was crying or not, he wasn't giving up.

"How about I meet you at—at—" she paused long enough to blow her nose again "—Bluebonnet Ice Cream?" She sniffed. "I'll buy."

Forrest didn't give a fig about ice cream or who was paying, but he did want answers. At the moment, a whole mess of bad, worse and don't-even think-it scenarios were play ing through his head and he couldn't seem to shake it. "On my way." The sooner he heard what, exactly, was going on with her, the better.

"Don't s-speed." She hiccupped. "I'll have to write you a ticket. And don't drive and talk on your phone. I'll have to give you a ticket for that, too."

"You know me—I follow the rules, not break them."

"I do." She sighed. "I'll see you there." And she hung up.

Ticket or not, Forrest had a hard time keeping his speed under control. Hattie was the one constant in his life—the one person he could count on to stay the same. Steady. Reliable. Levelheaded. Positive. She was the most can-do person he'd ever met. If there was a problem, she took it apart and found the solution without getting too rattled. Whatever was troubling her, they'd figure things out and then things would go back to normal. *And I'll never have to hear Hattie cry again.*

CHAPTER THREE

"THANK YOU." HATTIE took the ice-cream cone from Forrest. "Also, you and I both know there's no way you made it here that fast if you were going the speed limit."

Forrest shrugged, taking a lick off his strawberry ice cream. "I found a shortcut."

Hattie's nose was stuffy, her eyes itched, her throat was raw and she was still teetering on the edge of another full-on tantrum, but Forrest showing up, being sweet, being here, was helping.

Wait. *A shortcut?* There was no shortcut—unless he'd driven across Crawley's *and* Williams' land, all their fences, and leapfrogged across the Colorado River. She smiled, his well-meaning lie making the lump in her throat double, forcing her to swallow. She blinked away the tears and took a tiny lick of her mint chocolate chip ice cream. "I didn't mean to scare you."

"You didn't." He sat beside her. "I was already headed this way to check on—what did you call him?—Mr. Snappy-Pants?"

"Snappy-Shell." She had to smile. "Turtles don't wear pants. They teach you that the first day at the academy."

Forrest grinned. "Day one, huh?"

She nodded, so grateful he was here. "It's right up there with 'Standing still doesn't make you invisible and that skunk will still totally spray you,' and 'Bambis look sweet but they can kick you into next week so keep your guard up.' You know, the basics."

"Good to know." Forrest's blue eyes met hers as he chuckled.

She winked, taking another lick of her ice-cream cone. It'd always been gratifying to make him laugh—now was no exception. They sat side by side on the tailgate of her truck, perfectly content to enjoy their ice cream in silence.

Forrest finished his ice cream and gently bumped her shoulder with his. "Anything else exciting happen? Besides Mr. Snappy-whatever."

Yes, but I can't tell you. She'd been eaten up with guilt ever since she told Mabel and Brooke—since she'd promised Billy to keep it a secret. "No." Her voice wobbled, so she cleared her throat before adding, "Just the turtle rescue and ice cream with you." She slipped off the tailgate. "I should probably get back to patrolling." As nice as this was, she had work to do. The upside of work? It kept her busy—too busy to think about *other* things.

"Oh." Forrest's brow furrowed. "I was… I was hoping you'd let me in on whatever it is that's tearing you up inside." He glanced her way, clearly uncomfortable. She was still pulling herself together. Talking about it would undo the laughs and ice cream and… calm. She tried to smile.

"You seemed fine last night," he said mildly.

"I *am* fine."

"Hattie." He shook his head and looked down at her. "I guess it's time I confessed the truth. I wasn't heading this way to check on your turtle. I wasn't heading this way at all until you called."

"I sort of figured as much," she whispered.

"What I'm saying is I'm here…well, for you."

And he'd come running—speeding—to get here.

"I'm sorry I worried you." If she could go back and start this morning over again, she would. Minus the tears and drama. "You've got enough on your plate right now."

He stared at her, considering, before he finally said, "I've got room on my plate, Hattie." He sighed. "You're okay, aren't you? You're not..." He swallowed, his gaze darting from her truck to the ice cream shop to the field beyond. "You're not sick or something? Nothing is wrong with you, physically, I mean."

"Oh, Forrest." He was *that* worried? Her tears had shaken him more than she'd ever imagined. And she felt terrible. "I'm fine. Healthy as a horse. Nothing to worry about."

"Good. That's good." Until then, she hadn't realized how tense he was. As she spoke, he seemed to unknot a bit. He stretched out, his posture easing so that he seemed an inch or two taller. "But those tears were about something." He cleared his throat. "Or someone?"

Yes, they were. Definitely a *someone*.

"It's none of my business and we don't normally talk about this but...well, if some fella is involved—"

"What?" Hattie was lost now. "Forrest,

what on earth are you talking about? A fella?"

He frowned. "Well, I don't know, do I? You're keeping secrets. You don't keep secrets. What am I supposed to think?"

"I don't have time for that nonsense, and you know it." She rolled her eyes, ignoring his smile. If only it were that easy. She'd rather have her own heart break than know her brother's was in jeopardy. An image of Courtney Hall popped up.

"Do you…" She took a deep breath. "Do you remember how I was bullied in high school? I mean, I was younger than you so you might not—"

"I do." He looked more confused than ever. "Of course. And I remember Mabel talking about it."

"It's just that *that* person is coming back to Garrison. Courtney… And I… I have to be nice to her." She would be nice to her because she was nice. To everyone. "But I don't want to be. And I don't want her coming back here, making me feel…" *Awkward. Unfortunate. Ugly. Pathetic.* All of that, and more? How could she possibly explain the havoc Courtney had wreaked upon her self-esteem? *You'd think I'd be over it by now.*

She shook her head, grappling to control the emotional roller coaster careening around inside her stomach. "I want her to go away and stay gone."

Forrest continued to look confused. "Why do you have to be nice to her? Why have anything to do with her?"

"I have to." *Because my brother has gone and gotten engaged to the woman.*

"You don't have to." Forrest shook his head. "She was mean to you, so you don't owe her kindness. Civility, maybe, but not kindness."

Hattie smiled up at him. "You think?" How would that go over? In her hug-loving, share-everything, talk-on-the-phone-every-day family could she get away with being *civil* to her new sister-in-law? *Sister-in-law?* The thought… The reality… *Oh, no.* Family holidays. Get-togethers. Eventually, nieces and nephews. With Courtney always there? *No.* There'd be no escape. And her parents' home would no longer be a sanctuary. Nausea rolled over her so hard and fast, she bent forward and braced her hands against her thighs.

"Hattie?" His hand was warm on her back. "You sick?"

At the moment, answering him was impossible. *Breathe.* Don't picture Courtney's perfect face smiling that nasty smile. Her stomach clenched tight, bile stinging her throat. *Breathe.* She closed her eyes. *Come on, Hattie. Breathe.* She shook her head.

"Why am I not believing you?" Forrest's voice was low, almost like he was talking to himself.

This was exactly what couldn't happen. Letting that woman get to her this way. Letting past hurts turn her into some awkward, insecure teenager all over again. That's not who she was anymore. She had a respectable career, she was respected and she liked herself. *Courtney can't bully me anymore.*

She took a deep breath and opened her eyes. *I can do this. I will do this.* The nausea was ebbing. *Better.* She drew in a deep breath. Much better. "I'm fine." She rose quickly, smacking the back of her head into the front of his face with a crack that echoed across the Bluebonnet Ice Cream parking lot. The pain was jarring. She reached back to rub at the back of her head. If it hurt her this bad, he must…

Forrest was pinching the bridge of his nose, his face a deep red. Head tilted back, eyes pinched shut, jaw locked tight. *He was hurting, all right*. And then a trickle of blood came from his nostril.

"Oh, no. Forrest." She pulled her red handkerchief from her back pocket and reached up to dab beneath his nostril. "You're bleeding."

He pulled away. "Let me." The words were muffled.

"Right, sorry. Here." She pressed the handkerchief into his hand. "Ice. You need ice." She winced as he blinked away tears. "Stay here. Sit." She jumped up into her truck, opened her ice chest and pulled out one of the gel packs inside. "Here."

"I'm fine, Hattie." He pressed the ice pack against his nose. "Fine."

"You're not fine. Your face is swelling—your eyes." She froze. "Oh, Forrest, your nose. What if I broke your nose?" She had hit him, the full force of her skull bashing into his much more fragile face. "We're going to take you to town to see Doc Johnston. Just in case."

Forrest didn't argue. "Fine."

Hattie's heart was thumping like mad, then. It was worse than she thought. She'd expected him to argue, in true Forrest fashion. Instead, he'd agreed. *Immediately.*

"Do you need help?" she asked, taking his arm. "There's a step up, into my truck."

Forrest glared at her. "I know, Hattie."

"I *know you* know." She waited for him to get situated in the passenger seat, then closed the door. She ran around the front of her truck, climbed in and backed up, flipping on her lights and siren.

"Hattie Carmichael," Forrest mumbled. "That's not necessary."

"I don't care what you think, Forrest Briscoe." She shifted gears, in no mood for his sass. "Here you came to cheer me up and feed me ice cream after I blubbered like a baby, and what did I do?" She did a quick scan of the highway before she pulled onto the road and stomped on the gas pedal. "I went and broke your face, that's what I did. So, you hush now and keep that ice on it." Forrest needed help and she was going to get it for him. *Fast.*

"GET KICKED BY a bull?" Doc Johnston asked, his blasted penlight making Forrest's eyes burn.

It hurt to blink, but the light shining

back and forth between his eyes left him no choice. He blinked, winced, which made everything hurt all over again. The stars were long gone and the throb had subsided to a constant, blistering pain that extended from his upper lip to the middle of his forehead. "Something like that."

"Whelp." Doc Johnston let out a long, slow sigh. "Happy to say, it isn't broken much—just a bit displaced is all." He stepped back. "I can fix you right up, don't you worry. Let me get Aurelia in here." He opened the door. "Aurelia," he yelled.

From Forrest's seat on the paper-covered exam bench, he saw Hattie jump out of her waiting room chair and hurry to meet Doc Johnston at the door.

"Now, now, Officer Carmichael, he'll be just fine. You don't need to stick around. I can call one of the other Briscoes to come get him." Doc Johnston assured her, then he stopped. "Unless, you need him to fill out some sort of injury report or something?" He paused, looking back over his shoulder at Forrest. "You said a bull did this to you? I'm assuming it wasn't one of yours, then?"

The last thing Forrest wanted to do was laugh but…Hattie's face. She was beet red.

He could almost see the steam coming out of her ears. He was laughing all right and it hurt something fierce. There was no stopping it. The whole time he was laughing, he pressed the cotton pad against his nose, while his eyes teared up from the pain.

Hattie went from narrow-eyed and riled up to open concern. “Forrest, stop it.” She crossed to him, giving his arm a quick squeeze.

Doc Johnston looked back and forth between them. “I miss something?”

“Forrest’s just having a little fun. At my expense.” Hattie sighed, her hands on her hips. “There was no *bull*. At least, I’ve never been called a bull before.”

Doc Johnston’s white eyebrows rose high. “Ah, I see. What’d you do, Forrest, mouth off or get fresh with Hattie? Don’t you know better?”

Forrest was still laughing and wincing. “I’ve learned my lesson.” He leaned forward to nudge her, but the slight shift seemed to add a good ten pounds to his swollen face. And his nose? It felt about ready to pop off.

Doc Johnston made a disapproving sound.

“I can’t stay mad at you when you’re banged up like this.” Hattie’s hazel green eyes swept over his face. "I figure you need me to be extra nice to you since your brothers are going to have a field day with this. You, getting your nose broken, by me." She sounded all sympathetic, but he detected the tiniest gleam of mischief in her gaze.

I deserve that. "When you put it like that." Forrest didn't want to think about his brothers right now—but she was right. There'd be no end to the teasing. "It's more displaced than broken." He saw the confusion on Hattie's face and shrugged. "Just repeating what Doc Johnson said." He eyed the long cotton swab Doc Johnston's nurse placed on a metal tray—beside other equally torturous-looking paraphernalia. "What's the plan here, Doc?" He'd had more than his fair share of bumps, bruises and breaks and liked to think he was tough, but that didn't mean he wasn't ready for this part to be over and done with. "And how long is this going to take?"

"You got somewhere to be?" Doc Johnston asked, sliding on a wide headband with a bright light mounted in the middle. "You're not going to be up for any hot date tonight, Forrest, that's for sure. Unless your date doesn't mind two black eyes and a nose packed full of cotton."

"You might want to give us a minute, Miss Carmichael," Aurelia said. "We'll get Mr. Briscoe some pain relief and then set his nose."

"I'll stay." Hattie patted his hand. "I'll even hold your hand, if you want?" But then her gaze fell to the syringe the nurse was picking up.

It wasn't the syringe that bothered him, it was the look on Hattie's face. She took one look at the shot and turned the same shade of pea green she'd been wearing when she'd bent over in the Bluebonnet Ice Cream shop's parking lot. "Nope." Forrest pointed at the door. "Hattie, you need to leave. Now."

Hattie managed to stop looking at the shot. "But..." Her gaze bounced back to the nurse, walking toward him, with the syringe in hand.

"But nothing." Forrest sighed. "Doc, look at her."

"Oh, my." Doc Johnston frowned. "Hold on now, Aurelia." The nurse froze and Doc Johnston patted Hattie on the shoulder. "You heard the man, Hattie. No need for you to stay and make yourself ill. Or worse, pass out cold on this floor. You've done all you can do here. I'll call someone to get him when we're done here."

Hattie swallowed, steadying herself. "No, I landed you here. I'll take you home—"

"I don't want you getting sick, *but* I'm more than ready for some pain relief." If he snapped, it was intentional.

"I was going to say I'll take you home but I will wait outside." She patted his knee.

Forrest smiled. "Good plan."

Hattie's big eyes bounced from him to the shot and back to him. "Yay, pain relief." But her voice was tight and she was looking queasy as she pulled the door closed behind her.

"Hattie Carmichael." Doc Johnston chuckled. "That one, there, is an original."

Forrest spent the next few minutes getting poked and prodded. When Doc Johnston put some long plier-looking things inside his nostril, Forrest was grateful Hattie was waiting outside. A few tugs and nudges later, all with Doc Johnston's headlamp shining in his eyes, and he was even more grateful for the pain shot.

"Now." Doc Johnston stepped back, after taking the squares of gauze his nurse offered—and packing them up Forrest's nose.

"You'll need to leave this for a week. No earlier, you hear me?"

"Yes, sir." Forrest blinked.

"I know, I know, it's a nuisance, but you don't want this getting infected and wind up back here." Doc Johnston sat back on his stool. "You don't want me to splint this or perform surgery. You take it out too early and that could happen. Or your septum could go crooked and that can cause a whole other set of problems. You could end up whistling when you breathe." He paused then, chuckling. "Wouldn't that be something."

Over Doc Johnston's shoulder, Nurse Aurelia looked like this wasn't the first time she'd heard this joke.

"I guess it would," Forrest murmured.

Ten minutes later, Forrest walked into the waiting room to find Hattie talking to a little boy. He headed to the front desk to schedule a follow-up, but he—and everyone else in the waiting room—could hear their entire conversation.

"No, I don't think it's rabid," Hattie was saying to the boy. "Most animals growl or hiss because they're saying 'leave me alone.' Especially grown raccoons."

"Grampa Buck says the best thing to do is

trap them." The little boy was a spitfire, animated and using his hands and talking five times louder than he needed to. "What sort of trap? Like a mousetrap or a bear trap?" He clapped his hands together loudly. "Do they make a raccoon trap?"

"A catch and carry trap would be best." Hattie sounded and looked concerned. "And then you can call *me* and I can take your raccoon and find a new home for him."

"How do you know it won't come back?" The little boy didn't sound happy. "I don't want him to come back."

"Any date you can't make?" The schedule clerk asked, looking up from her computer for his answer. "Oh, my." Her lips pulled down and her forehead creased as she studied his face.

He suspected he was going to be getting a lot of stares and winces—or laughs—over the next several days. *Might as well get used to it.* "Whenever Doc Johnston says is fine by me." He took the appointment card she offered and slid it into his pocket, resisting the sudden urge to rub his nose as he walked to Hattie and the little boy.

About that time, Buck Williams came

over and sat beside the little boy. "You telling Warden Carmichael stories, Levi?"

"About the raccoon, Grampa." Levi stood, acting out the next bit. "How he's mean and hissing and bad and needs to go." He showed his teeth, using his hands like claws.

Buck chuckled. "Never met a nice raccoon, Levi."

"I know one." Hattie smiled. "His name is Peanut and he lives over at the big Colton County Wildlife Rescue Ranch on the county line. You should go see him." She turned her attention on Buck then, "I have a catch and carry trap in my truck, Mr. Williams. Call me and I'll come take care of your raccoon. I'd be happy to relocate the animal if he's a nuisance."

That was about the time Forrest reached their little group and Buck caught sight of him. "What in the Sam Hill happened to you, son?"

Forrest turned to Hattie. Hattie stared up at him. "An accident." He didn't elaborate.

"Glad you're all right." Buck shook his head. "You want a beer, come on over to my place and I'll make sure they're on the house. Looks to me like you could use one. Or two."

Buck owned Buck's Bar and Honky-Tonk,

a pool hall and bar that offered up live musical performances now and again. Not exactly Forrest's stomping ground, but he appreciated the offer. "Might just take you up on it." Forrest said his goodbyes and followed Hattie out of the clinic, the bright Texas sun brutal on his sensitive eyes. He was thankful for the cool—and shaded—interior of Hattie's truck.

"That little boy is something." The way Hattie said it, he couldn't decide if this was a good thing or a bad thing. "I'm sort of afraid for the raccoon."

So, a bad thing. He grinned—and instantly regretted it. The pain was dull, but there. He didn't want to think about how he'd feel once that shot wore off.

"I'm hoping Junior Rangers will make him appreciate nature a little? Maybe?" She shrugged. "Could be I'm fooling myself."

One of Hattie's extra duties was running the Junior Rangers program. It was an outdoor adventure club that included lessons on animal husbandry, conservation and general cooperation amongst the troop members. He'd never participated, but he remembered his younger siblings had and loved it. Now Mabel helped Hattie at the meetings. With kids like Levi Williams in the troop, Forrest understood why Hattie was always looking for extra hands to help out.

"You know what might help?" Hattie glanced his way, turning on the ignition. "A male role model. Maybe I can recruit someone to help out at meetings?"

Forrest knew what she was getting at. "It's like you were reading my mind." There was no chance—none at all—he'd have anything to do with the Junior Rangers. "Beau would probably do it."

"Ha ha." Hattie's sigh was long and loud. "I'll ask him." She glanced his way. "While you were with the doc, I got a text from my mom." She pulled onto Main Street. "You mind stopping by there real quick? Then I can drop you off and see if Mabel will ride over to get your truck?"

"I never mind seeing your folks." Bart and Gladiola Carmichael were good people. Not long after Forrest's parents died, Bart had told Forrest and Mabel to consider he and Glady—what Hattie's mom went by—their stand-in parents. And ever since then, that's how Forrest saw them. Family.

"I'll keep it short." Hattie glanced his way. "I'll try, anyway."

Forrest chuckled. "No hurry on my part." Glady couldn't tell a short story. "The shot should last a while yet."

They reached the Carmichael homestead in no time. "Come on in," Hattie said, waving him out of the truck. "They won't give you a hard time." She pointed at her own nose.

He followed her up the well-kept front path to the modest two-story pale blue house with navy trim. Glady and Bart loved to garden so it was no surprise to see vibrant flowers spilling out of planters that lined the porch railing—as well as several hummingbird feeders hanging along the covered porch's eaves.

Hattie waited, holding the door open for him. "Momma? Dad?" she called out, stepping inside.

Forrest heard the low rumble of conversation then. Hattie's parents had company.

"No." Hattie stared up at him, her hand resting on his arm. "Oh, no. Forrest." All the color drained from her face.

He caught her hand, instantly alarmed. "What's wrong?" he asked, stepping closer to her. She held her finger up to her lips, hushing him so he whispered, "Hattie? Talk to me."

"She's here," Hattie whispered, eyeing the still-open front door like she was considering escape.

"She?" he echoed.

"Courtney." Hattie shuddered, her gaze sliding to the open door again.

Courtney? *Who was... Oh, wait.* He remembered. The bully. The one who had made Hattie cry. The one Mabel went on and on about, spending hours on the phone trying to undo all the hurt and damage this Courtney person had inflicted on Hattie. It'd chapped his hide to hear Mabel reassure Hattie that there was nothing wrong with her. *And there wasn't. Not a thing.* Hattie was... Well, he didn't know a handful of people he thought more highly of than Hattie.

Why was the woman here? In Hattie's home?

Hattie took a step toward the open door, tugging him with her, when he stepped on a squeaky board. A very squeaky board. He frowned. Hattie froze, holding her breath—

"Hattie?" Glady's voice carried down the hall. "I heard something. Hattie? Is that you?" Footsteps. "Bart, did you leave the front door open? It's open, I tell you."

Forrest watched as Hattie steeled herself for what was to come.

Hattie squeezed his hand and then called out, "It's me, Momma."

"Oh-hoo." Glady's excited cry was followed by her arrival, practically running down the hall to meet them. "You scamp. I can't believe you kept it a secret. You." She hugged her daughter and kissed her cheek. "Can you believe it? A wedding."

"I know." Hattie's feigned excitement was winceworthy.

"I am over the moon. Billy getting married. As soon as possible, he said." Glady sighed. "Isn't that romantic?" She barely glanced at him. "Hi, Forrest, darlin'. Gracious. Is your nose okay?" She waited for his nod, then gave him a one-armed hug. "Come on, come on, you two. Have you two met before, Hattie? Courtney Hall. I think she went to high school here but, for the life of me, I don't remember her. I sure don't remember you ever mentioning her."

All at once, everything slid into place. The girl talk and tears and ice cream and going green. All of it made sense. Billy was

Hattie's favorite person in the world. Her favorite person in the world was about to marry her only enemy. No, *enemy* wasn't right. Hattie didn't have enemies. *Tormentor* was more like it. That's why she'd have to be nice to this woman—because she loved her brother and wanted him to be happy. But Forrest had to wonder—if Billy knew the pain and anguish Courtney had caused his little sister, would he be so fast to marry her? *Not that it's my place to say a thing.*

His gaze fixed on Hattie. Her tight smile, rigid posture, nervous glances down the hall. She was scared and it gutted him. He wanted to assure her it would all be okay but…he couldn't promise that. All he could promise was he wasn't going anywhere. As long as she was with him, he'd make absolutely certain this Courtney Hall person treated Hattie with nothing but respect—or she'd answer to him. He took a deep breath, hooked Hattie's arm through his and followed Glady into the kitchen. "We got this," he whispered. Whatever she needed, he'd do it.

Hattie's hand was ice-cold on his arm, but she rallied. At least, she was trying to. Hattie was Hattie, after all. When they set foot into the kitchen, he was pretty sure he was the only one who knew Hattie's heart was breaking.

CHAPTER FOUR

HATTIE HAD NEVER felt more like an outsider. Here, in her mother's kitchen, surrounded by the same blue-and-white china, framed prints of Dutch windmills and familiar cookie molds. The faces were the same, too, all the people she loved most. And, yet, nothing felt right. They sat, as usual, around the whitewashed farm table that was the heart of her mother's kitchen and her parents' home. This was where they spent most of their time. Snapping beans. Making bread. Rolling out sugar cookie dough. Doing puzzles. Playing board games. All good memories—times Hattie treasured.

Unlike now. Her throat was too dry to swallow. No matter how much iced tea she drank from one of her mother's treasured heirloom daisy-covered glasses, it didn't help. The lump that had formed the moment she'd realized Billy and Courtney were here, that this was really happening, hadn't budged. If anything, it seemed to grow every time her gaze bounced into Billy. Billy, who was all lit up like a Christmas tree.

Hattie swallowed again, beyond bewildered. If *anyone* else had put that smile on her brother's face, she would have been ecstatic. She wanted him happy, she did. But how could he be happy with…*her*? Hattie couldn't help thinking that, at any moment, Courtney would turn to her and make some derogatory comment about her clothing, call her "Hillbilly Hattie" or "Hattie Hayseed"—all while wearing that mean-eyed smile. And those were the kinder insults. The others still made Hattie's stomach churn.

She pressed her hands against her thighs and did her best not to panic.

Her mother was charmed, of course. Courtney had always done that. One smile, one laugh, and Courtney would have all the adults wrapped around her little finger.

I'm an adult. Hattie drew in a deep breath, clearing her too-tight throat. She shifted in her seat, oddly aware of everything. From the chipped tile on the edge of the kitchen counter to the cobweb in the far corner of the room to how the last family photo they'd all taken together hung just a hair crooked.

She felt uncomfortable, antsy. A big part of that? Her uniform. Not embarrassed so much as…aware. Painfully so. How many times had Courtney pointed and teased and laughed over her less-than-girlie clothing choices? And now, here she sat, in her khaki polyester pants and shirt, black steel-toed boots, and khaki baseball cap—with all the required game warden accoutrements attached to her belt and breast pocket. She rubbed her hand against her thighs, her palms sweaty. It seemed hot in here. Was it? *More likely, I'm just freaking out.*

If anyone was aware of her unease, they didn't let on. Her father, thankfully, wasn't acting any differently. He sat, sipping his tea, smiling indulgently as Momma and Courtney chatted excitedly and flipped through a bridal magazine Courtney had had tucked into her purse.

Hattie tore her eyes from the starry-eyed models in white flounces and giant skirts and resisted the urge to shudder. Courtney could have walked out of that magazine. While Hattie had managed to avoid making eye contact with the woman, it was impossible not to *see* her. She was, if possible, even more blindingly beautiful than she'd been in high school.

Tall and graceful, with the same husky laugh that had Hattie's stomach clenching and flipping over and over like clothes in a dryer. Blond hair styled just so. Huge brown eyes with thick lashes. A dimple in one round cheek. Bright pink nails. Dangling earrings with sparkling stars.

Hattie tucked a wayward curl behind her ear and adjusted her cap. No earrings. No pink nails… She glanced down at her hands. At least she didn't chew them off anymore.

Forrest's leg nudged her under the table. Maybe he understood how shaky she was—not just her hands, but all of her—because his leg stayed, solid and comforting against hers. She shot him an appreciative smile.

He winked back. Well, he tried. The attempt had him reaching for his nose and his whole face going red.

Under the table, she patted his knee. "Sorry," she whispered, meaning it.

"It may be none of my business, but what happened?" Billy asked, nodding at Forrest. "Momma says Mabel's engaged to Jensen Crawley and I remember you two going at it a time or two—"

"Jensen didn't do this." Forrest cut in. "It was an accident. Hattie, here, came to my rescue."

"That's my girl," her father said, giving her an approving nod.

Her daddy had no idea how much that meant to her—now, more than ever.

"An accident?" Her mother pressed a hand to her chest. "Forrest, darlin', thank goodness you're okay."

"I'm fine."

"He's tough," her father added. "Always has been."

Forrest's awkward shrug made Hattie smile. He was tough all right, but he couldn't stand praise or compliments or flattery. It made him uncomfortable—like now.

"So, how did you two meet?" Forrest asked, taking a sip of his tea.

"Oh, it's the sweetest thing." Her mother patted Courtney's hand. "Just the sweetest. I could see a movie being made out of it. With, hmm, Julia Roberts and Matt Damon, maybe?"

Hattie took another sip of tea, offended on Julia Roberts's behalf.

"Now, Glady..." her father cut in, chuckling. "Go on, Billy."

"My boss was supposed to go to his daughter's school for Career Day, but he was held up in court and asked that I go fill in for him." Billy covered Courtney's hand with his. "Lucky for me, his daughter was in Miss Hall's second grade class."

"You mean, lucky for *me*." Courtney practically cooed.

Hattie glanced at the two of them. Her brother, doe-eyed and flushed, with Courtney staring into his eyes… All pretty and feminine and… "You're a teacher?" Hattie croaked, horrified. *Those poor kids.*

Courtney's brown eyes landed on her, her smile fixed. "I am. I love children."

Loved making them cry, you mean.

Under the table, Forrest nudged her again, a little harder this time.

"Hmm," Hattie murmured, sipping more tea.

"She's amazing with them, too," Billy said, lifting Courtney's hand to press a kiss against her knuckles. "I was only supposed to cover for one class but I wound up staying the whole day."

Courtney's cheeks turned a pretty color of pink.

Hattie went back to staring into her almost-empty tea glass. *Courtney even blushed prettily.* Hattie got all red-faced and blotchy—there was nothing pretty about it.

"I don't think we've spent a whole day apart since." Her brother was clearly head over heels for the woman.

"How long ago was that?" Forrest asked.

"How long?" Billy asked.

"Oh, gosh," Courtney paused. "Almost two months ago?"

Did she just say gosh? The Queen of Mean said *gosh*? As far as she remembered, Courtney had a far more colorful and less parent-friendly vocabulary. In fact, it was thanks to Courtney that Hattie had learned all sorts of new and horrible insults—mostly because they'd been used against her.

"Two months?" Forrest asked. "Well, now, that's awful fast, isn't it?"

Hattie stared up at him, in shock. He was right, of course, but she'd never have gotten away with asking such a thing. *My hero.* Even with his swollen nose and bruises popping up under his eyes– Hattie couldn't help noticing how especially handsome he looked.

"Sometimes, it doesn't take long," her

mother gushed, not in the least deterred by Forrest's question.

"What is that Emily Dickinson quote?" Courtney asked, her eyes on Billy. "The heart wants, what the heart wants, I think that's it."

Hattie managed to cough over her groan.

Forrest did not.

Hattie was still coughing, to stop from laughing, when she nudged Forrest—hard—under the table. She thought she heard her father chuckle, too, but she didn't dare look his way to confirm it. There'd be no stopping her laughter then.

"Oh, don't let this group get to you. Romance isn't high on their priority list. What matters is you two have found each other and there's going to be a wedding." Her mother shot them all disapproving looks before turning back to the bridal magazine. "So much to do." She flipped the page. "When did you say your family was arriving?" Her mother pointed at a picture. "I like this."

"That is lovely." Courtney nodded. "My mother and aunt will be here Thursday afternoon. My sister's not sure when she'll be here. Everyone else will wait until the rehearsal dinner and the wedding."

"Anyone else?" her mother asked.

"My father left when I was young and we've lost contact over the years. So, no, it's just us Hall women." Her sigh was soft.

As much as Hattie didn't want to, she felt for Courtney. Other than Billy, her father was the most important man in her life. Well, and Forrest. So, to be without a father? Hattie couldn't quite wrap her mind around it.

"Which brings me to a question." Billy sat up and turned to face their father. "Dad—"

No. She knew what Billy was going to ask. After everything Courtney had just shared, everyone had to know where her brother was going. Hattie set her glass on the table a little harder than necessary, the thud drawing all eyes her way. "Sorry." She stood. "I'll be back." She headed down the hall and up the stairs, past her old room, to her bathroom. It was still pink and white—her mother's decorating, not Hattie's. But Hattie didn't care about the pink or the frilly shower curtain or the embroidered towels or bowl of potpourri; she cared about space. Needed it, desperately.

Of course, Billy would ask their father to walk Courtney down the aisle. It was the right thing to do. The kind thing. Logically, Hattie knew this. But she wasn't feeling all that logical at the moment. *He's* my *father*. Hattie pressed her eyes shut, hating how angry and selfish she sounded. It was awful. She felt awful. *Take the high road, Hattie*. She sat on the edge of the bathtub, tugged off her cap and shook out her mop of curls.

I can do this. She covered her face with her hands. *This isn't about me. This is about Billy.* She pressed her fingers against her temples and the building ache. So far, Courtney had acted like a normal person. *People change*. Maybe Courtney had. She groaned, pressing her fingers harder and willing the ache away.

She knew how to separate her feelings from the facts. As a law enforcement officer, it was an important skill. One she could use now. *Fine*. What were the facts?

The facts. Being a teenager was horrible for everyone—Hattie firmly believed that. Even Courtney… Still, Hattie remembered the entourage of girls trailing behind the Queen of Mean. All of them were either desperate to be Courtney's friend or terrified to be on the receiving end of her wrath. Hattie shook her head. Maybe the mean thing had been a… A coping skill? It was a stretch. A big one.

Back to the facts. Fact: Courtney wasn't glaring or hurling insults at Hattie or giving her all-knowing-mean-girl smiles.

Fact: Billy was in love with Courtney.

Fact: Billy and Courtney were getting married.

Fact: Hattie needed to get over it. All of it. No more Queen of Mean, crippling insecurities and doubts, the insta-nausea and clammy palms, or avoiding eye contact. *It's not like Courtney can shoot laser beams out of her eyes and disintegrate me.* She rolled her eyes.

Fact: *This is my home and my family.* Nothing could change that. Nothing and no one.

She stood and splashed cold water on her face and neck. *I'm going to go down there, smile and stop acting like...like this is the end of the world.* It wasn't. It was more like a fresh start. All Hattie had to do was set the past aside, pretend *that* Courtney wasn't *this* Courtney and move forward. *I can do that.* Hattie stared at her reflection. *I can.* Her reflection wasn't convinced.

Her hair stuck out in wiry corkscrews,

untamed and frizzy—with no sign of the sleek and almost-glamorous 'do Brooke had managed the day before. Maybe she could ask Brooke to re-create it? *No. Stop. This* was who she was. Khaki uniform, steel-toed boots, and out-of-control hair. *I'm me.* Hattie. Warden Carmichael. Forrest said everyone liked her. If that was true, that meant Courtney would like her, too. As is, no smooth hair or dangly earrings required.

With a final deep breath, she dried her hands and face, and opened the bathroom door.

FORREST GLANCED AT the kitchen door, again. No Hattie. He figured she needed a minute to herself, so he didn't go after her. But he wanted to. Real bad. The longer she didn't come back, the harder it was to stay in his chair.

"Oh, I think that's my favorite," Courtney Hall gushed, pressing her hand against one of the pages of the magazine.

He leaned back in his chair. It might be, now that his pain shot was wearing off, he wasn't in the best of moods, but he didn't get it. He remembered how Mabel and Hattie had gone on about this girl—the things she'd said and done and got away with. How people had treated her special, even if she was one hundred percent rotten on the inside. That's what Mabel had said, anyway. Hattie had mostly turned green and clammed up when Courtney Hall had come up in conversation.

Sure, she was something to look at—though he'd never liked all that fuss and gloss—and she seemed charming enough, but she'd just about broken Hattie's spirit, so what was Billy Carmichael thinking? If *he* knew about Courtney, Billy had to know. Hattie told him everything.

"It is pretty." Glady folded up another slip of paper and tucked it into the thick magazine. "Oh, no, what about this?"

"She's already picked out her dress, Mom," Billy piped up.

"You did?" There was the tiniest hint of disappointment to her voice. "I can't wait to see it."

"She looks like a movie star." Billy kissed the back of her hand again.

Forrest shook his head. After today, he appreciated that neither of his attached siblings carried on like this. There might be a little hand-holding or hugging now and then, but this sort of carrying-on was flat-out unnecessary. Watching Billy and Courtney making eyes at one another, plus the hand kissing and touching and I love you's and sugar-sweet compliments was more than a man could stomach.

Maybe he should go after Hattie—it'd get him out of here and away from all this. Otherwise, he wasn't sure how long he'd keep his no sarcasm or teasing promise. When Billy brushed Courtney's hair from her shoulder and Courtney dissolved into a high-pitched girlish giggle, Forrest was done.

"Excuse me," he mumbled, as he stalked from the kitchen, then headed down the hall. There was a guest bathroom downstairs—he knew that. But he wasn't looking for a bathroom; he was looking for Hattie. *And to get away from the lovebirds.*

He took the stairs two at a time and paused in Hattie's childhood bedroom door.

Pictures of Hattie showing lambs at the stock show. Ribbons and trophies, too. Newspaper clippings about her winning an orienteering challenge, her prizewinning barbecue sauce recipe, how she saved a baby alligator—with Mabel's help—from a storm drain, and a whole bunch more.

"Forrest?" Hattie asked. "What are you doing up here?"

He turned. "Getting some air." She'd fixed her hair, smoothed it evenly under her cap until there was no sign of her curls.

Her nose wrinkled up. "Your face. It's hurting?" she asked, stepping closer and peering up at him. "It looks like it hurts."

He shrugged, continuing his perusal of her accomplishments. "I've said it before and I'll say it again, I don't think there's anyone I'd rather be dropped down in the middle of nowhere with." He tapped one of her blue ribbons.

She smiled. "I bet you say that to all the girls."

He was so surprised, he burst out laughing. "Ow." He reached up to cover his nose, but stopped himself. "Oh, ow, Hattie..." He chuckled, wincing.

"Oh, no, Forrest." She rested a hand against his chest. "I'm really sorry. About everything. Today has been...horrible. Look at you." She shook her head. "Look at your nose. You're all but crying because of me." Her hand lifted, flailing a little. "And now, this..."

His hands settled on her shoulders. "Hattie, come on, now. This was an accident." He stepped close enough that she had to look up—or stare at his chest. "Besides, you can't help it that you're extra hardheaded."

She looked up then, her outrage turning into a reluctant smile. "Ha ha." She slumped a little. "I should get you home."

"I'm fine, but if you need to get out of here and carting me home will do that, then yeah, I need to get home." He rubbed her upper arms. "If there's anything I can do, Hattie, you know I'm here. Ask, all right? Whatever you need, we'll figure it out."

"I could use a hug." Hattie's arms slid around his waist and she buried her face against his chest, hugging him tight. "You can hug me back, you know," she murmured after a minute, her voice muffled. "So, is this getting weird? It's weird, right?"

He and Hattie didn't make a habit of hugging but...Hattie was wrong. *There's nothing weird about this.* It was all too easy to wrap his arms around her and hold her close. His chin knocked her cap off, freeing the strawberry-blonde curls she was always fighting to tame. They tickled his nose, but he did his best to ignore it. Not so easy when his nose was one mass of raw nerve endings.

Still, broken nose and swollen face aside, he liked having her close. *If this is what she needs, this is what I'll do.* Truth be told, Forrest was in no hurry to let her go. *That* part was weird.

"I'm going to try to pretend she's a different Courtney," she whispered.

Good luck with that. He closed his eyes—it eased the throbbing somewhat—and tried to think of something supportive to say. "Okay," he mumbled, hoping it was enough.

"I don't know if that's stupid or not but… If I don't, there's no way I'll be able to be okay with this, Forrest. And I need to be okay with this…for everyone." She sighed, leaning more heavily against him.

He understood what she wanted to do, but there was no way he'd be able to manage it. "Okay," he murmured, reaching up to move her curls from beneath his nose.

"I mean, people change." She turned, resting her cheek against his chest. "Right? And Billy's a good judge of character."

He absentmindedly wound a curl around his finger. It was soft, clinging to his work-calloused finger. *Maybe it was possible Courtney had changed.* His arm tightened a little, wishing she wasn't in this predicament. Wishing there was something he could do to make it better.

"Forrest?" She rested her chin on his chest and stared up at him.

He searched those hazel eyes, the soft curl sliding from his finger, as he smoothed her hair back. He'd always thought her hair was her best feature, but now he wondered if it wasn't her eyes. They were a mossy green. Unusual. Pretty, even. Right now, Forrest was hard-pressed to ignore that all of Hattie was pretty. More than a little. And he wasn't sure what to make of it. Hattie was...Hattie. Her being pretty didn't matter, not one bit. But now that he'd noticed how pretty she was, he couldn't un-notice it. Having her in his arms, looking up at him, had a powerful effect on him—one he wasn't the least bit prepared for.

There was a soft knock on the door.

"I'm sorry to intrude. Glady told me to put my things in the room to the left, at the top of the stairs?" Courtney was wide-eyed, her gaze bouncing between the two of them.

"Oh." Hattie stiffened, immediately stepping back. She stooped for her cap, twisted her curls and tucked them up and under, once the hat was back in place. "This is it. My room."

Forrest watched Hattie's jerky movements, more than a little shell-shocked. He wasn't holding on to Hattie anymore. His arms had never felt so empty. He swallowed hard. Any minute, he'd stop thinking about how pretty her eyes and hair and smile were and go back to thinking of her as…Hattie.

Courtney pulled her wheeled suitcase behind her, scanning the very articles and clippings, ribbons and trophies he'd been inspecting not ten minutes before. "Where should I put this? My toothbrush and such." She held out a smaller bag.

"The bathroom is through here." Hattie waved her over. "I'll show you."

Courtney glanced at him again, one eyebrow raised, before following Hattie into the bathroom.

He couldn't help but wonder what the woman was thinking. She had to know who Hattie was. *You didn't forget Hattie, period.* If she knew who Hattie was, she knew what she'd done to Hattie. Surely? He was half tempted to follow them into the bathroom, for Hattie's sake. Now *that* would *be weird.*

"Where'd they go?" Billy asked, leaning in the bedroom doorway.

Forrest nodded at the door.

"I have some extra towels," Glady said as she walked in, giving the room a once-over. "Bart? Did you change the lightbulb in the bedside table lamp like I asked?"

"I'm coming," Bart's voice drifted up the stairs. "I'm coming."

Forrest stepped aside, watching as Glady talked Bart through the lightbulb change—as if he'd never changed a lightbulb before—then exchanged a smile with Billy. Bart, being Bart, didn't seem the least bothered. He nodded, did as he was told and accepted Glady's grateful kiss on the cheek.

When Courtney hurried back into the room, she was all smiles. "Hattie just told me, Forrest."

Hattie trailed after Courtney, the strain of her smile putting him on alert. Hattie wasn't green, but she looked ready to bolt and run. He almost tuned Courtney out until he heard what she said next.

"I didn't know the two of you were dating." Courtney hooked arms with Billy. "Billy said you were *friends*, but they say friendship is the best foundation for any relationship."

Forrest blinked, his pulse tripping over itself. *What, now?* He and Hattie, what? If it hadn't been for the stricken look on Hattie's face, he'd have laughed. She'd told Courtney they were dating? He and Hattie? It was downright silly. Any minute now, everyone would start laughing. Any minute… He tugged at the collar of his shirt, unease clogging his throat.

There was absolute silence in the room.

"Well…" Billy gazed back and forth between them, grinning. "You two are an item, huh?"

Forrest resisted the urge to tug at his shirt collar again. *What are you up to, Hattie?* As much as he wanted to ask, now was obviously not the time or place. Hattie was looking a little green all over again, which meant she was no more okay with this than he was. One thing he knew for certain, Hattie wasn't one for telling tales. If she'd told Courtney they were a…a couple—he swallowed hard—she'd have a reason. A good reason.

"We…we didn't want to take any of the focus off your special day." Hattie's words came out in a rush, her gaze finally meeting his.

He saw the plea in her hazel green eyes and took a deep breath.

She was serious. Okay. Fine… He'd roll with it. He swallowed again. *I'll try. But what were the chances her parents would buy this? Or Billy? It seemed pretty far-fetched—*

"I knew it." Glady clapped her hands. "I just knew it." The woman was beaming.

"She did know it." Bart nodded, but he wasn't convinced. Not yet.

Join the club.

"You didn't need to keep this a secret, Hattie." Billy put his hands on his hips and stared back and forth between Forrest and Hattie. "This is nothing but good news."

Forrest had to smile at that. *Good news, huh?* It was definitely news. Maybe it'd be an easier sell than he'd thought—which didn't make a whole lot of sense—but what was he supposed to do? How was he supposed to act?

"This is so great. Billy worries about you," Courtney added. "You have *no* idea."

"I can't say I'm all that surprised. I just figured, after all this time, if it hadn't happened by now, it wasn't going to happen." Billy grinned.

But Forrest was still mulling over what Courtney had said. Billy worried about Hattie? Why? Hattie was the most capable and independent woman he'd ever met. Billy didn't need to worry about his sister, not one bit. And he should know that. Plus, there was something about Courtney's tone that rubbed him the wrong way. Forrest shrugged. "Some people figure things out in two months, others take a…few years."

That had them all laughing.

"We're *still* figuring things out." Hattie cleared her throat, staring at him. "It's all…"

"New. Unexpected." Forrest crossed to her side and, after a brief pause, took her hand. "A surprise, even." When Hattie smiled up at him, he figured he'd hold her hand as long as she needed.

Glady hugged him, clearly delighted. "I love surprises."

Hattie's laugh was all nerves. "Well, surprise. We're dating." She looked up at him, turning a deep red, and added, "Happily." It sounded like a question.

Forrest chuckled. "Very happily." He squeezed her hand until she looked up at him again. She was wide-eyed and pink cheeked with nerves. As ridiculous as this whole thing was, he'd go along with it. *If this is what you want.*

"Hattie," Courtney murmured, her smile bright. "Since we're all here, I wanted to ask you something? You and Billy are so close, and I know it'd mean so much to him—to both of us—if you'd consider being a bridesmaid?"

The shock on Hattie's face tugged at Forrest's heart. He knew she was struggling—with all of this. This whole *dating* thing was further proof of that. Poor Hattie. She was torn up over Billy marrying this woman. Now she was supposed to be excited to be one of Courtney's bridesmaids? *She's tougher than I am.*

"Of course." Hattie looked more uncertain now than ever. "I'd love to."

There was a whole bunch more hugging, but Forrest had just about reached his limit. "Hattie, you're still on duty." He tapped his watch.

Thankfully, Hattie seemed to be on the same page. "You're right. I'm sorry, I have to get back to work." Hattie took a deep breath.

"I'll come by tomorrow, if I can. I work late tonight."

Ten minutes and one "far-too-long Glady goodbye" later, they were sitting in her truck cab and Hattie was starting the ignition.

"So..." Forrest said, glancing at the Carmichael home. "*That* was...*something*."

Hattie nodded, turning onto Main Street. "I know." She glanced at him. "Don't be mad at me, please. I didn't mean to but... I don't know, she sort of implied she wasn't surprised that I was single and I... I just... I lied." She shook her head. "And once it was out and she was *so* surprised—shocked even—that I couldn't take it back. My pride got the better of me. I'm sorry."

Listening to her, it made sense. Heck, he was riled up just picturing it. Right or wrong, it was done and there was no going back.

Hattie tugged off her cap and shook out her hair. "You're mad, aren't you?" Curls fell about her shoulders and down her back. One particular curl rested on her forehead, dangling over her left eye. "You have every right to be mad."

"Not mad—at you, anyway. But I am... working through it," he murmured, watching the curl blow in the stream of refrigerated air blowing from the dashboard vents. This was eating her up; he could see it on her face. "I get it, Hattie. I do. And it'll be okay. We'll figure...*this* out." They would, too. She might have thrown him a curveball, but it didn't shake his faith in her.

"You're the best friend ever, you know that?"

"I do." He nodded, grinning. "Guess I need to work on being the best boyfriend for a while?" *Hattie's boyfriend.* Oddly enough, the more he thought about it, the less *odd* the idea became. Still, this wouldn't be easy. Hattie wasn't one for misleading people or lies. "You're sure this is what you want to do?"

She nodded slowly. "Yes, I guess... I'm sorry." She reached over and squeezed his arm. "I think that's about the millionth time I've apologized to you today. I'm whining about me, dragging you smack-dab into my mess, and you're over there in real pain."

He covered her hand with his. "If you want, when your shift is over, you're welcome out at the ranch. I can't promise Mabel won't be making lists or Webb won't get into trouble or Beau won't be carrying on about

Tess or something, but you're welcome." He left it at that. A lot had happened during their short visit to the Carmichael household, but two things stuck out above the rest. First, for all her "I'm fines," Hattie was a long way from okay. And second, he was a little too okay with the idea of being—pretending to be—Hattie's boyfriend. It was pretend, though. He'd be a fool to even think about risking his friendship with Hattie. Right now, Hattie needed someone to look out for her and, as far as he was concerned, he was the man for the job.

CHAPTER FIVE

"YOU CAN'T AVOID me forever. Meet me at the Buttermilk Pie Café for lunch," Billy said, his voice flooding her truck cab through the speakers. "Even *incredibly* busy game wardens like yourself have to take a lunch, Hattie."

Hattie eyed the pack of peanut butter crackers she'd tucked into her backpack before she'd left the house. It might not be the most appealing lunch, but it was far more appealing than having lunch with her folks, Billy and Courtney. For all her big talk with Forrest, she wasn't ready to face the reality of more Courtney time. Or questions about her and Forrest, either. Her mother was bound to have questions—questions Hattie didn't have answers to. *Because it's a lie.* So far, she'd managed to dodge dinner the night before and this morning's breakfast—even though her mother had made her absolute favorite chocolate cinnamon rolls—using a backlog of paperwork as her excuse.

Billy wasn't buying it.

"I don't know—"

"Come on, Hattie, it's what we do. Burger, onion rings, milkshake." He sighed. "I get that you're extra busy right now, but I'm only asking for an hour."

It's what we *do*. Meaning she and Billy? That sounded nice. A loud screeching had her sitting up, scanning the traffic on the roadway around her. In the opposite lane, a shiny sports car slammed on the brakes to slow down. That happened a lot. Drivers saw her black-and-white truck with lights on top and, all of a sudden, everyone was obeying the traffic laws.

"What was that?" Billy asked.

"Someone speeding, hoping to avoid a ticket." She loved that Billy had always taken in an interest in her work.

"I don't hear any sirens." Billy perked up. She'd let him ride along with her a time or two, and he'd been like a kid in a candy shop—all excited.

"I didn't get a speed on them, Billy. Too late." She sighed, glancing in her rearview mirror. As far as she could tell, Mr. Sports

Car was still going the speed limit. *At least until he was out of my line of sight, that is.*

"That's disappointing." He paused. "So, how about it?" Billy asked. "Lunch, I mean."

If it was just her and Billy, then sure. But she couldn't figure out how to ask that without coming across rude or stirring up her brother's suspicion.

"Mom and Courtney are going to the florist and, honestly, I could use a little break. Especially since Courtney's mom and aunt will be here tomorrow. Things are bound to get more interesting."

More interesting? "I can hardly wait." Hattie felt sick.

"Come on, now. I need some Hattie time." He chuckled. "If you can squeeze me in?"

And just like that, Hattie's nerves eased and she was smiling. "I think I can manage it."

"Good." He sighed. "I was beginning to think something was up. Something that had you dodging me. Or maybe you knew I'd get the whole Forrest-thing out of you."

Her big brother knew her so well. "That's just plain silly. I'll see you in an hour?" She hurried to add, "But I'm not talking about Forrest with you." Billy would see right through her and then how would she explain any of this?

"Uh-huh. Don't hold your breath," Billy said. "Love you. Stay safe. And prepare for me to beat your milkshake record."

"Ha. We'll see about that." She had the fastest time for downing a large vanilla milkshake. It'd left her with a beast of a brain freeze, but it'd been worth it to have bragging rights. Billy had been trying to beat it ever since. But, for the last three years, her one minute, four seconds time still stood. "But you're welcome to try." She pressed the disconnect button on her dashboard and ended the call, looking forward to her lunch with Billy. If she were braver, she'd pry a little. As Forrest had pointed out, two months wasn't a whole lot of time to get to know someone. How well did Billy really know the woman he was going to marry?

No. People change—Courtney *might* have changed. She hoped. *If I keep saying it, maybe I'll eventually believe it.*

She turned off the farm-to-market road and onto the river rock road that led to Buck Williams's patch of land. When Gretta Williams had called to accept her offer of a trap, Hattie couldn't have been more surprised.

Apparently, their conversation in the doctor's waiting room had made quite an impression on Levi. And his mother, much to Buck's amusement, had decided it was a teaching opportunity.

She pulled up in front of the large log cabin, parked and went around to the rear of her truck for the live-trap cage.

"Warden Carmichael." Buck Williams came out onto the front porch, toasting her with his coffee. "Gretta will be out in a minute."

"Good morning." She pulled out the metal trap. "I hear Levi's had a change of heart."

"Thanks to your little talk the other day." Buck smiled. "It's a good thing, too, or I feel for what might have wound up happening to the raccoon." He tipped his straw cowboy hat back on his head. "I love my grandson, but that boy has a way of getting himself into all sorts of mischief. But I'm guessing you know that since you're his Junior Ranger leader and all."

Hattie didn't answer, but she couldn't hold back her smile.

"How's Forrest?" Buck asked, waving her to follow after him. "I've been in plenty a bar brawl in my day. That wasn't an accident. That boy'd been fighting. To get a man riled up like that, it'd have to be something big. A woman, probably. Or some trash talk about his family. He is a Briscoe, and those Briscoes are fierce about their family." He looked back her way, waiting for her input. "We were placing bets at the bar. Of course, most folk seem to think it's something to do with the old Briscoe-Crawley rivalry."

Poor Forrest. First, she cried all over him, then busted his nose, dragged him into a fake relationship *and now* people are talking about him at Buck's bar? *Because of me.*

"Hattie," Gretta Williams called, hurrying to catch up to them. "Thanks so much for coming out this morning." She glanced back and forth between her father and Hattie. "Daddy, what did you say?"

"Nothing. I was just asking her about Forrest being all busted up." He grinned. "Everyone knows how *close* the two of you are." Buck shrugged, but Hattie thought she heard him murmur something like, "It's a matter of time," under his breath, but couldn't be certain.

"Daddy, really?" Gretta sighed, looking pained. "Please, don't mind him, Hattie. He likes to get the inside scoop on everything—

he and that Dorris Kaye could go toe-to-toe on who knows something on just about everyone in Garrison."

Hattie had to chuckle at that.

Buck stopped beneath a massive oak tree a short walk from the cabin. "He's up there, I think. At least, this is where he runs when Levi lets Scooter out."

"Scooter?" Hattie crouched, setting the trap and placing a large red apple inside.

"His hound dog." Gretta shook his head. "I've tried to stop him before he lets the dog out—"

"Scooter could give one lick about that old raccoon." Buck waved off her concerns.

"That's good. A raccoon can put up a fight, if it needs to." When it came to animals, she didn't mince words. "Scooter doesn't need to be anywhere near that raccoon. Levi, either." She didn't like thinking about the raccoon or poor Scooter getting hurt. "This should take care of it." Hattie made sure the trap was good, and stood. "Here's my number. It shouldn't take long for him to come down. In my experience, it's hard for a raccoon to resist apple."

Gretta took her business card and tucked it into her pocket. "Thanks for coming all this way, Hattie. Country living is a far cry from what Levi and I are used to… Where we came from…" Her smiled wavered.

It was thanks to Dorris Kaye that Hattie knew about Gretta Williams's marriage to some big-time record agent and how bad things got—bad enough that she packed up Levi and moved in with the father she'd never been all that close to. "I'm glad he's in Junior Rangers. He'll get a lot out of it."

Gretta nodded. "He already has. Levi said he wants to grow up and be a game warden, too."

"I told him it's a right honorable profession and a good choice." Buck scratched his temple. "I can't help thinking you might have something to do with that."

Hattie couldn't have been more surprised. "Oh?" Levi? A game warden? "He's still young. At his age, I wanted to be an astronaut. Or a singer." She shook her head. "But this was what I was meant to do. It's a good thing, too, since I'm not so good with heights and I can't sing."

"No?" Buck chuckled. "I'll be the judge of that. Come on by for some karaoke sometime."

"I'll say no now—your ears will thank me

for it, I promise." She smiled, holding out her hand. "Thank you for letting me do this."

"Thank you for giving Levi a focus outside his cartoons and comic books." Gretta smiled.

She had a nice smile—she seemed like a nice woman. Hattie made a note to invite her next time she, Mabel and Brooke got together. It wasn't always easy to make friends in a small town.

"He needs to do something other than hide firecrackers under my bed or put superglue on his teacher's chair or try to shave the cat." Buck shook her hand. "Now when he does something like that, all I have to do is remind him a game warden wouldn't do such things."

Hattie laughed and said her goodbyes before making her way back to her truck and driving into town. She parked a few blocks down from the Buttermilk Pie Café and enjoyed her walk. Garrison Main Street was lined with proud small business owners. That pride was evident in their spotless storefront windows, newly tended planter boxes lining the street and swept sidewalks. Garrison might be a small town, but there was *always* something going on. And today,

Hattie noticed, that something was being planned around several pushed together tables inside the Buttermilk Pie Café.

"Morning, Hattie," Miss Patsy said. "You here to make any arrests?"

Hattie grinned. "Anyone here needing arresting?"

"Well now..." Miss Patsy took inventory of the women gathered around the table. "Let's see. Pearl never does anything so she's a no."

Pearl Johnston, Doc Johnston's wife, gave Miss Patsy a stern side-eye, but held her peace.

"There's a chance Dorris should be locked up. If gossip is an arresting offense, that is." Miss Patsy glanced at Hattie questioningly.

If that was the case, all of the Garrison Ladies Guild would be in trouble, but Hattie kept that to herself and said, "No, ma'am. Gossip doesn't constitute breaking the law."

"Good news for all of you, and most of the Ladies Guild members, come to think of it." Miss Martha Zeigler spoke up, turning the page on her date book. Out of all the Ladies Guild members, Miss Martha was the queen bee. She was a master organizer, a genius at fundraising and had an opinion about everything—normally one she didn't bother to sugarcoat for niceness. "Or Hattie, here, wouldn't have enough jail cells." She paused. "Do you have jail cells, Hattie? As a game warden?"

Hattie managed not to laugh. It was close, but she managed it. "Not my own, no, ma'am. But I am considered a state police officer and, if the need arises, I can arrest someone and take them to the local jail for holding." Hattie glanced at the papers each woman held, curious. "What is the Ladies Guild working on this fine day?"

"Well, the Founders Day Festival is coming up soon and we need to make it bigger and better than ever." Miss Martha ran her fingers along the calendar in her book. "But, before that, we need to have a fall gardening day. All we need to do is recruit some volunteers."

"I bet Beau Briscoe could help with that," Barbara Eldridge said. "That boy is always volunteering for something or other. And it's his senior year, don't forget, we need him to help train up some new recruits for us."

Hattie nodded in agreement—an idea taking shape. "I can bring the Junior Rangers." Beau would have some energetic football players to lend a hand with the Junior Rangers, so it *might* be a perfect opportunity to get her little troop outside and doing something helpful.

Miss Martha stared up at her. "As long as those young'uns can use a spade and take direction, I'd be happy for the help."

Hattie nodded, making a mental note to touch base with Beau and make sure he'd have backup. "Let me know the date and we will be there."

The front door opened and Billy came in, causing the entire Ladies Guild to hop up. Hattie stood aside, smiling, while her big brother was hugged, had his cheek patted on, one bright purple lipstick was pressed to his cheek and a whole lot of women were talking over one another. Everyone loved Billy. They always had.

It took her a minute to see Forrest, bringing up the rear, and edging his way as far from the gushing elderly women as possible. He was smart to do it, too. If the women of the Ladies Guild saw his bruises, there'd be no end to the questions or clucking over the state of his face.

His discolored and swollen face.

Forrest looked so awful, Hattie was hard-pressed not to stare. It was one thing when he'd been all red and puffy, but now… Now it was more a deep purple, with hints of black and blue beneath his eyes. His skin seemed stretched—too tight—over his nose, between his eyes and his upper lip. She hurt just looking at him.

"All that?" he asked, once he'd reached her side.

"What?" She couldn't stop staring. He looked miserable.

"That." He pointed at her. "Staring. Making that face. All sad-eyed and grimacing."

She tried to clear her features.

"Yeah, that doesn't help." He sighed.

"You joining us for lunch?" she asked, steering him toward the booth in the back—away from the Ladies Guild.

"Is that an invitation?" he asked, chuckling when she shoved him into the booth with his back to the rest of the restaurant. He took off his cowboy hat and hung it on one of the handy hooks mounted along the wall beside each booth.

Hattie sat and pulled a menu from behind the metal napkin holder. She held it up like a shield, so she wouldn't stare and make him, or her, uncomfortable. "Yep," she whispered.

"Oh, and I told Billy I'm not talking about you—us—you know, not *us*…us."

"Right. *Us*." Forrest sighed.

Hattie glanced up at him then, guilt twisting her insides.

"Thanks for the rescue," Billy said, sliding in beside Forrest. "I never expected you to leave me unprotected like that, Hattie." He nodded at the menu. "Whatcha doin'? Having a hard time making up your mind?"

"No?" She ducked down behind the menu again. "I just—"

"She's hiding." Forrest tore the top of the straw wrapper off, put the straw to his lips, and blew—shooting the paper wrapper across the table to bounce off Hattie's forehead. "From me."

Hattie tucked the menu back into place, wadded up the straw wrapper and set it aside. "I am not."

"See?" Forrest murmured. "She can't look at me."

"I see that." Billy was laughing. "I get it, though. I'd have a hard time seeing Courtney banged up like…*that*." He waved a hand at Forrest's face.

Luckily, Miss Lucille arrived, her tablet in one hand and a pencil in the other.

"What'll it be, kids?" She smiled around the table. "Land sakes, Forrest Briscoe, I heard you were in a brawl. Over in Austin at a horse auction? Is that right? Who were you tussling with? You're all beat-up and then some."

Hattie smoothed the straw wrapper and carefully rolled up the strip of paper. Austin? Where had that come from?

"Sounds right," Forrest agreed. "Whupped but good."

Hattie pressed her lips together. First, he was kicked by a bull. Then, he was in an accident. Now, he was jumped in Austin? The Ladies Guild was going to be all kinds of confused when stories were swapped.

"You know, my sister's boy, Jerry, was jumped by surprise, too. Not that Jerry's all that smart, mind you, but it wasn't his fault. He'd been minding his own business, taking the dog for a walk, and someone knocks him over, takes his wallet and gives him a shiner." Miss Lucille tsked, then lowered her voice. "Things like this don't happen in Garrison, Forrest. In Austin, well—it's sort of expected. Still, it's mighty upsetting seeing you all beat-up. They got any idea who did it?"

"Hattie is on the case." Forrest propped an elbow on the table and rested his chin. "Aren't you, Hattie?"

Hattie glared at him. "Yep." Still, it was hard to stay angry when he was enjoying himself so much.

"Well, then, there's nothing to worry about, I'm sure." Miss Lucille nodded. "Now, what can I get you three?"

SO MUCH FOR not teasing. Forrest had picked and pushed until Hattie was all squinty-eyed and tight-lipped. But he couldn't help it. He couldn't help hoping it'd keep her distracted from this whole Courtney mess. Last night, with his face throbbing and before his pain meds had kicked in, Forrest had pondered Hattie's situation for some time. He'd decided that, if any of his siblings were about to walk down the aisle with someone like Courtney, he'd tell them. Sure, it might not change their mind and there was a chance—albeit slim—the person had changed, but at least they'd know and he'd have done all he could do.

The whole pretending Hattie was his girlfriend? That part he wasn't sure about.

"What are you feeling like today, Forrest?"

Miss Lucille asked. “We’ve got a Texas-sized chicken fried steak special today.”

“I think I can manage it. My jaw doesn’t hurt.” He glanced at Hattie, who rolled her eyes. “Much, anyway.”

“Well, now, if it’s too much for you, I’ll send it on home for you to eat later.” Miss Lucille patted him on the shoulder.

Hattie was still trying not to make eye contact with him. “I’ll have the usual, please, Miss Lucille.”

“Make that two.” Billy held up two fingers.

“I know what that means.” Miss Lucille shook her head. “You two.” With a sigh, she headed back to the counter.

“I’m going to do it this time.” Billy cracked his knuckles, rolled his head slowly and shook out his arms.

“Is the stretching really going to help?” Hattie had the most infectious giggle. It was all delight with a few uncontrollable snorts thrown in. Even now, with his face all bruised, he had to chuckle in response.

Most drinking games involved alcohol. The Carmichael siblings’ drink of choice was a milkshake, but the concept was the same. Who could down the most the fastest?

Last he'd heard, Hattie was the champion. "You two still doing that?"

They both looked at him, full-on judging him.

He held up his hands in surrender. "Okay, geez, didn't mean to ruffle any feathers."

"Oh, no?" Hattie's brows arched high. "I'm pretty sure that's all you've been doing since you walked through that door this morning." Barely glancing his way, she added, "Maybe I shouldn't have protected you from the Ladies Guild—"

"I see how it is," Billy interrupted, pointing at Forrest. "You'll protect him, but not your one and only brother?"

"Look at him, Billy." Hattie finally looked at him—really looked at him.

He wasn't sure whether her wince-y expression was from empathy or just because it was hard for her to look at him in his multicolored state.

"You're right." Billy sighed, leaning forward to inspect him. "I guess he's earned a little reprieve. For now."

"Yeah," Hattie murmured, inspecting his face slowly. When her gaze met his, those hazel eyes of her narrowed. "It seems to me, appearance aside, Forrest is feeling just fine."

Forrest shrugged. "Better than I was yesterday." Which was true.

"You two going to tell me what really happened?" Billy asked, lowering his voice and leaning in. "I know there's more to it than an *accident*." He used air quotes when he said *accident*. "Or we could start with when this—" he pointed back and forth between them "—started. Either works for me."

Hattie's gaze returned to the straw wrapper she kept toying with. "It was an accident, plain and simple."

One she was still feeling guilty over, Forrest heard it in her voice. "It was. One hundred percent."

Billy sighed, sitting back. "Fine, don't tell me. I'll figure it out, though. I always do." He chuckled. "I'm glad we're getting to do this before Courtney's mom and aunt get here." He shook his head. "Her aunt Velma could charm the bees out of their honey. Funny, too. But Courtney's mom takes a little getting used to. Lucky for me, she adores me." Billy leaned forward to whisper, "Let's just say, Rebecca Hall could give Miss Martha a lesson on being uppity."

Forrest had never met anyone as opinionated, self-righteous or outspoken as Martha Zeigler. Then again, knowing all he did about Courtney and her venomous tongue, it made sense.

A child takes his cues from the people in his life. Whether he aims to be like them or the exact opposite, you can bet he's influenced one way or the other. Forrest couldn't remember if his mother or father had said that—or something close to it—but he'd held on to it. Whatever the context, the notion still held up. Courtney hadn't been born hateful and full of spite. She'd have to learn it from somewhere. *Like her mother.*

He had a few memories of his parents—all good—that he'd tucked away for safekeeping. His mother and her patience and smiles, frequent touches and hugs and words of praise. His father and his eager laugh, words of wisdom and strong work ethic. He was grateful for the time he'd had with them and the lessons they'd imparted. He might not be the most affectionate of men, but he liked to believe those he cared about knew it.

"Thanks for giving Courtney your room." Billy smiled at her. "You always had the comfiest bed."

"I wish I'd known. I'd have cleaned up, packed away some of the clippings and pictures Momma's kept up—"

"She's proud of you." Forrest cut her off. "Of course, she wants to show off all you've done." The idea of taking it all down and putting it in a box for Courtney felt wrong. "Besides, it lets Courtney get to know you a little. See how awesome you are." Since he was her *boyfriend*, there was no reason not to reach across the table and pat her hand. So he did.

Hattie's eyes went round at the touch.

Billy grinned. "Look at you two. This is going to take some getting used to." He sighed. "But Forrest is right. Momma is proud of you, Hattie. We all are." Billy paused, then leaned forward. "I need to ask you a favor, Hattie—"

"Milkshakes first." Miss Lucille put the milkshakes on the table. "One for you, too." She slid an extra-large one onto the table for Forrest. "My treat."

"Why, thank you, Miss Lucille. That's mighty kind." Forrest nodded his head in thanks. "What's the record? Let's do this."

"You realize yours is almost twice as big as ours?" Hattie asked.

"Severe brain freeze coming your way," Billy said, eyeing the oversize fountain cup.

"Never had one before." Forrest stirred the massive milkshake with the red-and-white straw. "Maybe I'm immune."

Hattie snorted. "Fine. Go ahead. Make yourself sick. Don't say I didn't warn you."

Billy sat back, watching them. "I'll take on the winner—next time." He put his smartphone on the table and opened the timer. "Ready, set, go."

Forrest wasn't a huge fan of sweets or ice cream or milkshakes especially. Why he'd decided to challenge Hattie—the record holder—at gulping down a full gallon of ice cream was a mystery. And when he was a little more than halfway through, he began to seriously regret making this into a thing. Hattie was a woman with a mission. Her cheeks were hollowed out and she didn't appear to be breathing. Or pausing. Or batting an eye. He wasn't surprised when she finished her cup and held up her hands, smiling in victory.

"A minute flat." Billy sighed, shaking his head.

Forrest groaned. "Next time, we'll get the

same size." He still had a third of his milkshake left.

"Sore loser." But Hattie was still smiling.

Miss Lucille showed up with food then. "And?"

Hattie pointed at herself.

"I never doubted you, sugar." Miss Lucille laughed. "Y'all don't race through this, now. I don't want to have to call the paramedics over one of you choking."

"Yes, ma'am." Hattie stared down at her burger with pure anticipation. "I'm starving."

Forrest loved Hattie's appreciation of food. She ate. She didn't pick or poke or eat salads all the time and only a bite of something sweet.

"Turns out Courtney's sister is flying in tomorrow morning, Hattie." Billy took a huge bite of his burger.

"How's the sister?" Forrest asked. "More like the mother or the aunt?" He poured a healthy dollop of ketchup onto his plate, hoping for Hattie's sake the sister was more like the latter.

"More like Courtney, I'd say. Only met her once. She's younger—finishing up her first year teaching. She thinks Courtney hung the moon. Kinda like you feel about me, huh, sis?" Billy grinned.

"You know it." The thing was, there was nothing teasing or condescending about Hattie's quick response. She meant it. She adored her big brother. "You'd said something about a favor?" Her hazel eyes darted from Billy to Forrest and back to Billy.

"I know this is all last minute, Hattie." Billy paused, reaching across the table to take one of her hands. "And I know you have a life and work and asking you to take some time off is asking a lot. But I'm asking, not too long—a few days is all. Selfish or not, I want you be a part of this, Hattie. Next Saturday is the wedding and that's that. I know you. You haven't taken a vacation in..." He looked at Forrest. "Help me out here."

Forrest sighed. "I can't remember Hattie ever taking a vacation." Because she loved her job.

The look of betrayal on her face made him regret saying a word.

"Could you take a few days off? Leading up to the wedding?" Billy gave her hand a squeeze. "Please. It would mean more than you can know, sis. I want you and Courtney to get to know each other. You two are like the most important women in my life. I love you both, so I know you'll become good friends. She needs more of those and I don't know a better friend, or sister, than you."

There's no way she could say no to that. After hearing all that, there was no way Hattie would ever bring up Courtney's bullying days now. Billy had just backed his adoring little sister into a corner and there was nothing Forrest could do to help her out of it.

"What do you say?" Billy asked.

"I'll call my supervisor when we're through. I've got the days so…I'm sure it'll be great." She glanced Forrest's way, seeking reassurance.

I'm here. He resisted the urge to take her other hand, to give her a comforting squeeze. *We can do this.* Now that they were *dating*, he had a reason to hang around all the time. Which was good, because that was exactly what he was going to do. She was looking to him for reassurance, so he needed to be there to give it to her. And even though it felt like his skin would split and his eyes were stinging, he managed to wink—just for Hattie.

CHAPTER SIX

"IT'S MORE OF a blush than a pink." Courtney's mother, Rebecca, waved the somehow offensive garment at Judy Eldridge, the owner of Bluebonnet Brides on Main. "We want *pure* pink. Not too dark, not too light." She waved the gown for emphasis, as if the dress she was holding wasn't pink. "Classic pink."

How is that not pink? Hattie eyed the dress. *Pink was pink, wasn't it?* Not that she wore pink.

Judy, ever the diplomat, blinked and said, "How about I let the bride browse our selection. Remember, we can order most styles in almost any shade imaginable. When is the ceremony?" When the woman looked Hattie's way, Hattie was tempted to mouth "I'm so sorry," but decided that might not go over well if someone saw.

"Next Saturday." Rebecca Hall brushed

past Judy and headed for the rainbow of colored bridesmaid dresses.

"Oh. Well." Judy's smile wavered. "I'm afraid that's not enough time for a custom dress to be made."

"I'm sure we'll find something here that will work just fine." Hattie's mother offered up. "Lead the way, Courtney dear."

Courtney smiled and followed her mother.

"This is...*fun*." Lena Hall, Courtney's younger sister, sat between Hattie and Courtney's aunt Velma on the red velvet-covered couch. "Who knew pink was so controversial?"

It was news to Hattie.

"Hush now or your mother's likely to start spitting fire." Velma giggled. "She is in a *snit* this morning."

"Gee, Auntie, I hadn't noticed." Lena laughed, too.

Hattie wanted to laugh—more from nerves than anything—but she managed to not make a sound. While Rebecca Hall was *exactly* the way Hattie remembered Courtney in high school, Lena and Velma were delightful. Quick-witted and lively. Sure, their humor was a bit more bracing than Hattie was used to, but they'd kept things interesting so far.

"Why pink, anyway?" Lena asked. "Courtney hates pink." She leaned closer to Hattie. "I mean *hates* it. Remind me to tell you what happened when she got a pink Kate Spade purse for her birthday."

Hattie made a mental note *not* to remind Lena to tell the story. At the moment, she was trying very hard to think and see only good things about Courtney. She suspected the Kate Spade story wouldn't help with that. "Pink is a neutral enough wedding color," she offered.

"I guess." Lena sighed, crossing her legs and propping her elbow on her knee.

"Hattie. Lena." Rebecca waved them over. "Come on, girls, don't just sit there like bumps on a log. We need your input." She held up a hand. "No, you're fine where you are, Velma."

Hattie was horrified.

"Fine by me. Bernardo is about to ravish Lady Priscilla on board his pirate ship." Velma grinned, pulling a thick paperback novel from her oversize knit bag. "Now that's what I call a man." She held up the picture so Hattie could see. "Don't you think?"

Hattie studied the picture. The man, who needed a haircut something fierce, was wearing a big white shirt that appeared to be missing all its buttons. And no shoes. The woman's dress seemed also to be missing fastenings as it was falling off her shoulders. But neither one of them seemed overly distressed by their clothing malfunction—or that they were stuck in a wind tunnel—they were both staring at one another. Staring in a way that made Hattie acutely uncomfortable. "Well...enjoy."

"Oh, darlin', you know I will." Velma adjusted her thick black cat-eye glasses and leaned back against the velvet couch.

At least one of us is having fun.

"Hattie," her mother called.

Hattie swung around as soon as she heard the brittle edge to her mother's voice. One of the things Hattie had always admired about her mother was her calm. It took a lot to get her mother's feathers ruffled—more than the average person. But this morning had tested her patience, and then some.

The sunny, albeit warm, Texas morning had taken a turn for the worse when she, her mother and Courtney had met the Hall women at the Hilltop Inn. Breakfast was deplorable, Rebecca's bed was uncomfortable, her room was too hot, and a slew of other complaints had been aired on the five-minute walk from the B and B to the bridal shop. Which was another bone of contention for Rebecca Hall. Why walk when it was already over eighty degrees at 9:00 a.m.? What did people in this town have against air conditioning?

"What do you think?" her mother asked now, holding out a very pink dress.

Hattie was acutely aware of the fact that every eye in the shop—well, maybe not Velma's—was on her. And while the dress was a dress and pink, there wasn't much else Hattie thought about it. The longer she stood there, the more pressure swelled up inside her. Like a teapot—on the verge of boiling. "I'm fine with whatever Courtney chooses." The words sort of erupted, making everyone blink. "Courtney?"

Courtney smiled at her. "Thank you, Hattie. Are there two?"

Thank you? And a smile. Hattie braced herself, waiting for the punchline. *Stop it, Hattie.* Old habits die hard.

"There are." Judy pulled out the other

dress. "But they are different shades of pink."

Rebecca sighed, then opened her mouth and, from the corner of her eye, Hattie saw her mother stiffen.

"I'm fine with that," Courtney cut in. "I think the lighter color would suit Hattie's complexion better anyway."

Judy nodded. "I agree."

"Well, *fine*, if that's what *you* want." Rebecca Hall was not pleased.

"Let's try them on?" Judy suggested. "I'm certain I can get Kitty Crawley to make any alterations needed. She's magic with a needle."

Hattie nodded, then felt a moment's sympathy for Kitty. It felt wrong to pull Kitty, her friend, into the path of Rebecca Hall. The woman was a—

"Let's get you two set up." Judy stepped back, arm extended, to the back of the shop. "Do you need any foundation wear? Since this is strapless?"

Hattie didn't own foundation wear. She owned practical, functional underwear. She was on the chesty side so she tended to wear snug sports bras or wide-strapped support bras—neither of which would work for a strapless dress. "I guess," she admitted.

"I'm good." Lena took the dress from Judy and disappeared behind one of the velvet curtains that separated the dressing rooms.

"You okay, Hattie?" Judy's voice was low. "You seem a little out of sorts."

"That obvious?" she asked, nodding at the dress. "All this is a little outside my comfort zone, Judy. I'll be honest. You're going to have to get me set up with whatever foundation wear you think will work because I've never shopped for such a thing." She shrugged. "It's not likely I'd wear something like that under my uniform."

Judy smiled. "I'll take care of you, Hattie, I promise."

When it was all said and done, Hattie wondered what she'd done to wrong Judy Eldridge. As far as she could remember, she'd always been kind to the woman. And yet, that hadn't stopped her from hooking Hattie into some constricting band of spandex and wire that pressed and squeezed and lifted until Hattie wondered what might happen if she took a deep breath. Would the whole thing pop off and slingshot around the room—like some skin-colored boomerang?

Would her lungs collapse or a rib break beneath the pressure?

"That corset is a perfect fit. Look at you." Judy stood back. "Why, Hattie Carmichael, you have quite the figure."

Hattie did her best not to glare at the woman. "Is it supposed to be so…so…"

"Supportive?" Judy asked, nodding.

Supportive? That was the last word Hattie would have used to describe how she was feeling.

"Arms up," Judy said, sliding the silky-smooth fabric of the bridesmaid dress over Hattie's arms and head. "I think this will be a near-perfect fit."

"Uh-huh," Hattie murmured. As perfect as the corset? Which had to be three sizes too small.

"Let's zip you up." Judy stepped behind her, zipping up the dress, then smoothing out the slight flare of the skirt. Her hands rested on Hattie's shoulders as she whispered, "Rebecca Hall isn't going to take too kindly to this. You looking as pretty as a picture, that is. She won't like anything or anyone taking the focus off Courtney."

Hattie was fairly certain none of her group, especially her mother, needed more of Mrs. Hall's vitriol. She frowned. "Then I'll change—"

"You'll do no such thing." Judy patted her. "You look absolutely lovely, Hattie. And, as you said, Courtney picked this out so let's see what she has to say first." She cocked her head to one side. "Allow me? I'm not as talented as Brooke, of course, but…" She held up some bobby pins.

Hattie sighed. "Whatever you think." *And good luck.*

Another five minutes and Judy stepped back, nodding. "Perfect. What do you think?"

Hattie refused to look at her reflection. She could only imagine how ridiculous she looked. She wasn't the girlie sort, so just *thinking* about how she looked—strapped into a corset *and* some sleeveless pink floor-length dress—had her on edge. "I'll take your word for it." She shook her head, pushing aside the bombardment of nasty Courtney images that flooded her brain. "Let's get this over with."

Judy shook her head, chuckling, and held the curtain back for Hattie.

That's when Hattie faltered. It was bad enough to have to face Rebecca and Court ney, but now… Now Billy and Forrest and her father were here.

"Hattie?" Judy whispered.

"I just…" She took a deep breath. *I'm just making a mountain out of a molehill, is what I'm doing.* Right now, she needed to be the levelheaded, clear-thinking Hattie Carmichael she was. Not quick to tears and nausea and panic as she had been a decade ago. She took another deep breath. Luckily, nothing popped off or caused any internal injury she could feel. It's not like they weren't going to see her looking ridiculous at some point during this whole wedding fiasco. The sooner this was over and done with, the better. "Nothing."

"All right." Judy patted her shoulder. "When you're ready. I'm going to check on Lena." She brushed past her and headed into the shop front, where everyone was gathered.

Whenever she was ready? Hattie was pretty sure that time would be never, so… Straightening her shoulders, she marched out to face them. There'd be teasing and laughing, to be sure. After all, this was about the most un-Hattie she'd ever looked. Ever.

"Harriet Ann Carmichael," her father whispered.

"I know." She shook her head, feeling hot. Blushing. *Not the pretty way.* "Don't—"

"Sweet girl." He was hugging her. "You just about stopped my ol' heart," he whispered, kissing her cheek. He held her by the shoulders, giving her a long look before shaking his head.

Were those tears in his eyes? All she could do was stare. Her daddy?

"Oh, Hattie." Her mother was crying. "You look…you look…"

"Like a girl." Billy's eyes narrowed and he leaned in closer, inspecting her. "That is you, isn't it?"

"Ha ha." Hattie scowled at him.

"William Bartholomew," their mother chided. "You behave. This instant."

"Hattie knows I'm teasing." Billy chuckled. "No need to bring out the middle names." He hugged her. "You look good."

She rolled her eyes.

"You do," he pushed. "Tell her, Forrest."

Hattie sighed, bracing herself for Forrest's reaction. He hadn't taken to the hair straightening so there was no way he was going to be okay with this. *I'm not okay with this.*

First, his eyes were looking more colorful than ever. Almost like a raccoon—the deep bruising almost masklike. Second, he was wearing the strangest expression she had ever seen. Like he was sucking on something sour or on the verge of sneezing. Third, he didn't say a thing. He just nodded, stiffly, before looking at his watch.

What was that? *Did she look that bad?* Her throat felt tight then. She blinked, surprised how much his reaction stung. Then again, he couldn't come right out and say she looked silly—even if she did. *If you can't say something nice, best not to say anything at all.* Her mother's advice rang in her ears. Which is exactly what Forrest was doing.

"I think you look great," Lena said, looking pretty as a picture and totally at ease in her pink bridesmaid dress. "Courtney was right, that's a good color on you. Do we have your stamp of approval, oh bride-to-be?"

Courtney. Never in her life had she thought she'd look to Courtney Hall for approval. Courtney who, with one look or smile or twitch, would likely have Hattie running back to the dressing room. Maybe she'd change her mind and let Hattie off the hook and she wouldn't have to be a bridesmaid or wear something this fancy after all.

"Yes," Courtney said, oddly excited. "You both look lovely."

Lovely? A compliment? Forrest couldn't look at her. Billy had poked and teased. Rebecca Hall was scowling at her. Sure, her parents were emotional but she was in a dress—that was enough. Was the plan to send Hattie out, looking horrid in a long pink dress she'd likely trip on, and humiliate her in front of the whole town? It wasn't hard to imagine.

Hattie started giggling, a snort slipping out. *What is wrong with me?* Oxygen deprivation due to her corset. She took a wavering breath and swallowed down another bout of laughter, her gaze colliding with Forrest's.

As soon as Hattie had walked—well stomped—out of her dressing room, Forrest had been spiraling. He'd tried to assure himself nothing unusual was happening. She was still Hattie. Who wore a warden uniform, favored caps and jeans and too-big shirts on her days off and had never cared a lick about dresses or getting her hair done or looking... Looking like *this*.

While everyone else had moved on to discussing what shoes or hairstyles or whatever other wedding *things* they could think of, Forrest was too distracted by Hattie to think about much else.

He shook his head, feeling a fool. *This* was his Hattie. Sort of. That was her laugh, all right. That snort was all Hattie. But he couldn't process the rest. Maybe it was because he'd never seen her in clothes that fit her—let alone something that made her look one hundred percent woman—that had him rattled. More likely his muddled state had everything to do with how soft and feminine and beautiful she looked. She was, too, even if she had no idea that she *was* beautiful.

Forrest wasn't sure what to do with that. His Hattie. Beautiful.

Her hair was mostly twisted up. The few curls that had escaped were shaking. From nerves. She was flushed and nervous, her giggle revealing so much.

Even though the curl dangling down her neck to rest on one bare shoulder was awful disconcerting, he did what needed doing and walked to her side. "You good?" he whispered.

She nodded but didn't look up at him.

"You sure?" he whispered.

She shook her head.

"What's wrong?" His hand rested against her back.

"Nothing," she whispered back. "Why are you here?" Her glance darted his way. "I know I look ridiculous. I don't need you making that face—" she pointed up at him "—to make me feel even worse."

Ridiculous? His brows rose. "Who said you look ridiculous?" He was already looking for Courtney—the entire group of women having migrated across the shop to inspect a wall covered in shiny things. Of course, it could have been Mrs. Hall. She'd taken one look at him and asked if he'd come into town straight from working the ranch, since it was *obvious he hadn't had time to change.* Forrest had chuckled, astounded the woman thought he'd value her opinion. But, like mother, like daughter.

"I did." She crossed her arms.

He looked at her, stunned. Had she looked at her reflection?

"See." She sighed. "You keep looking at me like I've grown a second head or…or…" She broke off, her cheeks going a darker pink.

Forrest was in a quandary. He should

speak up and tell her she looked beautiful, but he didn't say things like that—normally, he didn't *think* things like that. He didn't consider a whole lot worthy of the word. His land was beautiful. A sunset was beautiful. He swallowed hard. Hattie Carmichael was beautiful. If he kept silent, she'd go on thinking he thought she looked ridiculous. *That's not right.* "Hattie, you don't look ridiculous." He paused, working up the courage to say the rest.

She rolled her eyes. "I've known you for as long as I can remember, Forrest Briscoe, and I have never seen that expression before. Not ever. So don't you try to flatter me because you feel obligated to or you feel sorry for me."

"I don't say things I don't mean." He frowned.

"So don't start now." There was hurt in her eyes. Hurt he'd put there. "Don't say anything."

"You're out of luck, Warden." He drew in a deep breath and turned to face her. "I've got something to say. And, as always, it will be the truth."

She faced him, jaw locked, eyes narrowed, bristling from his gruff tone. "Go on."

He cleared his throat, keeping his voice low as he said, “Ever think it might be hard for me to see you…like this?” He gestured from her head to her feet.

Her anger fizzled into confusion. “No. Why?” The curl on her forehead swayed as she shook her head.

“Because…” *Say it. Spit it out.* It doesn’t have to be a big deal. It’s not a big deal. *Just say it.*

“Forrest?” Hattie waited, growing impatient.

Over Hattie’s bare shoulder, which was far too distracting, Billy and Bart Carmichael were watching them, talking softly.

“Never mind.” She sighed. “I guess I’m grateful you’re here. I can’t bring myself to look at my reflection. Seeing your reaction, I have all I need to know.”

That did it. “Hattie.” He blew out a slow breath. “You should look. At your reflection.” If she did, she’d see for herself, and he wouldn’t have to say a thing.

“I’m trying to stay positive here.” Hattie snapped.

“Hattie.” He scratched his jaw. “Just look.”

“I don’t want to.” She frowned, hands on hips.

He faced her, scowling. "Well...you should." Was it his imagination or were Bart and Billy laughing?

She stepped closer. "I already know. I'll look like a fish out of water standing up there beside Courtney and Lena, Forrest. I'm not like that...like them." She stared up at him, angry and hurt. "It'd be nice if you could be on my side here—"

Forrest rested his hands on her shoulders and, carefully, turned her around to face the full-length mirror. "I don't know what you think you're going to see, Hattie, but all I see is you." *In a way I never saw you before.*

Hattie's gaze locked with her reflection. After a few seconds, she moved closer. She lifted a hand to her hair but didn't quite touch the twist or the curls. She frowned as she gave herself a slow head-to-toe inspection.

Why wasn't she smiling? He couldn't account for her reaction. "So?"

"So?" She shook her head. "I look—"

"Beautiful," Forrest spit the word out, then took a deep breath. "You look beautiful, Hattie. You do."

"There now, it didn't hurt much, did it?" Bart murmured.

Forrest shot the older man a look.

"You do, sis." Billy nodded, his arms crossed over his chest. "I should have said that, instead of teasing."

Forrest's thumb trailed along the ridge of her bare shoulder, silky-soft and oh-so warm beneath his touch. It was a light touch, but it was enough to have his lungs empty and his heart take off.

Hattie's gaze met his, her eyes wide, and she froze.

For a second, Forrest forgot about her brother and father and the whole bridal shop. He'd never been so caught off guard. So uncertain. All tangled up inside. But, staring into Hattie's eyes, he felt all of that. And more. Specifically, the urge to turn Hattie Carmichael around and… And what? *Kiss her.* He wanted to kiss her.

"Should we leave you two, alone?" Billy chuckled, nudging Forrest.

It was just the thing to knock some sense into him. What was he thinking? Kissing Hattie? *Not gonna happen.*

Without a blink, Hattie turned back to look at her reflection again, puzzled. She moved away from them and closer to the mirror, her head cocked to one side, giving herself what appeared to be a thorough inspection.

Didn't she see how beautiful she was? Didn't she know what a treasure she was? She looked so skeptical, he wasn't sure she did. Who knew what was going on in that head of hers? He grinned, watching as she grasped the sweetheart neckline and tugged it up. But the dress fit like a glove, so it didn't move. It fit like it was made for her. He swallowed once, then again, tearing his gaze from Hattie and her dress.

"That's the thing about Hattie, she's never seen herself." Billy shook his head, his voice low. "I never understood it."

Forrest didn't think as he murmured, "She *was* bullied something fierce in high school." The words were out now; there was no way to take them back. And Hattie would be fit to be tied if she heard them.

"I remember she had a rough time of it." Bart glanced his way, frowning. "I always chalked it up to Billy being off at college—the two of them being so close and all." He crossed his arms over his chest. "Bullied, you say?"

With his jaw clenched, frowning the way

he was, Billy looked like a younger version of his father. "Who could bully Hattie?"

Your fiancée. Forrest glanced at the woman in question. "Who, indeed?"

"I wish she'd said something." Bart was upset. "How did I not know?"

I've gone and stuck my foot in it now. If he didn't smooth things over, and quick, Hattie'd be spitting nails at him all over again. He was supposed to have her back, not add to her stress. "It was a long time ago. She's come out all right. Anyone can see that." His gaze drifted back to Hattie. She'd turned around and was looking back over her shoulder, eyeing the lacing that ran the length of her dress. "She's something." Something special and funny and unique. He'd always known that. The other stuff? How beautiful she was... The *urge to kiss her* thing that was happening? That was new. And it'd caught him by surprise. Forrest couldn't remember ever being so surprised.

"That's not real," Hattie announced.

"What?" he asked, thoroughly shaken by his thoughts.

"The laces." She pointed at her reflection. "There's a zipper underneath. I wonder why they did all that? Seems like a waste of time."

Forrest chuckled.

"She's something all right." Billy grinned. "Some girls like all the—what do you call it, Hattie—froufrou and bells and whistles."

Hattie shrugged. "I guess if there was ever going to be a dress that had all that, it'd be for a wedding." She peered around until she saw the others were out of earshot before saying, "I think I'd go the Brooke and Audy route and go down to City Hall."

"That's my practical little sister." Billy winked at her. "Take note," he murmured for Forrest's ears only. "City Hall. No frills. Easy-peasy."

Forrest was speechless.

"Are you okay, Forrest? Your nose hurting?" Hattie's concern warmed him through.

He shook his head. "Fine."

Billy was laughing.

"Oh, you two." Hattie rolled her eyes. "All I'm saying is it seems like a whole lot of fuss for one day." She walked, taking each step with care, to Billy and hugged him. "But I want you to have what you want, Billy, so don't mind me."

"Oh, hold on." Glady rushed over, phone

in hand, to take pictures of Hattie and Billy. "I love seeing you two like this." She sniffed.

"Bart." Forrest waved him over. "Let me get a family picture." He took Glady's phone. "Y'all smile." He took a couple of shots.

"What about Courtney?" Rebecca Hall demanded, standing close to him. "I think it's a little thoughtless not to include her, don't you?"

Forrest glanced at her. "I'm not known for being the thoughtful sort, Mrs. Hall." He enjoyed the surprise on her face a little too much. "Courtney, you want to get in there?"

"Oh, no—"

"Yes, now, come on." Glady waved her over. "You're part of the family."

It wouldn't have been so bad if Glady hadn't tucked Courtney right in the middle, between Hattie and Billy. As much as he'd like to think he was imagining it, he saw the way Courtney leaned toward Billy. And when her hand brushed Hattie's—Courtney pulled away like she'd been burned. Hattie noticed. Of course, she did. And the smile she'd been wearing went thin and tight.

He was done. From where he stood, it looked like Hattie could use a break, too. "We good here?" Forrest asked, handing

Glady back her phone. "I was hoping to steal Hattie for a couple of hours."

Billy's brow furrowed. "Oh?"

"We have a lunch reservation." Rebecca Hall shook her head. "The least you can do is wait until after lunch."

As much as he'd like to argue, he relented. "Of course." He managed a smile for the woman before turning to Bart. "Mabel needs a hand. Planning Webb's farewell party and all." Which was a complete fabrication.

"I'm sure it won't be a problem if we turn up with one less person. You two go do what you need to do." Billy nodded. "Of course." He glanced between Forrest and Hattie. "But you two will be back for dinner?"

"I'm sorry, how is Mr. Briscoe *family*?" Rebecca Hall asked Hattie's father, at a volume so that everyone heard.

"He just…is." Bart shrugged. "You two get. We'll see you at six sharp."

Forrest nodded. "Yes, sir."

"He and Hattie are a couple, Rebecca," Glady gushed.

"Let's get you set up with a fitting appointment." Judy grabbed a black book from the counter and followed Hattie to the dressing room.

"I'm glad you're coming," Hattie said, just loud enough for Forrest to hear. "There's no way I'm getting out of this contraption without breaking a rib or something."

Judy Eldridge was still laughing when they disappeared behind the fancy dressing room curtain.

"How are you holding up?" Bart asked, drawing his attention. "With Webb leaving?"

"I'm trying." Which was true. "Hattie's been a rock." Also true. "But I know sending him off Monday..." He didn't finish that.

"He's a good boy, Forrest." Bart clapped him on the shoulder. "I know he's a little accident-prone but he'll sort himself out in no time. I bet he'll make quite a fine soldier."

Forrest kept his thoughts and reservations to himself. "I appreciate that. You know you're all invited. You, Glady and Billy, I mean." He shot Bart a pointed look.

"Ah, well, I'll see what I can do." He chuckled. "Might not get Billy without Courtney, though."

Forrest hesitated long enough to sweep their surroundings. No one nearby, no one watching or listening. "What do you think of her? Courtney, I mean?"

"She and Billy are quite the couple." Bart

seemed to mull over the question. “I don’t rightly know about her yet. It’s still early on but, from what I have seen, I think she’s a good girl.” He glanced at Forrest, his brows dipping. “Why?”

As much as he wanted to tip off the senior Carmichael, he held his peace. No one else had seen the little exchange while he was taking pictures and he couldn’t think of a way to casually introduce Courtney Hall being Hattie’s high school bully into conversation. “No reason.”

Hattie came out not long after, wearing an oversize untucked button-down shirt, jeans and boots. She had her hair twisted up and clipped back—the whole sloppy bun hanging at an angle on the back of her head. Not that she noticed or cared. But Forrest was flummoxed when seeing Hattie in her normal every day off-duty attire didn’t diffuse the heightened awareness to her. He was still very aware of the soft curls that’d slipped free to hang around her neck and that the stripe of green in her shirt had her eyes reflecting the color, and he didn’t know what was happening to him. But deep down—in his chest—he felt more at ease with her at his side. He cleared his throat, refusing to ponder over this new, unsettling, train of thought. "You ready?"

"I am." Hattie nodded. "I'll see you tomorrow for the fitting, Judy." She blew her father a kiss. "See you later, Daddy."

"Tell Mabel to let me know if she needs anything," Glady offered.

"Will do." He held the door open for Hattie, then followed her outside. "You survived."

She nodded, tucking her curls behind her ears. "It wasn't easy—what with that whole corset thing."

Forrest had to laugh. "Now that you're free, what do you want to do with the rest of your afternoon?" he asked, opening the passenger door for her.

"I thought..." She stared at him, whispering, "Forrest Briscoe, did you just lie to my parents and my brother to get me out of there?"

He shrugged. "I guess I did."

She gave him a quick hug. "My hero." She climbed up into the truck cab. "I'll feel guilty if we don't go see Mabel, Forrest."

"I figured." He shut the door and walked around the hood of the truck to the driver's door. "We can have lunch at the ranch and then what?" He started the ignition.

"Hmm, well, if I've got you for the afternoon, I could use some help picking out the trim boards for my kitchen." She turned, waiting for his answer.

"A visit to Old Town Hardware and Appliances?"

"Yes, sir." She was noticeably excited. "I've been itching to get this done. And Rusty said he thought they had some trim board that was just right for me."

Rusty. Good ol' Rusty. Forrest didn't know what it was, exactly, that bothered him about the whole Rusty-Hattie thing. Not that there was a thing. Rusty had gone out to measure for cabinets is all. Nothing else. And if there was something else, he'd know when he saw the two of them together. "Lunch, then hardware, then home repairs."

"What about work?" she asked. "I didn't think a foreman could take a day off."

"This helps." He pointed at his face. "Audy and Uncle Felix and Webb have all stepped up. But I'll check in while we're there."

She nodded, appeased. "As long as you're sure I'm not getting in the way."

He shook his head. "You're not." He liked

it when she came to the ranch. Uncle Felix thought she hung the moon and she got on with Webb and Beau—well, everyone. Hattie was one of those rare individuals everyone liked. His thoughts shifted to earlier and how quickly Courtney Hall had jerked her hand back from Hattie. Well, almost everyone. But not counting Courtney Hall as a friend didn't seem too great a loss to Forrest. The only person losing out there was Courtney Hall.

"Forrest?" Hattie asked once they were headed for the ranch. "Did I… Did I really look pretty? In the dress?"

He glanced her way, taking note of her flushed cheeks and the way her hands were clasped in her lap. "No, Hattie. You didn't look pretty." He nudged her. "You looked beautiful."

"Forrest Briscoe, I'm not used to all this flattery." She smiled at him. "Keep it up and I'll start to get a big head."

"Right." He chuckled. Hattie? Vain? No way. "I wasn't flattering you, either. I was just telling the truth." And even though Hattie laughed and brushed his words aside,

Forrest was forced to consider another truth. If he wasn't careful, before long, he wouldn't be faking things.

CHAPTER SEVEN

"I DON'T KNOW." Hattie rested her elbows on the countertop, watching Mabel slice into a delicious-looking pie. "I feel…like I should give her a chance." Courtney hadn't done or said anything mean or acted anything but civil—if not cordial—since she'd arrived in Garrison.

"Well, that's good. I guess?" Mabel served up a piece of pie on a white china plate. "It's not like she hadn't given you plenty of reason to be suspicious."

Hattie didn't argue. Yes, her past with Courtney was nothing but bad, but, so far, she'd seemed like a normal human being. "Her mother, though… Well, I almost feel sorry for Courtney."

Mabel shook her head. "You know you're too kind, don't you?" Mabel asked. "I'm not telling you to hold on to your high school years, but I'm saying it's okay for you to remain cautious."

Hattie took the plate. “Thank you.”

“Now, on to the important stuff. How was the dress?” Mabel asked, carrying her pie to the table and pulling out a chair to sit. “What color was it? What design? Did it have a sweetheart neckline?”

Hattie sat and scooped up a bite of pie. “Pink. Sleeveless. Long?”

“Okay.” Mabel was laughing. “And how did it look? How did you feel?”

She shrugged. “Like a little girl playing dress-up. In a corset.” She wrinkled her nose. “I was all tucked in and pushed up and worried I’d pop a lung.”

Mabel was laughing harder now.

“Forrest acted weird over it at first.” Hattie appreciated how supportive he’d been, but it’d been a struggle for him to compliment her. No matter what he’d said about her being beautiful, she knew she looked ridiculous. She knew the dress didn’t suit her. She knew he’d only said it because her father and brother had said it—and he was a good friend. But for reasons she couldn’t quite pinpoint, it bothered her that he had struggled so much.

“Like how?” Mabel frowned.

“He just sort of clammed up and looked

like…he was sucking on a lemon drop or something. All pinched up and strained." She shrugged. "It could have been worse. He could have out and out laughed at me."

"Sucking on a lemon drop?" Mabel repeated.

"He said it was hard for him to see me that way." Which only made the whole thing more awkward.

"He said that?" Mabel's eyebrows rose.

She nodded. "It's like he doesn't know I'm a girl."

"Do you want him to see you as a girl?" Mabel crossed her arms over her chest.

"I am. Aren't I?" She frowned. "I guess I'd never thought about it before, but it's weird, isn't it? That it's hard for him to see me in a dress?"

Mabel was giving her the oddest look.

"What?" Hattie stopped eating her pie. "What does that look mean?"

"To be fair, Hattie, you don't wear dresses very often—or ever." Mabel nodded at her. "You're more the jeans and T-shirt sort, is all."

"And that makes me less of a…a girl?" Hattie crossed her arms over her chest.

"No, Hattie, no, of course not." Mabel

sighed. "Don't get upset. I'm not siding with him—at all. I bet he was just…surprised to see you all decked out. I mean, he got all in a dither over your hair being straight."

He'd mentioned the hair thing to Mabel? Next time Brooke asked to test some new styling something out on her curls, Hattie would have to think long and hard about it.

"I think he's used to you being his friend, not so much a…a girl," Mabel added.

"Well, that's just about as ridiculous a thing as I've ever heard." Hattie scooped up a bite of pie. "I'm the same Hattie, whether I'm all strapped into a corset, wearing my uniform or my favorite jeans. I'm…me. I don't get why it's such a big deal."

Until now, she hadn't realized how much Forrest's attitude bothered her. "Can't he just look at me and see me and like me without getting all caught up in the window dressing?"

"He, who?" Forrest stood in the doorway to the kitchen, a deep frown creasing his forehead. "Who are we talking about?"

Hattie shook her head. "Nothing."

"It doesn't look like nothing." He walked over to the table, his gaze falling on her plate. "Hey, hey, now. No one told me there was pie."

"I didn't send out a pie memo, Forrest." Mabel chuckled. "It's over there. Help yourself." She pointed to the glass cake stand. "Don't make a mess."

He shot her a look.

"Don't glare at me like that. I don't know how you manage it but you get crumbs and pie filling all over the place." Her eyebrows rose. "All over. And I get to clean it up."

Forrest was pretty bruised, but Hattie thought she could detect a hint of red on his cheeks.

Hattie chuckled. "It's delicious. Peach pie."

"Uncle Felix came home with a basket from a roadside vendor, so we have jam and pie and muffins and there's enough for at least one more pie." Mabel smiled. "Uncle Felix believes buying in bulk makes it cheaper and that's fine when it's paper towels or canned goods but when it's fresh fruit—" she shrugged "—you have to do something with it before it goes bad."

"Pie works." Forrest carried the pie plate to the table. "You should make more."

Hattie and Mabel stopped eating.

"What?" he asked, taking his usual spot at the head of the table.

"Forrest, that's the whole pie." Mabel pointed at the pie with her fork.

"No, it's not." He shook his head, using his fork to point at their plates. "It's a whole pie—minus two pieces." He glanced between them. "Who is the 'he' you two are not talking about?"

"Look at you, being all nosy." Mabel stood. "I forgot the whipped cream." She hurried to the refrigerator. "Who do you think?"

"I don't know." He stabbed the pie, his brow still creased. "If I had to guess, I'd say Rusty Woodard?"

"Rusty?" Hattie was beyond confused now.

Mabel carried the can of whipped cream back to the table, looking as confused as Hattie felt. "What makes you say that?"

"Nothing." He gazed Hattie's way, leaning back so Mabel could put a huge dollop on top of his pie. "Thank you. What have you two been up to?"

"Talking about the rodeo tomorrow night—Beau's riding. Are you and Rusty?" Mabel asked, adding whipped cream to both Hattie's pie and her own.

"Mhm." He scooped up another massive bite.

Hattie wasn't sure what to make of that sound. Forrest was… Out of sorts. He wasn't exactly making the sucking on a lemon drop face, but it was close. She took a big bite of pie and shot a pointed look at Mabel, nodding at Forrest and mimicking his expression.

"What's that face about?" Forrest asked, his fork paused midway between his plate and his mouth.

"Hattie was telling me how much you like the bridesmaid dress." Mabel was trying not to laugh.

"Mhm." Forrest shoved a huge bite of pie into his mouth.

Hattie finished her pie and put her fork on her plate.

"And she said Courtney seems to have changed?" Mabel added another dollop of cream on top. "Actually, I think Hattie said something about feeling for Courtney, now that she's met her mom."

Forrest started coughing.

At first, Hattie thought he was joking, but

then she realized he was turning an alarming shade of red and hopped up from her chair. "Forrest?"

"Water." Mabel jumped up, too, sprinting across the kitchen to the sink.

"Are you okay?" Hattie asked, patting on his back.

Forrest held up one finger, a barely audible, "I'm fine," slipping out between coughs.

"Here." Mabel shoved a glass of water in front of him.

Forrest took a long sip, swallowed and took another long sip. When the glass was empty, he turned to Hattie, "You feel for her?" He shook his head. "For Courtney?"

Hattie sat in the chair beside him. "You saw how it was today." She grabbed his fork and started eating out of the pie plate Forrest had claimed. "Can you imagine growing up with all that…negativity?"

He shook his head. "I'd like to think that if I had a mother like Rebecca Hall, I'd go out of my way to do and say the exact opposite."

"Or not. I guess I… It's been eye-opening, is all." Hattie shrugged and took another bite of the cinnamon-peachy goodness. She hadn't eaten breakfast this morning—she'd been too nervous. Now that the whole fitting thing was over, her hunger kicked in full force. She scooped up another bite, making sure there was plenty of whipped cream on it.

Mabel returned to her seat, using her fork to point at Hattie. "I told her she's too big-hearted."

"That's a good thing." Forrest reached across the table for Hattie's fork. "That shouldn't change. I'd say be cautious is all. I don't know why but she's got my guard up."

"Maybe you're just being superprotective of Hattie?" Mabel offered up.

He *had* gone out of his way to be there for her. Hattie smiled at him, took the fork from him and scooped up another bite.

Forrest shrugged, frowning when he took in the state of the pie. "Are we sharing?"

Hattie swallowed her especially large bite of pie. "I didn't have breakfast." She sighed. "I didn't realize how hungry I was. Plus, I can't remember the last time I had peach pie." She wasn't about to apologize. "Mabel, this is heaven. I agree with Forrest on this one—you should make another one."

"But make sure it's when Hattie's not around next time, okay?" Forrest said, pushing the pie in front of Hattie.

Hattie grinned, swallowed the last bite and pushed the pie back. “I’m done.”

He peered into the almost-empty pie pan. “Uh-huh.”

Hattie started laughing then, a snort slipping out.

He leaned forward. “Hold up.” He chuckled, reaching over to wipe her cheek. “How you got whipped cream up by your ear, I’ll never know.”

His fingertips were calloused and rough from working with his hands. Hattie considered it a badge of honor—strength and hard work and grit. That was Forrest, to a T. But she’d seen those hands be gentle when needed. Untwining a deer’s leg from a barbed wire fence. Holding baby Joy. *Wiping whipped cream from my face.*

His eyes seemed especially blue at the moment. Maybe it was because of how bruised his face was or the light was hitting them just right. Whatever the reason, his steady blue gaze seemed to be looking for something. Normally, she knew what Forrest was going to say before it came out of his mouth. But today… Well Forrest wasn’t acting right.

“Are you going with Hattie to dinner?” Mabel’s voice cut through Hattie’s musings.

"You don't have to." Hattie patted his arm. "I know your time with Webb is short and—"

"Webb's going out," Forrest cut in, his gaze falling away.

"Still." Hattie shrugged. "Mabel might need your help for this weekend. Or Uncle Felix. Or Beau."

"You trying to get rid of me?" He was frowning again.

"No." She frowned right back. "But I… I know you have better things to do with your time than follow me around—"

"Doc Johnson told me to take it easy, remember?" He sat back in his chair and pointed at his face. "Besides, your father invited me to dinner and your mother said she was making au gratin potatoes just for me. And oatmeal raisin sheet cake with raisin cream cheese icing. Since you ate all the pie…"

"Fine." Hattie sighed and sat back in her chair, eyeing him. "If you're all right with it, I'll go get my trim boards another time?" She could use some time with Mabel here on the ranch. It was one of the few places she'd always felt at ease—something she desperately needed.

He nodded, crossing his arms over his chest. "If you're sure?"

"I'm sure. I'm sure there are things I'm keeping you from doing here, too." She sighed.

"Hattie." He was frowning again. "Anyone ever tell you you're stubborn?"

"Just about everyone." Hattie laughed. "A time or two."

"One of your many charms." Mabel smiled. "What about your fitting in the morning? I'm dying to see the dress. I know Brooke is, too. We could go get breakfast afterward?"

"I don't know about breakfast." She frowned. Between her mother and Courtney, the wedding to-do list kept on growing. "I think Rebecca had something lined up. But y'all are welcome to come to the fitting. As long as you don't laugh."

"Why on earth would we laugh?" Mabel put her elbows on the table and rested her chin in her hands. "Hattie, I hate to break it to you, but Brooke and I both know you're pretty—*and* a girl."

Forrest looked nervous. "What's that supposed to mean?"

"Hattie might have mentioned your reaction to the dress." Mabel's eyebrows rose.

"That I said she was beautiful?" Forrest almost snapped.

"I didn't get that far." Hattie wasn't sure what to make of his tone. Or his scowl.

"You did?" Mabel pushed off the counter, staring wide-eyed at her brother. "*You* said *beautiful*?"

"I…did." Forrest grunted and stood. "I should go make sure Webb's…well, being careful." He left the kitchen.

"See what I mean?" Hattie asked. "He's acting all…like that." She pointed after him. "You mention the dress and he gets all… like that."

Mabel kept right on smiling. "Hattie, could it be that Forrest liked seeing you in that dress? Like, a lot? And, maybe, he likes you? A lot?"

Hattie stared at one of her oldest, dearest friends in shock. Then, she burst out laughing. It was a good thing she and Forrest had decided not to mention the whole pretend dating thing. What would Mabel have thought about that? "Oh, Mabel." She kept right on laughing. Where in the world did Mabel get such a…an outrageous notion?

FORREST SHAVED, PUT on fresh-starched jeans, and one of his rodeo pearl snap button-down shirts before heading into the kitchen to meet up with Hattie. He wasn't out to impress anyone, but he didn't exactly want to be in the line of fire, either. "You ready?" he asked, smiling when he saw the two of them were still at the table. Only now, Mabel had her legal pad out and was flipping through the pages. *How many pages?* He was pretty sure he didn't want to know.

Hattie did a double take. "What are you wearing?" She stood. "You can't go like that, when I look like this." She smoothed a hand over her curls. "There's no time for me to get home and change."

Forrest didn't see a thing wrong with the way she looked. She was all wild curls and too-big clothes—as Hattie should be.

"You can borrow something of mine." Mabel offered.

"Do you own something that isn't a dress?" Hattie asked, concerned.

"Not really." Mabel stood. "But I'm sure I can find one that doesn't have too many ruffles or lace." At the look on Hattie's face, she added, "I'm teasing, Hattie. We will find something. Come on."

Forrest was still smiling when he walked out into the Great Room.

"Was that Hattie I saw Mabel dragging down the hall?" Uncle Felix asked, coming in through the back door. "Been a while since she stopped by for a visit."

Forrest nodded.

"She staying for dinner?" Uncle Felix asked. "I'll grill something, just for her. I know she's partial to ribs—"

"I see how it is. Hattie gets ribs?" Forrest grinned.

"Hattie is special." Uncle Felix brushed aside Forrest's teasing. "I'll get the grill going—"

"We can't." Forrest stopped him before he could get the large barrel grill going. "She's got some family thing for Billy's wedding."

Uncle Felix gave him a once-over. "And you're going, too?" He sighed. "Mabel might have mentioned a little something about this fiancée of his. Is she as bad as she sounds?"

Forrest scratched his jaw. "I don't know. I get the feeling she's hiding something, Uncle Felix. She's cagey—barely looking at Hattie. I can't figure it out." If he could, he'd know what to expect. "I can't help but feel like the other shoe is going to drop. I don't want Hattie getting hurt."

"What are you thinking?" Uncle Felix looked concerned. "I've no problem putting this highfalutin miss in her place, now, son—you just say the word. I don't take kindly to meanness."

Forrest didn't remind his uncle about the long-standing feud with the Crawley family that'd lasted for the better part of Forrest's life. If Mabel and Jensen weren't getting married, he suspected it'd still be going on—eating them all up with *meanness*. Now the only feuding between the Briscoes and Crawleys was centered around Barbara Eldridge. Both Uncle Felix and Dwight Crawley had set their caps for the woman but, so far, they'd each been properly courting the woman without incident. Forrest hoped it'd stay that way.

"I appreciate that," Forrest said. "I'll tell you, the mother is a piece of work." He shook his head. "I don't know how the younger sister turned out so…so normal." He hadn't exchanged a single word with Courtney's sister, but she didn't have the same overly stiff posture or tight-lipped expression. She was all smiles and open conversation—including Hattie, instead of snubbing her.

"Normal, huh?" Uncle Felix shook his head. "Well, I'm glad you've got her back. Our Hattie's too gentle a soul to fend off a den of lions on her own."

Forrest didn't disagree. "Webb get the order placed?" He almost hated asking but it needed doing. And since his uncle and brothers had chased him out of the barn to rest, he could only hope what needed doing was getting done. Like ordering feed, mineral and salt blocks, and getting some of the hay stacked into the barn for the leaner winter months.

"The order got placed. The hay..." Uncle Felix shrugged. "Webb had a little trouble with the tractor."

Forrest ran a hand over his face. "Damages?"

"To the tractor, the hay or Webb?" Uncle Felix asked.

Forrest stared at his uncle. "What now?"

Uncle Felix chuckled. "Audy's already fixing the fence, Forrest. It's all fine. I was funnin' you a little is all."

"Fixing the fence?" Forrest repeated, not in the least bit amused.

"Well, now, Webb might have backed up a little more than he needed." He was still chuckling. "That boy's never been too good at gauging distances."

Before Forrest could respond to that, Mabel came in the room and said, "Hattie's ready." Once she reached his side, she whispered, "Hattie is wearing a dress, so don't make your prune-y face thing or I'll be forced to kick you."

Forrest sucked in a deep breath and turned. Not all dresses were like the one Hattie'd been wearing earlier. This would be different. She was wearing one of Mabel's dresses so it wouldn't twist up his insides when he looked at her, surely. "Where is she?"

"She's still fiddling with the belt." Mabel shook her head. "After all this time, it still surprises me that she doesn't get how pretty she is. She is, too, you know it." She glanced up at him. "And when you get back, we're going to talk about this Rusty thing."

"What Rusty thing?" Uncle Felix asked.

Mabel leaned forward around Forrest to whisper, "Hattie and Rusty—"

"Rusty? Rusty Woodard?" Uncle Felix's brows shot up. "You don't say."

Forrest's mood darkened. "There is no Rusty and Hattie." He tried not to snap. "She said so." And he was going to take her at her word. She'd even laughed when he'd mentioned it. Still, he'd been mighty relieved when she canceled their trip back into town. Like it or not, he was afraid of what he'd see between Rusty and Hattie. He wanted to believe Hattie, he did, but he'd never heard of Rusty making house calls before and…

Uncle Felix and Mabel were both staring at him.

"What's eating you?" Uncle Felix asked.

"Nothing," Forrest barked.

"Uh-huh." Uncle Felix kept right on staring.

"I don't get why this is necessary." Hattie came into the room, fiddling with the braided rope belt around her waist. "I mean, do I have to wear it?"

Forrest swallowed. This was easier. Somewhat. Yes, she was feminine. Soft. Pretty… No, *more* than pretty. But he wasn't blindsided this time. His heart might be a little fast and his chest might feel a little heavy, but it was… Fine. Sort of. He swallowed again. Not exactly what he was hoping for.

"Yes." Mabel stepped forward and adjusted the belt. “You have a waist, Hattie. A teeny-tiny waist. Technically, you have an hourglass figure.”

Hattie’s look of concern had Forrest smiling. She really had no idea. *None*. Here she stood, pretty as a picture, with no awareness. The thing was, it was sort of a huge revelation for him, too. He’d always known Hattie was pretty—but it’d been like knowing the sky was blue or grass was green. He’d sort of taken it for granted. But now he was seeing things differently.

“It’s not as bad as the corset.” But Hattie didn’t look happy as she smoothed her hands over the chambray shirt dress she’d borrowed. It hung to her knees, giving a slight glimpse of creamy skin and muscled calves that disappeared into her black leather cowboy boots.

“Hattie, darlin’.” Uncle Felix chuckled. “I don’t know much about corsets but I do know a pretty woman when I see one. And I see one.”

Hattie’s rolled her eyes, but her cheeks turned pink and the ghost of a smile touched her lips.

It felt like a fifty-pound sack of feed

landed on Forrest's chest and knocked the air out of his lungs.

"See." Mabel hugged her. "I told you."

Hattie shrugged, her cheeks going red now. With a deep breath, she met his gaze. "Go on."

"You look nice. Ready?" His tone calm and steady even though his heart was pounding away and he was struggling for breath.

She blinked, her hazel green eyes flitting across his face before she sighed. "Let's go, then." She turned and headed for the door.

Mabel elbowed him, hard, in the side. "That's all you're going to say? She's in knots over tonight," she hissed. "Forrest Briscoe..." She broke off with a little groan and shook her head.

As they drove into town, Forrest was still mulling over what to say. If Hattie was worried about tonight, he should say something, shouldn't he? What, he had no idea. "Hattie," he started. Out of the corner of his eyes he saw her playing with the rope belt. "About tonight." He cleared his throat, feeling a fool. She'd gone completely still now. "Don't you let those Hall women get to you. You hold your head high and be proud of who you are. Your work. Your family. Your friends." He was carrying on too much now. “Like me.” He grinned, beyond uncomfortable. “I think you look beautiful—I think you are beautiful.” He hadn’t meant to blurt the last bit out, but it was out there now.

“I think you do just fine with your words, Forrest.” She glanced his way. “And I think you’re just about the best friend, ever.” She swallowed. “I admit I’m worrying a bit, but it’s not about Courtney, it’s about…us.” She turned to look at him. “Tonight. What do we do? How do we act?”

He was smiling then. “Like we always do.”

“So we…” She waved a finger between them. “We don’t have to be like them? Courtney and Billy. All affectionate?”

He looked at her then, understanding. While the idea of being affectionate with Hattie held significant appeal, he figured it was the wrong way to go. “Probably best not to do anything that can’t be undone… When this is all over.” His heart raced like he was running a marathon.

“Right.” She nodded. “Good point.”

The rest of the ride was completely silent, which did nothing to help his heart rate slow. By the time they pulled in front of the Carmichael house, he had to remind himself that he was here for Hattie. He couldn't drop her off and leave—no matter how tempting the idea. He parked, went around and opened the passenger truck, offering her his hand to step down. But, once she was on the sidewalk, her hand tightened on his. He stared down at their joined hands. His heart was still clipping along, but his anxiety seemed to melt away.

"How's your face?" she asked, their hands swinging.

"It's there." He shrugged. "Better, I guess. Good thing I'm just as hardheaded as you are."

"Isn't that the truth?" She squeezed his hand.

He didn't miss her deep breath when they reached the front door or how her hold tightened on his, but he waited, without comment, until she opened the door and the conversation and music trickled out to meet them.

"You're here." Mrs. Carmichael hugged Hattie close.

Once Hattie let go of him, Forrest's hand felt empty.

"What can I do, Momma?" Hattie asked.

"First, let me look at you." Glady held Hattie by the shoulders. "Don't you look all dressed up." Her gaze bounced his way. "The both of you."

"It's not every day her brother's getting married." Billy came into the kitchen, sneaking up behind Hattie to grab her around the waist and spin her around.

"Billy!" Hattie squealed, laughing.

Billy set her down. "What's with the dress?" One eyebrow cocked up.

"It's Mabel's." Hattie shrugged, fiddling with the belt. "What's wrong with it?"

"Nothing is wrong with it." Billy shook his head. "I'm used to you in jeans is all."

I know the feeling.

"Forrest. Hattie." Courtney joined them in the kitchen, her arm sliding around Billy's waist. "You look nice, Hattie."

"Thank you." Hattie managed to smile. "You do, too...Courtney."

Forrest saw the tightening of Courtney's jaw when Hattie said her name but he couldn't make sense of it. Why did she act like she had some axe to grind with Hattie? She'd been the one with the axe.

"All right." Glady opened the oven. "Let's get everything to the table, shall we?"

It took a good five minutes to get everyone gathered around the barely used formal dining room.

"It looks so nice." Hattie surveyed the table wide-eyed.

Forrest noticed, too. Glady and Bart were casual folk—eating around the kitchen table and only pulling out their fancy china for holidays. But the china was out. Fresh flowers were in one of Glady's grandmother's pitchers, and there was even soft music playing in the background. "It does."

"I finally got to break out the table leaves," Bart said, sitting at the head of the table. "And Glady went and outdid herself with flowers and...all the trimmings." He winked at his wife.

Glady's strained expression said it all.

"It seems a shame you have such a nice dining room and never use it." Rebecca Hall said, glancing around the room. "A kitchen table's fine for breakfast, I suppose. Maybe even a light lunch. But it's all very...informal."

"I've always appreciated that fact, too." Forrest had to speak up. "I know you'll always make room for me—treat me like one of the family."

Glady beamed at him. Hattie smiled up at him with a grateful expression.

"Well, hello there, cowboy." Aunt Velma peered over her thick black-framed glasses. "Who are you and where did you come from?"

"That's Forrest, Aunt Velma," Lena said, laughing. "He was at the fitting earlier? Remember?"

"I was reading my book." Aunt Velma shrugged. "It's nice to meet you, Forrest. Why am I sitting all the way down here when I could be sitting next to him?"

Forrest wasn't sure how to react.

"Aunt Velma," Courtney snapped, horrified.

"What?" Aunt Velma peered around Lena and Billy at Courtney. "I might be old, but I still have eyes."

All that mattered was Hattie, and she was laughing. She was trying to be discreet about it, holding her napkin over her face, but a snort slipped loose and Forrest was done for. He and Billy started laughing then, the tension easing from the room. Maybe, just maybe, tonight wouldn't be so bad. With any luck Aunt Velma would keep things interesting and there'd be more laughter than snide comments. He glanced at Hattie, her green eyes meeting his. She rolled her eyes, still giggling—and snorting. Tonight was going to be just fine.

CHAPTER EIGHT

HATTIE CARRIED THE last of the dirty dishes into the kitchen, exhausted—but relieved that the evening had gone so well. Forrest's sarcasm might not always go over so well at home, but it had been the only thing stopping Rebecca Hall from commandeering the dinner with her negativity. For every pointed comment the woman made, Forrest managed to find just the right words to deflect it. Considering how many pointed comments the woman had made, she suspected poor Forrest had to be exhausted, too.

"Put on some, coffee, will you?" her mother asked as soon as she came into the kitchen.

"You okay, Momma?" She slid her arms around her mother and gave her a solid hug. "It was all delicious—and so pretty."

"It's nice of you to say so, darlin'." Her mother sighed. "I'm not sure I have it in my power to please her."

Hattie knew exactly who *her* was. "Courtney and Billy are happy, and they are the ones that matter." She hugged her again.

"How did I get so lucky?" She pushed the hair from Hattie's shoulder. "A sweet and thoughtful daughter, cheering me up when I need it most."

"Like mother, like daughter." Forrest came in. "Thought I could lend a hand?" His hand was warm against the base of her back. Warm and steadying.

"Oh, you two." Her mother smiled. "It makes me happy to see you two together." With a pat on the arm, her mother started pulling dessert plates from the cabinet.

"Glady?" It was Rebecca. "Glady, can you come here for a second?"

Her mother frowned. "Can you two—"

"Go on, Momma." Hattie smiled. "Forrest and I can take care of it." Once her mother had disappeared through the kitchen door, she looked at Forrest. "I know what you're thinking."

"That Mrs. Hall has two working legs and she could get up and walk in here, instead of sitting there expecting your mother to wait on her?"

"Well, maybe not exactly what you're

thinking." She grabbed his hand and tugged him over to the counter. "If you can take these out." She loaded him up with dessert plates. "I'll get silverware and the coffee stuff on a tray."

"I'll be back." He was glaring.

"Smile, Forrest," she urged. "Please."

The corner of his mouth kicked up as he backed out the swinging kitchen door.

Hattie stood there, warmth settling into her cheeks. And her chest. Forrest was… Well, he'd been amazing tonight. Without him at her side? Hattie couldn't picture it. Chances were, she wouldn't be doing so hot.

Hattie had plans to tell him that when the door opened and Courtney walked in. "Aunt Velma grabbed a hold of Forrest," Courtney said.

Hattie had to smile. *Poor Forrest.*

"I know you and I weren't really close back in high school, but I am glad you've… You seem happy." Courtney's smile was small. "Like you've really come into your own."

"Oh." Weren't really close? That's one way of putting it. Did Courtney really not remember? As much as she wanted to ask, she knew better. Instead, she counted out silverware onto the serving tray.

"Forrest is a nice guy," Courtney added.

Hattie nodded. "He's a good man."

"Have y'all been serious long?" Courtney leaned against the counter, while Hattie poured cream into the little porcelain pitcher from her mother's coffee service.

Hattie glanced her way. Courtney had one of those faces. Her expression was mostly blank, but there was just a touch of something else. She looked flushed. And she was fanning herself. "Are you feeling okay?"

Courtney pushed off the counter. "Of course. I'm fine." But she went back to leaning against the counter.

"Are you sure?" Hattie stopped counting silverware.

Courtney nodded. "Tired, I guess."

Considering how exhausted Hattie was after a few hours with Rebecca Hall, Courtney had every right to be tired. But Hattie couldn't shake the feeling that Courtney was holding something back. "Is there anything I can do? To help out with wedding plans?" The words were out before she thought about it.

"Oh, well, my mom seems to have everything under control, so that's not really necessary..." Courtney's voice faded.

"No, of course," Hattie murmured, feeling like a fool for offering. She took a steadying breath, her heart beating as she scanned the tray. Sugar. Cream. Cups. Silverware. Coffee? She glanced at the pot. Still brewing. "I think I've got things covered in here."

"Right." Courtney pushed off the counter. "I'm sure you do." But she stood there, staring at Hattie—almost like she was waiting for something.

Hattie wished she could translate what the tone and the odd "blank but not blank" expression all meant. It meant something; she knew it did. For a second, Hattie braced herself—waiting for the Queen of Mean to surface.

"But I appreciate the offer. Of help, with the wedding, I mean." Courtney opened her mouth, then closed it.

"Courtney Elizabeth," Rebecca called. "Bring me my purse."

"Where's the coffee?" Aunt Velma bellowed.

Courtney sniffed, then pulled Hattie into a tight hug. "I... I..." She released her suddenly and hurried out of the kitchen.

What had just happened? Hattie wasn't sure. Courtney had hugged her, but Hattie had no idea *why*. She made sure she had enough of everything, then picked up the tray and backed out of the kitchen and into the dining room, moving slowly. "Coming through," she said, turning and facing the room. "I'll get the coffee next—I don't have enough arms."

"I'll get it." Forrest winked at her—then winced—before heading into the kitchen.

"If I was thirty years younger, I'd fight you for him," Velma Hill said.

"Velma," Rebecca's tone was all condescension and impatience. "Stop making a spectacle of yourself."

"At my age, what else have I got to do?" Velma chuckled, not in the least discouraged by her sister.

But Hattie was feeling queasy on Velma's behalf. She knew that tone. It haunted her dreams. The Queen of Mean was here, but it wasn't Courtney. Not this time. Rebecca Hall sat across her mother's carefully set dining table, shooting daggers at her sister. It didn't matter that everyone else was amused—Rebecca was not. It was all so familiar and horrible that there was the distinct possibility that she'd throw up, here and now. *No, no, keep it together, Hattie.* She drew in a deep breath. This had nothing to do with her, so it shouldn't get to her. Not in the least.

But Forrest's arm slid, warm and heavy, around her waist. "Hattie?" He stared down at her, his gaze sweeping over her face to linger on her mouth. His brow furrowed. "You okay?"

Was she? At the moment, she wasn't so sure. Not because of Courtney or Velma or Rebecca, but because of Forrest. She was oddly aware of the weight of his arm around her waist and the press of his fingers along her side. Even more disconcerting was the alarming tingle that raced the length of her spine and caused a full body shudder. She should answer—say something—but his eyes were so blue and his touch was so warm that no words came out. She just stood there, oddly caught up in the closeness of Forrest.

"Have a seat." Forrest set the coffeepot on the table and pulled her chair out. "I can pour coffee. No matter what Mabel says, I don't always make a mess." He grinned.

Hattie managed a smile. "I guess we'll see." She sat, the place where his arm and hand had rested against her tingling. Tingles. From Forrest. Hattie wasn't a *tingle* sort of girl. Not ever. Even if she was, Forrest shouldn't be the one giving them to her. She swallowed, her throat tight.

"Ouch." Forrest sighed. "Here I thought you believed in me."

"I do." Hattie shrugged. "On just about everything. Maybe not messes, but everything else."

Forrest chuckled, carefully filling her cup of coffee. "See?"

Hattie rolled her eyes.

"How about you fill up my cup, cowboy?" Velma asked, holding out her cup. "I don't care if you make a mess."

Forrest obliged, chuckling the whole time—which made Hattie chuckle, too.

"I'm glad you're happy, Hattie," Billy murmured. "I like seeing you like this."

Like what? Was she acting differently? Was Forrest? She glanced his way.

"As far as I'm concerned, it wouldn't be right if it was anybody but Forrest." Her father clapped Forrest on the shoulder. "You two fit—there's no doubt about it." Her father's eyes searched her. "I was a little worried, to be honest. You work all the time—and it's good that you love your job—

but your mother and I don't want you going through life alone. I mean, without someone to share it with." Her father sighed, smiling broadly. "But now...well, I'm not worried anymore. My boy and my girl are happy and loved. I don't think a parent could ask for more." He sat at the head of the table. "What about you, Glady?"

Hattie couldn't remember the last time her father had looked so happy. Or her mother.

Forrest took his seat beside Hattie, leaning toward her and draping his arm along the back of her chair.

"No." Her mother shook her head. "I think you're right. At least, until we get some grandbabies."

Hattie was grateful she was sitting down. If she wasn't, she likely would have slumped onto the floor. As far as her parents were concerned, they'd just started dating. Now her mother was bringing up grandchildren? She didn't want to think about how devastated they'd all be when she told them the truth. She didn't want to disappoint them. *Or worry them.* Her gaze shifted up, looking to Forrest for reassurance. If only she'd kept her pride in check and her mouth shut, she—and Forrest—wouldn't be in this predicament.

Forrest stooped to whisper, "We'll figure this out," into her ear. "It'll be okay."

She was starting to relax when Forrest's lips pressed a featherlight kiss against her temple and everything seemed to tip sideways. *Again.* What was happening? This was Forrest. His blue eyes. His warm smile. Those were familiar and welcome. But his kiss? The sweep of his fingers, brushing a wayward curl from her forehead? Those were new. New and… Different. Forrest was her rock. He didn't send her heart rate skyrocketing or wake up each end of every one of her nerve endings. Not until today. Now. Right this very minute. She swallowed, certain that every single person in the room could hear the gallop of her pulse—but she couldn't seem to tear her gaze free from Forrest's to check.

She took a deep, steadying breath.

Maybe he was right and they could figure this out. Maybe. Not that she was worried, not really. Once Billy and Courtney and this whole wedding was over and done with, life would go back to the way it was—and she and Forrest would keep being what they had always been: good friends.

FORREST HAD ALWAYS left the talking to his brothers and uncle. He was fine with it that way. To him, the less a man said, the more power his words imparted. And with a houseful of boisterous siblings and one opinionated uncle, he'd learned to keep his thoughts to himself—unless they were worth sharing.

Tonight, had started out that way. He'd done a lot of watching and listening and watching some more. But the more he saw, the more he had a hard time keeping his mouth shut. At the end of the day, Forrest had deduced there were three types of people: those who meant well, those who were clueless and those who didn't mean well. There was no denying Rebecca Hall was the latter. Every word, look and sound she made seemed to pick, taunt or ridicule Glady Carmichael—in the most subtle of ways, of course.

It wasn't long before Forrest was speaking out. If there was ever a time for some good-natured sarcasm, now was it. The Carmichael table had become a battlefield and the lines were firmly drawn. For all her narrow-eyed glares and tight smiles, he suspected the older woman was enjoying the verbal sparring. She probably scared most people out of ever daring to take her on.

You don't scare me. And he made sure she knew it, too.

But he'd lost his firepower when Hattie's gaze had locked with his. Her father's words were meant to be supportive—he knew that. But hearing her father was worried over her, like Billy, wasn't easy for Hattie. She didn't want anyone worrying over her. And hearing it out loud, with an audience, had put hurt in her hazel eyes. One thing Forrest couldn't abide was Hattie hurting.

He'd told her it'd be okay and he'd meant it. But now that his nose was buried against the soft strawberry-blonde curls at her temple, he wasn't so certain he was telling the truth.

It wasn't the first time he'd struggled to make sense of the way his insides seemed to shift and warm when she was close. Or how one hazel-eyed look or touch made the air in his lungs too thin to breathe. Even though the room was full of conversation and people, he was wholly distracted by her nearness and the way she leaned into him. Hattie was causing this, only Hattie, and he wasn't sure what to do about it.

"Good coffee," Bart announced, holding up his cup.

"All of the meal was delicious, Glady," Forrest added. "As always, that is."

"You silver-tongued devil, you." Velma laughed. "Goodness, you'd give Bernardo a run for his money."

"Do I want to know who Bernardo is?" Forrest whispered for Hattie's ears alone.

"The hero in her book." Hattie smiled up at him. "He was on the cover, with his shirt falling off."

Forrest stared down at his shirt. "I'm not gonna try to compete with that."

Hattie was laughing and snorting then.

"When did this come about?" Glady cut and served pieces of her oatmeal raisin sheet cake as she spoke. "I mean, you two have been stuck together for as long as I can remember, but, well, that was different."

"You had to sit through our story." Billy toasted Forrest with his tea glass. "Now, you get to tell yours." He chuckled.

"I'm confused." Rebecca Hall's brows rose. "We're listening to what story? How the two of you are now a *couple*? Not an engagement? Just that…you two are…dating?"

"Mom," Lena cut in.

In all his years, Forrest could safely say he'd never met anyone like Rebecca Hall. What was wrong with the woman? Did she have something against folk being happy? Not that Hattie was all that happy at the moment, since she was caught in a lie. That's when he realized he was strangely okay with this. He took the extra-large piece of cake Glady had cut for him and picked up his fork.

Lena added, "Could you be any ruder, Mom?"

Forrest wasn't sure that was the right thing to ask the woman. *Don't want her thinking it's a dare.* He was grinning when he took a big bite of cake.

"Better hold on tight, Hattie." Aunt Velma cackled. "Don't rest until you get a ring on your finger. That's Rebecca's motto, anyway—isn't that right?"

Forrest's fork froze halfway to his mouth. It was on the tip of Forrest's tongue to ask how many rings the woman had obtained over the years, but he decided that might cross a line there was no coming back from. He ate his cake, instead.

Rebecca shot daggers her sister's way. "I swear, Velma, you make me sound awful."

He was pretty sure Velma was only telling it like it was but, again, he kept his opinions to himself and enjoyed his cake in peace.

"As nice as it is for you two, and I'm sure it is, you have to think long-term. At a certain age, there's no point in going slow or waiting," Rebecca Hall continued. "Both Hattie and Courtney are of that age. Time keeps ticking away—we all know that."

"Mom." Courtney frowned, almost apologetic.

"What?" Rebecca took her daughter's hand. "There's no harm in being romantic *and* practical. I'd never encourage you, or Hattie for that matter, to pursue a relationship that didn't have a future. That would be a waste of time."

When it came to Hattie, Forrest was already protective, but there was something about the woman's matter-of-fact and totally offensive assessment of things that had him feeling extra protective. Somehow, she'd managed to insult both Hattie and her own daughter without acting like she'd said a thing wrong. And, from the expressions of the rest of their dinner party, he wasn't the only one trying to decide what to say or do next. Manners were part of his upbringing. He couldn't say the same for Rebecca Hall.

"I'm okay with them not being engaged." Billy shot his future mother-in-law a disapproving frown. "I'm still getting used to the idea of them dating. Go on—when did this all happen?"

Hattie stared up at him. "Well…" She swallowed.

"The cake is delicious, Glady." He nodded his thanks, trying to give Hattie some time to decide what to say.

"I called him. I'd saved a snapping turtle." She turned the dessert plate in front of her.

"Right. Mr. Snappy-Pants?" Forrest grinned. "It didn't go well." Not because of the turtle, but because of Billy's engagement to Courtney. *Best to leave that part out.*

"But at least I came out with all my fingers." She took a deep breath, smiling slightly. "Anyway, he wanted to cheer me up."

Forrest swallowed another bite of cake. "I don't like it when she's upset."

"I don't, either," Glady agreed, sitting to enjoy her cake.

Forrest nodded. "Ice cream was in order."

"And we just...talked..." Hattie faltered.

Lying wasn't her thing. Or his thing, for that matter. It made sense to stick to the truth—for the most part. "And then, Hattie got sick." He shrugged. "And I went to help her and—"

"Forrest." Hattie looked horrified.

"What? You did?" He chuckled.

"Fine." Her hazel eyes narrowed. "*You* can finish the story." She took a big bite of cake.

There was a ripple of laughter around the table.

"I bent over right as she stood up and boom." He pointed at his face. "I was bleeding and she was panicking and she might have said a few things that told me she cared about me. More than she let on, I mean."

Hattie kept eating cake, trying to hide her irritation. It wasn't easy, he could tell, but she didn't go all red and there was no steam coming out of her ears.

"And, even though I was bleeding and hurting, I figured it was okay for me to go ahead and tell her how I felt, too." His hand shifted to rest on her shoulder. "Then she got me into her truck, threw it in gear and took me to Doc Johnson's."

"But that was…" Glady shook her head. "All this *just* happened?"

Forrest watched Hattie take another bite. Was she eating cake so she didn't have to answer questions with a lie? He was smiling all over again.

"You know Hattie's no good at keeping secrets," Billy pointed out. "I'd have known if it had been going on for long."

"Sort of snuck up on you, did it?" Bart was leaning back in his chair, his steaming coffee mug held in both hands.

"You could say that." Forrest reached up for his nose—earning more laughter and a sigh from Hattie.

"And?" Rebecca Hall pushed. "That's it?"

Forrest nodded.

"I think we should let the two of them work it out on their own." Glady spoke up, her smile more strained. "I'm glad you told us—"

"Technically, Courtney told you," Billy murmured. "Sorry about that, sis."

Courtney nodded, wincing. "I didn't want you two to have to pretend like nothing was going on just so you wouldn't ruin things for Billy and I."

Forrest finished his cake and sat back,

eyeing the half-eaten piece Hattie was poking on. He picked up his fork and stole a bite.

"Really?" she whispered.

"Getting even. For the pie?" He shrugged.

Hattie smiled—a real smile this time.

Rebecca sighed. "I don't see why all *this* was necessary? I'll agree Hattie is lucky to catch the eye of someone like Forrest but there are no guarantees, are there. It's important to be honest and accept we can't say how this will pan out." She gave Hattie a long, hard look. "No point getting your hopes up." She sighed. "It's not the same thing as getting married—in two weeks. I feel obligated to remind you that *that* is why we're all here and that's what we need to be focusing on."

"I agree." Hattie spoke up before Forrest could let the woman know exactly how he felt about her. There were things he'd never dreamed of saying before, not ever, but this woman... This woman needed to be reined in. And quick.

Hattie nudged him with her elbow, as if she knew he'd reached his breaking point, and went on to say, "This is Billy and Courtney's wedding. It's a big deal. This should be all about them—one hundred percent.

That's why we don't want to say anything. Not to anyone else, I mean, since you all know." She smiled at her brother with such love Forrest forced himself to stay silent. Hattie glanced up at him. "Forrest and I… we don't like attention. We don't want it. We sure don't want to detract from y'all's wedding."

Forrest marveled over her calm. He was still fuming, and she was trying her best to smooth feathers. She was right about neither of them liking attention, but that wasn't what she was worrying about. Right now, their lie was confined to the people in this room. It'd be easy enough to undo it. But if this got out and the Ladies Guild or Miss Lucille or some other story lover caught wind of it? It'd spread like wildfire.

"That's my girl." Bart nodded, but Forrest didn't miss the pointed way the man said, "Always thinking of others," or the side-eye he shot Rebecca Hall's way.

"I'm happy to help you two keep things under wraps," Aunt Velma volunteered. "We could pretend we're seeing each other, Forrest, just to throw everyone off track."

"Aunt Velma." But Lena was laughing. "You are incorrigible."

Aunt Velma's eyes widened. "What? What did I say?"

"I appreciate the offer," Forrest said, barely keeping it together. "I'll think it over and get back to you."

"I'll be waiting." Aunt Velma giggled.

"As I said earlier, sis, you're terrible at keeping secrets." Billy was watching the two of them. "All anyone has to do is see you two together to know."

"Well, that's just silly." Hattie frowned. "Forrest and I aren't looking or acting any different than we always do."

Billy made a dismissive sound. "Right, sure."

"You can try to keep it a secret," Bart said with a chuckle. "But it'll come out in the end. The truth always comes out."

Hattie stared at her cake.

Forrest squeezed her shoulder.

"Well, I, for one, appreciate your discretion, Hattie." Rebecca Hall pushed aside her uneaten cake. "After all, Courtney is only getting married once, and it should be everything that she wants—without distractions."

Hattie nodded.

"And, besides," Rebecca went on. "Keeping it quiet is the smart move." She was completely unaware of the looks she was getting. "It'll save you both a lot of talk and embarrassment and trouble down the road."

Because he and Hattie didn't stand a chance of making it... Rebecca Hall didn't say it, but she'd made sure everyone at the table was thinking it. Pretense or not, he wanted to show that woman she was wrong. She didn't know Hattie. She didn't know how Hattie worked or thought or what she believed in. If Hattie ever made a commitment to someone, it'd be ironclad until the day she passed on. He knew that, in his bones.

"How about we clear off the table?" Glady asked. "Now that everyone's done."

Plates were stacked, coffee cups and all the fixings were loaded back onto the tray, but Forrest was still metabolizing his anger. What happened to a person to make them think or say such things?

Hattie's hand rested on his arm, catching his attention. He glanced her way to find her wide-eyed and focused—on his hand. No, not his hand, his fork. The dessert fork he'd managed to bend while Rebecca Hall was filling the room with hot air and negativity.

"I'm sorry," he murmured to Hattie, resting the fork on his dessert plate. "I'll replace it."

She smiled, squeezing his arm again.

"Don't you worry about it." Bart Carmichael leaned forward, nodding at the fork. "If I didn't have arthritis in my knuckles so bad, mine'd look the same." He shot Rebecca Hall a hard look. "You two go on, now."

Hattie shook her head. "Daddy, I should help clean up."

"No, you and Forrest have done plenty. Go on, spend some time together." He patted her cheek.

Shortly thereafter, they were driving down the road in his truck, in silence. He didn't want to replay all that had happened, but the scene at the Carmichaels' house seemed to be stuck on Repeat.

"I've made a mess out of everything, haven't I?" Hattie mumbled. "I should have kept my mouth shut, but I was all flustered. My dad's walking Courtney down the aisle. My brother is marrying her. And even though this makes no sense, I started thinking she'd find a way to get to you, too. I couldn't bear the thought of giving you up to Courtney—somehow, someway."

Forrest smiled. *I couldn't bear the thought of giving you up?* "Instead, we're a couple."

"A couple that horrible woman doesn't think will last. And I'm so lucky to have caught your eye… Like no one would be interested in me." She covered her face with her hands, her voice strained.

"She doesn't know what she's talking about," Forrest assured her, his temper rising all over again.

Hattie made an odd noise before saying, "I know it's wrong, Forrest, but it got to me. Just like Courtney. I… It made me want to prove her wrong." She groaned. "Which is how I got us into this situation in the first place."

Wrong or not, he understood. More than that, he wanted to prove Rebecca Hall wrong, too. "It's only two weeks. We act just as lovey-dovey as Audy and Brooke, and Courtney and Billy until the woman leaves." He paused, glancing her way. "After that, we'll tell your parents the truth." He shook his head. "After seeing your father's reaction tonight, something tells me he'll understand."

"That I lied to him? To them all? I don't

know, Forrest." Hattie covered her face again.

Is it a lie? His pulse jumped up as he circled around to the truth. Did he care about Hattie? *Really* care? The question wasn't new… He'd done his best to ignore it for some time, but it'd been there—waiting. Maybe, pretending he and Hattie were a couple would give him a chance to see what kind of couple they'd be… *Who am I kidding?* He already knew. He and Hattie, together? It would be good. Better than good. But this wasn't about him. Deep down, he knew where his heart lay. This was about Hattie. Pretending they were a couple would give him a chance to *prove* to Hattie they were meant to be together. Solid. True-blue. Unshakable. A near-perfect match.

CHAPTER NINE

HATTIE HAD TOSSED and turned, her dreams jolting her awake—again and again. Worse, when she woke up, her thoughts wandered right back to the subject of her dreams. Specifically, Forrest. When she made her morning coffee, she remembered the brush of his lips against her temple. As she was brushing her teeth, she was caught up in the memory of the warmth in his gaze when he smiled her way. When she drove into town for her fitting, she could almost feel the gentle sweep of his work-roughened fingertips along her jaw. She couldn't help but blame Mabel—she was the one who had suggested Forrest had feelings for her. Which was silly—she'd told Mabel as much. But then dinner and the whole performance at her folks' and the stress of lying... Well, it made sense that her mind was a little muddled. By the time she'd reached town, she'd calmed down and convinced herself that everything was going to be fine.

Just like Forrest said.

Hattie's day was busy enough to keep her mind occupied and off Forrest and her beyond-silly dreams. Her fitting went off without a hitch. Mabel and Brooke gushed when she walked out of the dressing room—without teasing or acting like it was strange—and Kitty hemmed the dress so it hid her boots from sight. She'd met her mother at the florists' to finalize Courtney's flowers, then picked up cake samples for Courtney and Billy to try around her mother's dining room table. By the time they'd settled on a flavor, Hattie was so full of cake her stomach hurt.

Now she stood beneath the tepid spray of her tiny shower, rinsing the soap from her face, relieved to be done with all things wedding and ready for some rodeo-centered fun. Fun—as long as she didn't let the Hall women get to her. She shook her head, wrapped herself up in a towel and headed into her tiny bedroom.

She'd laid her rodeo outfit on her bed before her shower but wondered if she shouldn't try something new. Her starched faded jeans and tooled leather boots were her go-to, but the shirt had a small hole in the seam beneath her left arm and it was missing a button. Fine. A new shirt might be in order. A new shirt that had nothing to do with her insecurity over the Hall women and everything to do with the hole and missing button.

She reached to the back of her closet to peruse the clothes her mother continued to buy for her. No matter how many times Hattie had tried to tell her mother she wasn't a girlie girl, her mother refused to listen. She'd show up at Hattie's with a bagful of pastel-colored, embroidered, detailed cutouts, or sparkly tops or dresses that were "too good a deal" to pass up. Hattie had checked the price tags, and *none* of them were a good deal, but her mother said they were nonreturnable, so they hung, the whole pastel-hued rainbow, at the rear of her closet—with the tags still on.

But the more she looked, the more overwhelmed she became. *I'll wear the first thing I pick.* Easy. No thinking or worrying, just grab and go. She closed her eyes, reached into the closet and grabbed the first hanger her fingers touched. She kept her eyes closed, refusing to look at other options.

and pushed the door shut behind her before allowing herself to see what she'd picked.

"Oh, no." She frowned at the dress hanging off the hanger. *Another* dress? Unlike Mabel's plain blue shirtdress with the weird belt-thing, this was... This was way more dress-y. It was lavender, with a fancy stitched top and a skirt that didn't look like it'd hang past her knees.

She held the hanger out, frowning at it.

Maybe the second thing?

A rising wave of cricket sounds had her dropping the dress and reaching for her phone. "Hello?"

"Hattie? It's Gretta. Gretta Williams."

"Hey, Gretta, did you catch your raccoon?"

"I did, but I'm afraid he might be a she, and there are babies in the tree she's been taking care of." Gretta sighed. "How do I let her out?"

Hattie walked her through the door release. "It's pretty easy. Just make sure you wear some thick gardening gloves—in case she's feeling extra protective.

Gretta repeated what Hattie had said. "Okay. I can do that. I feel so bad."

Hattie sat on her bed, eyeing the dress.

"If it's easier, I can come over and do it for you?"

"Oh, no, I can get it. I'm sure you're going to the rodeo?" Gretta asked. "Dad's taking Levi so I'm going to, you know, have some quiet time here."

"Why don't you come to the rodeo? With me?" Hattie asked.

"Oh." Gretta paused.

"You don't have to." Hattie laughed. "If you were looking forward to some alone time, I get it. I've been running all over the place for my brother's wedding, and I'd be fine to stay home and do nothing but… I can't." If Forrest was riding and she wasn't working, she was there. It was just the way it was. Plus, she knew her parents, Courtney and Courtney's family would be there. Hattie had had more than her fair share of Rebecca Hall, but she didn't feel right about leaving her mother to fend for herself. "I'm sitting here trying to decide what to wear. Normally, I just put on jeans and a shirt and go."

"Why not do that now?" Gretta asked.

"Honestly, I'm not sure." She glanced at the dress. "I guess I'm feeling…insecure."

Gretta made a sympathetic noise. "Oh,

Hattie, I know all about that." She sighed. "Well, then, I recommend you put on what you feel prettiest or strongest in. If that's jeans and a T-shirt, wear that. If you feel good in it, it'll come across to everyone that sees you. A lot of it isn't the clothes you wear, it's the attitude."

"I'd never thought about it that way," Hattie murmured.

Gretta was a lot like Courtney in that she never looked anything but perfect. Tall and willowy and fashion savvy, Gretta knew how to dress and carry herself. Unlike Courtney, her smiles were real, if hesitant, and she had an air of sadness about her. Probably because of her not-so-nice marriage and divorce. "Can I ask if it's a someone or a something that's making you feel insecure?" Gretta hurried to add, "I've always envied how self-assured and comfortable you are in your own skin."

Maybe when she was in warden mode—she knew who she was and what she had to do every second she had that uniform on. Without it? "I guess it's a little of both." She'd never been one to speak ill of someone else so she didn't elaborate.

"Gotcha. I can come over and help you

pick something out, if you like?" Gretta paused, then added, "Or not—I mean—"

"I'd like that," Hattie agreed. "Come on over. We can go to the rodeo after?"

"Okay." Hattie thought she heard a smile in Gretta's voice.

"Okay. See you soon." Gretta hung up.

By the time the two of them had just the right outfit put together, Hattie's bedroom looked like it'd been hit by a tornado. Tops, shirts, jeans and dresses, covered her bed, draped over the back of the chair in the bedroom corner, and hung from the hinges and doorknob of her closet.

As they were driving to the stockyard, Hattie felt confident. Jeans, boots and one of the tops her mother had purchased. Cap sleeves, buttons up the front, a pretty pale mossy green—that Gretta said matched her eyes—with a vine pattern stitched into the fabric. After Gretta had smoothed some yummy-smelling hair stuff into her curls, Hattie had almost regretted putting her straw cowboy hat on. For once, her curls looked shiny and soft, not frizzy. She'd taken a picture of the hair stuff with her phone.

They parked and walked to the front gate.

Gretta looked like a rodeo angel. Her long

blond hair fell straight down her back and her white sundress and boots fit her to perfection. Hattie couldn't imagine wearing earrings that big, but Gretta pulled it off.

"You two are going to turn many a head tonight," Miss Martha Zeigler said, taking their cash and handing them the tickets. "I'm going to have to get to my seats pretty quick for a good view." She glanced at her watch. "Where is that Dorris Kaye?" She sighed.

Probably sidetracked collecting, or spreading, gossip. "Hope she gets here soon," Hattie said, waving.

"She scares me," Gretta whispered when they'd walked through the entryway of the fairgrounds.

"She scares everyone." Hattie shrugged. "It's what she does."

"She is very good at it." Gretta smiled.

Hattie glanced at the array of booths lining the dirt path that led to the stands on either side of the arena. "I'm thinking some cotton candy and a funnel cake might be in order before we find seats?" Hattie grinned. "And water, too. Have to stay hydrated in this heat."

Gretta laughed.

They were in line for funnel cake when

Hattie saw them. Courtney, hanging on to Billy's arm. Behind them, Aunt Velma and Lena—trailing last, was Rebecca.

"What's wrong?" Gretta whispered, her brown eyes going wide. "You just tensed up."

"Oh…nothing," she murmured, forcing a smile when Billy saw her. "Hey." She waved.

"I was wondering where you were," Billy said, walking toward her. "Loading up?"

"Don't want to miss anything," Hattie said. "You haven't met Gretta, have you? Gretta opened the only dance school in Garrison and has been running it now for…"

"A little over a year," Gretta answered, smiling at them all. "It's nice to meet you all."

"My brother, Billy. His fiancée, Courtney Hall. And this is Courtney's sister, Lena, Aunt Velma and her mother, Rebecca Hall," Hattie rattled off, noticing Courtney's hold on Billy tighten once she'd given Gretta a not-so-subtle once-over.

"Mom has mentioned the school in her letters," Billy said. "She says you've added only good things to Garrison."

"Your mother is a gem," Gretta answered.

"I've never heard her say a harsh word about anyone."

Billy nodded. So did Hattie. Courtney and Rebecca did not. If anything, they seemed to be making a more thorough inspection of Gretta. Hattie was all too familiar with that look—the judging one. Not that Gretta had done or said a thing out of line.

"We should probably get back to our seats," Courtney said, tugging on Billy's arm.

"We'll see you?" Billy asked, oblivious to the awkward interaction.

Hattie nodded. "Yep. If there's room." It wouldn't be a great hardship to sit somewhere else. She waved and turned, not in the least concerned the line had barely moved.

"So…that was on the icy side," Gretta murmured, watching them make their way to the stands.

"Don't take it personally." Hattie shrugged, wrinkling her nose. "Lena and Velma are fine. I have yet to figure out the other two."

"And Courtney is marrying your brother?" Gretta asked.

"Yeah." She sighed. "I guess you can see why I'm feeling a little…tense." *Tense* didn't quite express how she was feeling, but it was close enough.

"I think you and I are alike—we're both people pleasers. I've learned that there are some people you will never please. Ever. The harder you try, the more distance they will put between you. Those are the people that don't need to take up a lot of space in here." Gretta pressed a hand to her heart, then her head. "At the end of the day, happiness is a choice. They have to choose it. You can't choose it for them." She sighed. "I'll stop giving you unsolicited advice now."

"Feel free to do that anytime." Hattie shook her head, mulling over everything Gretta had said. "You're right."

Gretta smiled. "Thanks. It drives my dad crazy."

Cotton candy, funnel cake and water bottles in hand, the two of them made their way to the near-full-to-bursting stands. Mabel and Brooke waved, indicating a super small space they'd managed to save between the two of them. Her parents were seated on the opposite side of Billy and Courtney, at the far end of the row from Rebecca, so Hattie didn't mind being a row apart from them. She gave her father a wave and her mother a smile as she and Gretta reached the space.

"Everyone hold their breath," Hattie teased as they squeezed in, right as the flag girls came racing into the arena, carrying their flags high.

"I've always wondered how they do that without dropping it," Gretta murmured.

"Hours and hours and hours of practice," Mabel murmured back.

Bull riding started things off.

"It's weird not seeing Audy out there," Brooke said quietly, a tinge of regret in her voice.

Hattie knew it had been Audy's choice to give up rodeo. He'd said he'd found something better than the thrill of bull riding: his family.

"He is loving coaching the rodeo team, though," Mabel added. "I don't think those kids could ask for a better teacher."

After bull riding, calf wrestling and the always enjoyable mutton bustin' for the kids, team roping began.

"This is Forrest's event," Mabel explained to Gretta. "That's why Hattie perked up like a meerkat over there—all alert and wide-eyed."

"A meerkat?" Hattie laughed. "Where did that come from?"

"Baby Joy has a new animal book. With meerkats." Brooke was laughing. "It's her favorite. She'll make you read it over and over and over."

Hattie was still giggling when she spied Forrest guiding his horse into the chute. He'd always carried himself with a certain… Confidence. Not cocky, not like Audy, just a focused certainty in his actions. He sat tall and straight in the saddle with his chocolate brown cowboy hat sitting just right on his head.

"You can still see the bruises from here." Mabel winced. "Poor Forrest."

Hattie nodded. Bruises or no bruises… "He looks good. Handsome." In her eyes, there wasn't a better-looking man in the whole arena. He turned, looking over his shoulder, one hand on the pommel of his saddle.

"You know you said that out loud, don't you?" Brooke asked, laughing.

"What?" Hattie asked, her breath catching in her throat when Forrest's gaze scanned the stands.

"What's he looking for?" Mabel whispered.

"I don't know, but that's *some* look," Brooke whispered back.

Hattie heard them, sort of, but it didn't matter. She waited—until he saw her.

He touched the brim of his hat, the corner of his mouth cocking up.

"Oh, my," Gretta murmured. "My heart picked up and that look wasn't even for me."

It was for me. Hattie's heart hadn't picked up—it was racing. Pounding. Like it or not, Forrest Briscoe was the reason for it. It was the single most terrifying realization of her life. This big, strong, good man was her very best friend. She knew him like the back of her hand and vice versa. When she had a good day, he knew. When he had a bad day, she knew. Their friendship was solid and constant and necessary. And yet, here she was, smiling back at him—waving like a teenager—awash with a whole new spectrum of feelings, all of which went deeper than friendship.

He shook his head, still smiling, and turned his attention back to his horse.

"You breathing?" Brooke asked.

She nodded. Sort of.

"I don't think she is," Gretta said. "I wouldn't be. That was…something."

It was something, all right. Something everyone on the stands had witnessed. She shifted in her seat, acutely aware of the ripple of conversation and the number of curious eyes turning her way. Forrest's look had done more than jump-start her heart, it had made sure everyone who'd seen the exchange knew it, too.

LUCKILY, RUSTY HADN'T given him much grief for his lack of focus. Their time had been a solid 7.58 seconds. Nothing to write home about, but not too shabby. The upside was he was done and free to enjoy the rest of the evening. Which meant, he could go find Hattie. He'd tried to convince himself he'd scanned the stands to make sure she was out of range of Rebecca Hall's reach but… That would be a lie. Once he'd laid eyes on her, he hadn't needed further confirmation that what he was feeling was real. He was in love with Hattie. Plain and simple.

"You're for real about this?" Webb asked, his voice catching him off guard.

Forrest finished securing his horse, Lariat, to the trailer and turned to his brother. But it wasn't just Webb—Audy and Beau were there, too. "What are we talking about?" He scratched his jaw, waiting.

Webb, hands on hips, shot him a disbelieving look. "That little stunt you pulled out there. With Hattie? People are making assumptions. Some I'm thinking aren't too far-fetched, after that."

Forrest glanced at Audy, who held up his hands and chuckled. "I'm just here to watch and listen."

Webb pointed at the arena. "You're the one always telling me, keep your private life private and avoid the headaches of gossip, and you go and do that. Like I said, people are talking, Forrest."

Regret washed over him then. He didn't want Hattie worrying over anything else; she had enough on her shoulders right now. "Go on and speak your peace." Forrest glanced at Beau.

"He dragged me along." Beau nodded at Webb, then shrugged. "I'm cool with it. You and Hattie, I mean."

But Webb's muffled groan, his headshake, had Forrest asking, "What's eating you, Webb? Why is this a problem?"

"I… I don't know." Webb rested his hand

on Lariat's shoulder. "I guess I don't want you rushing into anything because I'm leaving."

Forrest blinked. "What now?" That was pretty much the last thing he'd expected Webb to say.

"You don't handle change all that well," Beau pointed out.

"They have a point." Audy held up his hands again. "Right. I have no opinion."

"Let me get this straight. You think, since I don't like change, that your leaving is why I'm starting a relationship with Hattie?" Forrest scratched his jaw. "You don't think that's a stretch?"

"Mabel was talking about stress and how it makes people do stuff they wouldn't normally do." Webb crossed his arms over his chest, glaring now.

"She was talking about me?" Forrest asked, surprised. Mabel wasn't one to keep her thoughts to herself. If she had something to say to Forrest, she'd say it to him—not Webb.

Webb stared at him. "No. She was on the phone, talking to someone..."

"To who? About what?" Forrest prodded.

"I don't know." Webb snapped back. "It was a private conversation."

"Not private enough, apparently." Forrest clapped his brother on the shoulder.

"Mabel did say Hattie's under a lot of stress right now, *and* that she was worried about her." Webb frowned. "I just think, maybe, you two should stop and think is all."

"He has a point." Audy nodded.

Forrest ignored Audy. "I appreciate the concern, Webb, but I know what I'm doing."

"And what, exactly, would that be?" Audy asked.

"I thought you were here to watch and listen." Forrest pushed his hat back on his head. "How about we do this at home? Later. When there's no chance of someone overhearing something that's private."

"Sounds good. I gotta go meet Tess over at the kettle corn booth, anyway," Beau said. "I'll see you at home." He waved, gave Webb a shove as he walked by and disappeared in the maze of pipe corrals, trailers and trucks.

Forrest gave Lariat a pat. "We'll talk about this at home?" he asked, glancing Webb's way.

"I guess." Webb shrugged. "I feel like I'm

going to come back and everything is going to have changed."

And that, right there, was the root of this whole conversation. Forrest exchanged a quick smile with Audy.

"Time never stops, Webb. Whether you stay or go, things change. It's the way it works. Garrison will still be Garrison. We will still be your brothers. Audy and Brooke might have a half a dozen more kids when you come back, but I don't see much else happening to make things all that different." Forrest wasn't sure what to make of the smile on Audy's face but it was mighty suspicious.

"Mabel's getting married," Webb pointed out.

Forrest nodded. "But you like Jensen and little Samantha well enough, don't you?"

Webb nodded. "I just… I don't want to miss anything."

Forrest's heart twisted hard. He didn't want to wake up and not see Webb bleary-eyed and propped up over his heaping bowl of cereal. He couldn't imagine a whole week going by without Webb making a mess of something that needed cleaning up. Webb and his goofy laugh over Uncle Felix's terrible jokes. Or the way he could fall asleep in five seconds flat just about anywhere. He'd miss all of that. *I'll miss you.* But he didn't say it. He couldn't. His throat was so tight, he could barely breathe.

"That's what letters are for," Audy said, his voice thick with emotion. "Between Uncle Felix and Mabel, you'll always know what's going on. Chances are, you'll know before the rest of us."

Webb grinned then.

"Come on." Audy waved them forward. "I've got a hankering for a corn dog or two… or three."

"Sounds good." Webb followed. "And a funnel cake."

"It's not a rodeo without one," Audy agreed.

Forrest trailed a bit behind, reining in his panic over Webb's imminent departure. He had to believe it was all going to be okay. Comparing Webb to Gene wouldn't help. Gene's accident was just that, an accident. He'd been overseas nine months when it happened. His supply truck had a flat and when he'd stopped to change it, he'd stepped on a long-buried land mine. The chances of something like that happening again were slim. Sure, Webb was accident-prone but… He'll be fine. He had to be.

"You want anything?" Audy asked, looking back over his shoulder.

"Nah." Forrest cleared his throat. "I think I'll go on…" He nodded at the stands.

"Uh-huh." Webb stopped and look at him. "Text if you or Hattie want something."

Forrest nodded. "Will do," he said, before taking the steps that led into the stands.

In a town the size of Garrison, it was impossible to go anywhere without knowing almost everyone. Now was no exception. He shook hands with Buck Williams, answered Levi Williams's questions about what kind of rope to use when roping, let the entire Ladies Guild cluck and praise his ride that night, plus a handful of others offering congratulations or comments before he spied the Carmichaels.

He was glad to see Glady and Bart were seated well outside Rebecca Hall's conversation range. With all the noise of the crowd, the emcee and the bucking bronc rides taking place, there was a chance they'd go the whole evening without hearing one nasty word from the woman. He hoped so anyway. They'd more than earned an evening out.

"You did good," Bart said, standing to shake his hand. "Clean ride, through and through."

"And you look so handsome," Velma Hall piped up.

Forrest touched the brim of his hat. "Thank you, ma'am."

Velma pressed a hand to her heart. "Land sakes, if I didn't like your Hattie so much, you'd be in trouble." She clucked. "I don't suppose there are any more where you came from?"

"A couple." Forrest chuckled. "Uncle Felix, for one. But he might be a little too old for you."

"A seasoned fella, huh?" Velma asked. "Does he wear a cowboy hat?"

"Velma, enough." Rebecca rolled her eyes. "Go read your book."

Velma's eyes, enlarged by her round lenses, regarded Rebecca. "Sister, darling, I'm being charming at the moment and making small talk. Why don't you go talk to one of those mean-tempered bulls? I bet the two of you would have lots in common."

From the corner of his eye, Forrest watched as Bart Carmichael covered his mouth to stifle his laughter.

"You do look handsome, Forrest," Glady agreed, struggling with her own laughter. "You're looking a little less purple now."

For the most part, he didn't think about his bruises. Not unless he tried to rub his nose or smile too big or… Make any sort of facial expression.

"Go on." Bart pointed. "Mabel and Jensen took Samantha to look at the horses, so there should be plenty of room up there."

Forrest did his best not to be too obvious, but he couldn't hold back his frown when he saw Brooke, Gretta Williams, Hattie and Rusty sitting, animatedly talking, in the stands. Hattie threw back her head, laughing at something. She must have snorted then, because she covered her nose and mouth and Rusty, Gretta and Brooke were all cracking up.

He grinned, making his way up the steps to their row. "What did I miss?" he asked, happy to find room for him on the row right behind Hattie. "Something was funny."

"Rusty was telling stories on you." Hattie smiled up at him. "Something about when you were young and you roped an old cow in the pasture, but you didn't let go of the rope so you wound up in the dirt with the cow looking down at you." She snorted, covering her nose again.

Forrest grinned. "I remember that. Knocked the wind clean out of me."

"How old were you?" Gretta asked.

"About nine or ten?" he asked, looking to Rusty for confirmation.

"Sounds about right." Rusty nodded, glancing at Gretta.

"When you were full of mischief," Hattie added, shaking her head. "I'm surprised you two didn't wind up with more broken limbs than you did."

Gretta chuckled, shaking her head. "Promise me you won't tell Levi any of this. He'd forget about being a game warden and get excited over rodeo." She sighed. "I'm not sure I'm cut out to be a rodeo mom."

Forrest noticed Rusty's quick inspection of Gretta's left hand. Looking for a wedding ring, maybe? *Interesting.* "Rusty, you know Gretta Williams, don't you?" Forrest asked. "Gretta, you know Rusty? He is co-owner of the Old Towne Hardware and Appliance."

"I should have asked," Brooke joined in. "I just assume everyone knows the Woodard family. Plus, Garrison's not exactly huge so...how could you two not have met?"

"I don't think we have." Gretta glanced at Rusty. "Then again, if you're not taking dance classes or your kids aren't taking dance classes, there'd be no reason to meet." She paused. "Or you're the elementary school principal. I get a lot of calls from him, too."

"Your son?" Rusty grinned. "I think my mom was on a first-name basis with my elementary school principal."

"Levi is a character." Hattie added, "He's one of my most...eager Junior Rangers. I'm counting on him to be a real help at the next meeting on Monday. We're helping the Ladies Guild clean up the flower beds." She glanced at Forrest. "We might need extra hands, so consider yourself invited." She elbowed Rusty. "You, too."

Rusty stopped staring at Gretta long enough to shrug. "As long as there's no emergency at Old Towne Hardware and Appliance, I might be able to squeeze it in."

"Are there often emergencies at Old Towne Hardware?" Gretta asked, surprised.

"Nope. Never." Rusty grinned. "But I like to be prepared."

Forrest watched the back-and-forth with interest. Hattie, too, seemed to be absorbing what was happening. When her gaze met his, her brows rose and her eyes widened. Maybe he was seeing things, but Hattie's eyes seemed especially green tonight. A warm breeze blew her hair against his hand as she turned, a silky-soft curl dancing against his skin. He ran the strand between his thumb and forefinger, the small contact as potent as a live wire.

Brooke pulled her phone from her pocket. "That's Audy." She stood. "We're going to head out now that both you and Beau are done."

"Good to see you, Brooke." Forrest nodded. "Y'all come on over early if you want, to set up for tomorrow."

"We'll be there. Tess is going to stay with Joy and bring her over later on—or I'd be no help at all." Brooke waved, carefully walking down the narrow wooden steps to the ground.

"I was going for a lemonade." Forrest nudged Hattie in the back with his knee.

Hattie glanced his way, saw the pointed look he shot at Gretta and Rusty, and said, "Sounds good. Maybe an ice cream?" She stood. "You two want anything?"

"Oh, I can come with you." Gretta glanced around her.

"No, you two can save seats, if that's okay?" Hattie asked.

"No problem," Rusty said, smiling at Gretta.

"Okay." Gretta's eyes bounced from Rusty to Hattie. "Water would be great."

"I really like Gretta," Hattie said, once they were walking down the aisle of food vendors and carnival games. "She wasn't sure about tonight but I begged her to come—after she helped me pick out something to wear."

"You look nice." Which was the understatement of the year.

"Thanks to Gretta. You should see the mess we left in my room." She shook her head. "But *that* looks promising."

"She and Rusty?" Forrest agreed.

"Isn't that why we're down here, getting ice cream? Because you, Forrest Briscoe, are playing matchmaker? Or did I somehow misread that look?"

He shrugged. "I wouldn't say matchmaker, exactly."

"No?" She smiled up at him. "I guess we'll see. He hasn't met Levi yet, and that little boy is something else." Her gaze seemed tangled up with his. "You… It was a good ride tonight."

He nodded, entirely sidetracked by her smile.

"Forrest?" she whispered.

He nodded again.

"Should you be looking at me like that? It's a lot." She stepped closer, whispering still. "I mean, other people can see you—looking at me like that. And Mrs. Hall isn't around. You're going to make people think you're…interested in me. I know better, of course, but…" She swallowed. "Still."

What would she do if he told her how he felt? If he said, "Hattie, I *am* interested in you?" Better yet, "Hattie, I love you." He swallowed hard. Would she laugh, thinking he was teasing? Or would she throw her arms around his neck and tell him she felt the same way? The idea was so appealing, the words started coming, "The thing is, Hattie—"

"There you are." Gretta came running up. "I'm so sorry, Hattie, but Dad found me. Levi started throwing up. I'm sure my dad let him eat way too much junk food." She sighed. "Anyway, I'm going to have to take him home and I didn't want to just disappear on you."

"I'm so sorry he's sick." Hattie hugged her. "I had fun tonight, Gretta."

"Me, too, Hattie." Gretta smiled. "Thank you for including me. It's been so long since I've gone out…" She shrugged, her smile fading. "It was nice."

"We will definitely do it again," Hattie promised, waving as the woman hurried back to her father. "Poor thing." Hattie waved at Mr. Williams then, Levi in his arms. "And Rusty." She frowned. "You should go back and sit with him. I can get lemonade, if you want."

He hadn't wanted lemonade. He'd wanted time alone with her. "I'm good."

"Then I'm going to call it a night. I'm beat." She seemed intent on not looking at him. "I promised Mabel I'd be over early to help, so I figure I'll turn in early."

Disappointment cut through him. But if she was tired, she should go. "I'll see you in the morning, then."

"Okay." She glanced up at him, then away. "Maybe, tomorrow, you could try not looking at me like *that* so much?" Her cheeks flushed. "Or we'll have to explain we were pretending to *all* of Garrison instead of just my mom and dad." She hurried off before he could answer.

Or finally admit that he wasn't pretending.

CHAPTER TEN

"EVERYTHING LOOKS AMAZING." Hattie ran her hand down the tablecloth, smoothing out the tiniest of wrinkles. She took Mabel's hand. "You can relax now." Advice she needed to listen to. So far, she'd managed to dodge Forrest at every turn, but she knew she'd have to face him at some point. After last night, she was more jumbled up and confused than ever. Her traitorous heart was ready and willing to jump ship and give itself over to Forrest Briscoe. And it was all Forrest's fault. He was a little too good at pretending. Last night at the rodeo, she could almost swear he cared about her. Searching her out. That smile. Her chest squeezed tight. *He does care about me.* He wasn't in love with her, though. Her fool heart didn't seem to realize that. And she was scared she would be in for a world of hurt when the pretending was all over and done with.

"I think keeping busy has made it easier

to cope." Mabel squeezed her hand. "And now, it's done and I'm not sure I'm going to make it through today without crying at least once."

"I don't think there's any rule that says you can't cry." Hattie tried to give her an encouraging smile.

"You know how my brothers are, Hattie." Mabel wrinkled up her nose. "They see tears and it's all over."

Hattie nodded. Wasn't that what had sent Forrest careening down the highway to the ice-cream shop—and the horrible bruises that followed? Her tears. "I think this is one of those times when no one will say a thing." She hoped. "If you want, I can pinch you or tell you the ending of *Old Yeller* or something really sad so you can cry now? Maybe it'll help?"

Mabel laughed. "I'll take my chances." She scanned the Great Room one more time, the distant sound of car doors slamming announcing the arrival of their first guests. "Here we go."

All in all, Hattie thought Mabel held up just fine. Her fiancée, Jensen, was amazing. He was never too far away from her side. His daughter, Samantha, adored Mabel, so she trailed after her like a tiny tiara-wearing shadow. Hattie did her best to be helpful. She carried platters of briskets, chicken and sausage to the massive barrel grill, where Uncle Felix was slow roasting the barbecue for dinner. She lingered a time or two, to hear one of his stories—or to keep Forrest at a distance. She kept the tea and lemonade full, made sure to refill things as needed and managed to stay on the move as much as possible. Now that Uncle Felix had mentioned the need for coffee, Hattie had a new task to keep her busy.

She set up the large percolator Mabel had pulled out of the pantry earlier and turned to find a plug. She frowned, dropped to her knees and lifted the tablecloth covering the serving table. “Where are you?”

“Who are you talking to down there?” Forrest was leaning against the doorframe, staring down at her.

“No one. Looking for a plug,” she said, crawling under the cloth-covered table. “Uncle Felix wants coffee.”

“That explains everything.” He crouched, lifting the tablecloth to see her. “You could have just asked me, Hattie. I realize you’re going out of your way to avoid me ”

"I am not," she argued, scanning the wall to hide her face. He'd know. He'd see it on her face. That's *exactly* what she'd been doing.

"Uh-huh." He sighed. "It's coincidence that every time I enter a room, you slip out?" He stood and held the tablecloth aside.

"I found one," she said, hoping to change the subject. "There." She slid back out from under the cloth and dusted her hands on her jeans-clad thighs. "I never noticed before, but you're awful full of yourself, Forrest." She tried to tease, while taking care not to look at him. "Avoiding you? Why on earth would I do that?"

"Uh-huh." He held out his hand to help her up and off the floor.

She didn't think. If she had, she wouldn't have taken his hand. Forrest staring at her was…a lot. It had kept her wide-eyed and staring at her ceiling for far too long last night. But touching him? The moment her hand clasped his, the air around them snapped and vibrated. His touch took the heart racing and the lung emptying and the whole "world tilting on its axis" to another level.

Once he pulled her up, he didn't let go

of her hand. Instead, he turned it over and clasped it in both of his. "I appreciate all of your hard work, Hattie. I do." His voice was low and just gruff enough to send a shiver down her spine. "But it'd be nice if you came out and spent some time with the family. Webb, too."

She stared at their hands, breathing slow breaths and concentrating on calming down.

"Hattie?" He pulled her closer, tilting her head back with one finger. "Can you look at me?"

She closed her eyes and shook her head. "No."

"Why?" He chuckled.

It wasn't like she could tell him the truth. That would lead to bad things—like losing her best friend forever. "I'm feeling..." she murmured, then paused. *What am I feeling?* "Emotional?"

"About what?" His voice lowered, softened.

"Webb." *Partly.* "All of you." *Partly.* "I know this is hard." *True.* She drew in a wavering breath. "I'm afraid I'll look at you and I'll start crying." *Also true.*

"Then, do not look at me," he whispered. "Please." His arms slid around her and he pulled her against him. "I can't handle your tears, Hattie."

She melted into him without thought. Her arms were around his waist and her face was buried against his chest and she was breathing in Forrest. "Besides," she murmured. "Last time I cried on you, it didn't go so well."

He chuckled again, one hand stroking over her curls. "I think the odds of that happening again are pretty slim."

"Well now you've gone and done it." She shook her head, her face still pressed against him. "You don't put things out there like that. It's like you're tempting fate. Next time, I could end up breaking your jaw or something."

He sighed. It was loaded with so much weariness, Hattie couldn't help but worry.

"Are you okay?" she asked, tempted to look up at him and stare into those sky-blue eyes.

"Mhm," he murmured against the top of her head. "Fine."

"You sure?" she asked, fitting herself more closely against him. When had being in his arms started feeling like this? Safe and warm and...right?

"I will be." His arms tightened the slightest amount. "In a minute or two."

Hattie could do this. If Forrest needed comforting, she'd give it to him. There was no harm in giving him a hug and sharing his burden. Hadn't he been doing the same? Since Courtney had arrived, he'd bent over backward to be a shoulder for her. Even before that, really. Hattie couldn't remember a time when Forrest hadn't been there. It was one of the things that made him easy to love.

Love. Forrest. She swallowed, finally accepting the horrible—wonderful—truth. *And I do love you, Forrest.*

"What?" Forrest asked. "Did you say my name?"

Her eyes popped open. Had she? "No." She shook her head. "Nope." Surely, she hadn't said that out loud?

"Forrest?" This time, Hattie heard it, too. A voice that was definitely not hers. Relief nearly brought her to her knees. "Forrest? Where is that boy?"

"Is that Uncle Felix?" Hattie wasn't sure.

"Don't know, don't care." His hold didn't ease.

"Forrest, we can't hide in here forever."

She leaned back, her gaze shifting up to meet his.

"Why not?" he asked, his eyes searching hers. "This is right where I want to be."

Hattie had no words. None. He was looking at her that way again, the way that made every inch of her warm and tingly. But now that there wasn't a sea of people between the two of them, there was nothing to dull the full force of his eyes. She went from hugging him, to holding on to him—certain the ground beneath her was about to give way.

"Oh, Hattie," he whispered, his fingertips trailing along her jaw as he bent his head.

His lips met hers and Hattie clung to Forrest. She had to. The brush of his breath against her cheek. The gentle hold of his hands cradling her face. She was wholly wrapped up in his warmth, his scent, his touch. Hattie didn't care where they were or who might walk in or anything beyond Forrest's kiss.

"Is the coffee ready—" Uncle Felix's voice came to a sudden stop. "What in the Sam Hill is going on in here?"

Forrest sighed, easing his hold on her slowly. "We were making coffee."

What were *we doing?* Hattie wasn't so

sure. The only thing she was sure of? She'd kissed Forrest. Rather, Forrest had kissed her. Really kissed her. Had he known there was an audience? Of course he had, why else would he have kissed her.

"Is that what you call it?" Uncle Felix chuckled.

"That's a new one." Her mother's voice. Amused—but still her mother. *My mother?*

Hattie's cheeks were burning when she turned to face them. "Um..." Uncle Felix. Her mother. Martha Zeigler. And, of course, Dorris Kaye, had all crowded into the kitchen nook. This wasn't supposed to happen. What *had* just happened? She shook her head, reeling. Forrest had kissed her...but none of this was real. Why he'd kissed her now, when neither Courtney or Rebecca Hall were present was a mystery, but... It was done. This beautiful, wonderful kiss was all part of the act. It had to be. It was the only thing that made sense. The momentary joy fizzled, leaving cold, hollow dread churning in the base of her stomach.

"I guess the cat's out of the bag, now? Isn't it, you two?" Her mother was grinning, eyeing the two of them. "Don't look so worried, now." She gave her shoulder a pat. "Billy is looking for you, Hattie."

"I didn't know there *was* a cat in a bag, but…" Martha Zeigler was wide-eyed with surprise. "I'd say so."

This was bad. Dorris Kaye giggling like that? Worse than bad.

"Billy?" Hattie croaked. Good. An escape.

"He was hoping you'd check on Courtney," her mother asked.

Of course, it was Courtney. Hattie managed to nod, even if her insides were twisting up. Not exactly the escape she was hoping for.

"She's in the bathroom. She wasn't feeling well." Her mother nodded. "We can finish up here—with the coffee."

Dorris Kaye giggled again.

Hattie nodded, on the verge of running from the room. There was no way—no way—she was going to look at Forrest. He had to be just as shaken up as she was. Now they weren't just lying to her family, they'd be lying to all of Garrison. This was bad. So, so bad. No matter how wonderful and right it might have felt, it had been a huge mistake. *What am I supposed to do?*

"I guess I see why you didn't answer me

calling," Uncle Felix teased as Hattie slipped from the room. She saw Billy, saw him point down the hall and mouth "Thank you" before turning his attention back to Rebecca Hall.

At least he'd asked Hattie to check on Courtney instead of occupying Courtney's mother. She walked down the long hall to the closed bathroom door, doing her best to box up what had just happened until later, and knocked softly. "Courtney?"

Through the door, Hattie could hear crying. Not just crying, sobbing.

"Courtney?" she whispered, jiggling the handle. "Are you okay? Please, let me in. Billy is worried."

The handle clicked and the door cracked. "I'm fine," Courtney said, before bursting into tears.

Any thoughts of a quick check-in before reporting back to Billy went out the window as soon as Hattie's gaze swept the room. Courtney was sitting on the bathroom floor a few feet from the toilet, a roll of toilet paper in her hands and mascara running down her cheeks.

Hattie closed the door behind her and sat on the floor beside Courtney. She didn't say anything—she didn't know what to say, but she couldn't just leave her. "Are you sick?"

Courtney nodded. "The barbecue, I think." She covered her mouth. "It's so strong."

The smell? It had to be the smell—the food wasn't ready yet.

"Hattie." Courtney looked at her, tears running down her cheeks. "I… I know what you think of me and I don't blame you," Courtney said on a wavering breath. "I know what I… I did to you. It was horrible. I thought I could pretend like it didn't happen, but it did." She was sobbing all over again. "I was horrible." She sniffed. "But I'm trying, Hattie, I am… I don't want to be that person." She tore off some more toilet paper and blotted her eyes. "My m-mother. I don't want to be her." Her gaze bounced from Hattie to the toilet paper. "I've spent the last eight years trying to put distance between us, because I know…she's not a nice person. And I don't want to be like that." She hiccupped. "But I'm getting married, so she—she has to be here. I couldn't *not* invite her." She blew her nose. "She's my mother." She frowned, then started crying again.

"You're not your mother." Since her arrival, Courtney had remained distant, but that wasn't the same thing as what her mother was doing.

"I could be. I know I could be. I *was*." She was sobbing again, covering her face with both hands. "Billy loves you so much and I wanted us to be friends, but then I saw you and I knew… I knew… I'd blocked all of that out, I had to. I hated myself. But there you were… And it all came back. What I did to you. What I said. You have to hate me." She shook her head. "Why haven't you told him, Hattie? I keep waiting and waiting… Just do it. I can't take it anymore. Just tell him."

It wasn't easy, but Hattie met her gaze. "That was a long time ago, Courtney. I'll admit that I was upset when I found out about your engagement, but… Billy is my brother. If he loves you, then there's a reason—"

"I'm pregnant," Courtney blurted out. "We're not rushing to get married because we can't stand to be apart. We're rushing so that he doesn't embarrass you or let you all down. You and your parents mean everything to him…"

Hattie was staring at her now. This was a surprise. A big surprise. *A baby?*

"I want to believe he's not marrying me

because of the baby, but… I know I'm not good enough for him. I *know* it. Coming here, meeting all of you—and this town. I don't fit here." She shook her head. "I never did. I was *always* the outsider. I knew it every day we lived here, too. I will be, even after we're married." She glanced at Hattie. "I'm so sorry, Hattie. So, so sorry. I hate what I did to you—who I was." She twisted the toilet paper in her hands. "I was so angry then, and I took it out on you, Hattie. If I could go back and change it all, I would. Please believe me. There is no excuse for how I was or what I did, but I was s-so alone and so, so jealous of you and your family and your friends…" She was sobbing all over again.

Hattie didn't doubt the grief or regret in Courtney's words. She felt it, deeply. Hattie couldn't begin to imagine how hard it would be to try to move into Garrison the middle of her high school career, after her father had left, and coming home to a bitter, judgmental mother every day. "Courtney—"

"No, now you're going to be nice to me, because you feel sorry for me. That's who you are, the nice girl that everyone likes. And I'm— I'm the mean girl. I am, I know it. Pregnant and…horrible. And when Billy hears what I did to you—"

"Do you love my brother?" Hattie already knew the answer. It was plain on Courtney's face every time she looked at Billy.

"I love him. He's the best man—the best person—ever. Do you think I'm pretending? I'm not, I promise." Courtney looked stunned. "I— I've n-never felt like this about anyone before." She sucked in a deep breath and pressed her hands against her stomach. "And now our baby. He seems so happy about it, but I worry he's doing what's noble. That he doesn't really love me, too." She stared down at her stomach. "The baby is a surprise, but I'm so grateful. Billy and I…" She glanced at Hattie. "I do love him, Hattie. He is everything. Everything."

"That's all that matters." Hattie swallowed. "I believe you, Courtney. Thank you for saying you'd go back and change things. And apologizing, too. That means a lot to me. I'm sorry I didn't reach out then—that I didn't try to be your friend." She'd never stopped to think about it from Courtney's point of view. Yes, she'd been horrible to Hattie, but that didn't matter. Not now. "Let's put all that behind us, okay?" She smiled, hurting for this woman in a way she'd never imagined. "I believe you'll be a good wife to my brother and mother to my niece or nephew. And I know Billy loves you and you're going to make each other happy."

Courtney stared at her. "Just like that?" She sniffed. "You mean it?"

"I mean it." Hattie nodded. "I want you to be happy, Courtney. I want Billy to be happy." From the sounds of it, up until recently, Courtney hadn't had a lot of happiness in her life.

Courtney leaned over and rested her head on Hattie's shoulder. "I'm sorry for crying and ruining everything...it's just..."

"The barbecue smell is pretty overpowering," Hattie agreed.

Courtney laughed. "Well, that, but there's more to it." She sniffed. "I never had this, you know? People who care about me, as is. You're all so close. And now I get to be a part of it. After everything I've done, I don't feel like I d-deserve it."

Hattie squeezed her hand, aching for her. "You're family now, Courtney."

Courtney squeezed back. "Thank you, Hattie. Thank you so much for giving me a second chance. I promise you, you won't be sorry." She sighed. "I don't think anyone has ever been so kind to me, Hattie, not ever. Billy was right—you're one of a kind."

Hattie rested her head against the wall, marveling at the turn her day had taken. She'd never imagined sitting on the bathroom floor littered with tear-streaked toilet paper to have a healing heart-to-heart with Courtney. Then again, she'd never imagined falling in love with Forrest. Or eagerly kissing him—in front of an audience. *One thing at a time*. She'd made peace with Courtney. Somehow, some way, she'd make peace with having all of Garrison know about her and Forrest's charade—and watching her deal with a broken heart.

FORREST WAS IN KNOTS. He'd kissed Hattie and she'd disappeared. It had been almost an hour and no one had seen her. All because he'd overstepped and kissed her. He didn't know what he'd been thinking. He hadn't been thinking. Yes, he was in love with her but she didn't know that. Here she'd been all worked up over Webb leaving and her brother's wedding and he went and planted some earthshaking kiss on her. It was earthshaking for him anyway. Other than being wide-eyed with shock, he wasn't sure how she felt about it.

How was he supposed to look her in the eye now? How was he supposed to be there for her when that kiss removed every doubt or hesitation he'd had?

He knew, with every fiber of his being, that Hattie was the one for him. Likely, the only one for him. And as wonderful and real and comforting as that fact was—it also threatened to be the end of the friendship he relied upon most.

What am I doing?

He headed out to the fire pit, away from the buzz of conversation and crush of people. He wouldn't touch a thing or Uncle Felix would light into him, but he needed space. A lot of space. He needed to clear his brain, work through the situation and figure out where to go from here.

The problem was, he had no idea. None. Did he speak from the heart and tell Hattie how he felt or did he stay quiet and protect their friendship? Either way, there was no predicting the outcome. And, either way, there were risks. Big ones.

He was standing there, staring into the open grill when Audy walked up and clapped him on the shoulder. "It's meat, all right. And it's cooking."

Forrest closed the lid and nodded.

"You look all pinched up." Audy pointed at him. "What's wrong? You eat something bad?"

Forrest shook his head. "I'm not in the mood, Audy."

"I know that face. And that tone." Audy nodded. "Woman trouble."

Forrest glared at his brother.

Webb was headed straight for them, Beau jogging to catch up.

"You said later." Webb nodded, hands on his hips. "It's later."

"I meant later, when we're alone. We still have an audience," Forrest grumbled.

"They're all busy." Beau's cheeks were surprisingly red when he looked Forrest's way. "Got plenty to talk about."

Forrest groaned and flopped into one of the chairs made from cedar boughs Beau and Webb had constructed a few years before. "That's why you're all here?"

"Well...yeah." Webb sat opposite from him. "After what I heard, I'm thinking that blow to the face caused some sort of brain injury or something."

Forrest shot him a look.

"You kissed Hattie?" Beau asked, taking a seat and propping his elbows on his knees. "I don't know why everyone's talking like it's such a big deal."

Everyone? Forrest ran a hand over his face. "It sort of is a big deal—a really big deal." His heart was on the line. "I think I made a mistake," he murmured. All three of his brothers sat and stared at him, waiting for him to go on. "She's my best friend..."

"You always told me Mom and Dad were best friends," Beau said, shrugging.

"They were." Forrest had to smile then. "They were a team." He did his best to talk about his parents with Webb and Beau. They'd been so much younger when their parents died, he knew they needed memories and stories more than he and Audy and Mabel did. He considered what Beau was saying before he said, "But they were on the same page."

Beau sat back, looking thoughtful.

And so much like Dad.

The knot in Forrest's throat wasn't just about Hattie now—it was about his father not being here, having this talk with him, giving him the guidance he needed not to make things ten times worse.

"Hold up." Webb pushed his hat back on his head, his eyes narrowed. "Just so we're clear… You and Hattie are… You want Hattie for… You—"

"Are in love with Hattie," Uncle Felix said, his voice making them all jump. "What? The four of you were all so caught up talking, I was worried the chicken would dry out." He regarded each one of them before he smiled. "I'm right, though, aren't I, Forrest?"

Forrest swallowed hard. He and his brothers didn't sit around and do this. Uncle Felix, either. They kept their business to themselves but… Things were changing. They were changing. Maybe this could be a good thing? This talking, as painful as it was, might be something they could all benefit from. "Yeah," he grumbled.

That set them all off then, laughing. Even Forrest joined it.

"Glad you're so happy about it," Webb hooted.

"You should know—that kiss? Everyone knows about it." Audy glanced over his shoulder at the porch and house. "Every single one of them. Dorris Kaye is like a kid in a candy store, sharing with anyone who makes eye contact."

Uncle Felix was chuckling again.

Forrest glared at them both. "Not helping."

"Brooke says she'll swap out your shampoo for hair remover if you hurt Hattie," Audy added. "Figured I'd toss that out there."

Webb eyed Forrest. "I don't think you could pull off being bald."

Forrest scratched his jaw, refusing to take the bait.

"I know you're stubborn, Forrest, but there are times when being stubborn isn't a good thing." Audy waved a hand in front of his face. "Are you listening to me at all?"

"About being bald? Everyone knowing about me kissing Hattie? Or how I'm stubborn and you think you have advice I'd want to listen to?"

Audy was laughing then. "Sounds like I hit a nerve."

"Or two," Webb agreed.

Beau just watched his brothers, wearing a half smile.

Forrest went back to glaring.

"Since you've gone and kissed her—" Uncle Felix flipped over chicken on the grill as he spoke "—and that was some kiss, boy…"

That had his brothers laughing again and Forrest covering his face.

"What are you going to do next?" Uncle Felix asked. "Other than sit out here and let your brothers get under your skin, that is."

"What am I doing?" Beau asked, holding up his hands. "I haven't given Forrest any grief."

"Nothing." Forrest smiled at him. "I appreciate that, too, Beau."

"I might poke a little, but that's what I do." Audy stopped and smiled as Brooke headed their way. "Just know, if I hadn't gone and made a fool out of myself before the whole town, I wouldn't have her." He nodded at Brooke.

Brooke slowed, aware that they were all staring at her. "What are you Briscoe boys talking about, all serious?" Brooke asked, smiling as Audy stood and offered her his chair, which she declined.

"You," Audy said. "How lucky I am."

"And don't you forget it." Brooke slid her arm around his waist. "It there a reason we're talking about how lucky you are?" She glanced at Forrest.

Forrest stared up at the clouds overhead. "Has anyone seen Hattie recently?"

"She's in the bathroom with Courtney." Brooke shrugged. "Courtney wasn't feeling well."

"What?" he asked, surprised. He couldn't exactly go charging into the bathroom, but he couldn't just sit by while Hattie was stuck in close quarters with Courtney. He didn't want to think the worst of Courtney, for Billy's sake, but he couldn't forget what the woman had done to Hattie or let his guard down. "Can you go check on her?"

"Sure." Brooke smiled. "I'll be right back. Joy is with Barbara." She pressed a kiss against Audy's cheek before heading back to the house.

"You act like she's gonna rip Hattie's eyes out," Audy murmured. "They were kids when all that happened. Neither of them are kids anymore."

"I'm lost," Uncle Felix said.

"Courtney used to bully Hattie in high school. Bad," Audy said, like it was no big deal.

"She did what?" Beau was upset. As a high-schooler himself, he'd understand the gravity of what Audy'd just said.

"That's not right," Webb agreed, frowning. "Billy know this? I'd wanna know."

"Calm down," Forrest said. "Hattie doesn't want this to be a big deal."

"But it is, isn't it?" Uncle Felix asked, not waiting for an answer. "Who could pick on Hattie? She's as good as gold—no denying."

Forrest loved that all four of them nodded at that.

The shrill cry of baby Joy set Audy in action. "That's for me." He pushed out of the chair. "Stop wasting time, Forrest. Isn't that what you told me? Tell Hattie, straight out. If she's not in love with you, she'll still be your best friend. Hattie is Hattie." He trotted to the back porch to scoop Joy out of Barbara Eldridge's arms. The crying stopped instantly.

Forrest watched, amused at the change in his brother. It wasn't all that long ago that Audy's only baby was his restored truck. The idea of a family and responsibility—was strictly avoided. And then, boom, everything changed and he's running across the yard to comfort his little girl. He couldn't be happier for his brother.

"Who'd of thought, huh?" Webb asked.

"It just takes the right woman." Uncle

Felix frowned. "Or so I hear," he grumbled. "Stop making those faces." He pointed at them with his long barbecue tongs. "Why don't you all make yourselves useful and get the fixin's on the table. The meat's all but done and I don't like eating cold food."

Just like that, they were up and in action. The large circular pavilion his father had built right on the edge of his favorite hill had been used for many an event on the ranch. Mostly casual, like now. They'd always thrown a big picnic for the ranch hands, their families and friends on the Fourth of July. The pavilion had also been where Brooke and Audy had cake and punch and a little impromptu dancing after their city hall wedding. It held a whole lot of folk and cast a whole lot of shade—exactly what they needed on a warm Texas day like today.

Forrest was glad to have something to do. He waved down Mabel, gave her the heads-up and went about setting up tables. All around him, activity buzzed. From Audy dancing with Joy and Brooke on the back porch, Rusty and Mikey Woodard were laughing with Velma Hall, while Mr. Woodard was doing his best to keep up conversation with Rebecca Hall. *Poor Mr. Woodard.*

He and Audy started setting up chairs while Webb brought out the red-and-white-checked tablecloths they had set aside for big gatherings just like this.

"What do you think of the rest of the Halls?" Audy asked, popping open a folding chair and sliding the seat beneath the table.

Forrest shrugged. "Velma is a hoot. Lena, the one making eyes at Webb, seems nice enough." So far, Webb had been surprisingly charming. "Mrs. Hall?" He shook his head. Some things were best left unsaid.

"She's something, all right." Audy shook his head. "She asked Brooke if she'd done Miss Patsy's hair like that on purpose. I don't know how Brooke managed to stay so calm but she did. She told Mrs. Hall that her job was to make her clients happy. If Miss Patsy wanted rainbow-colored hair, that's just what Brooke would give her."

"I get the feeling Mrs. Hall isn't all that familiar with happiness." Forrest stood, glancing at the back porch.

Hattie was there.

His heart kicked into overdrive.

She was smiling, more at ease than he'd seen her in some time. From here, it looked like she was smiling and talking with Courtney. Not the strained, forced way of the preceding few days, either. That was one of Hattie's real smiles. The kind that made his insides melt.

Once he figured out what to say to Hattie, he'd say it. But not here or now. Today was about Webb. Webb, who was sitting next to Lena Hall—smiling like a fool and would be gone come Monday morning.

The buffet table was a mix of potluck and family favorites. Barbara Eldridge had brought potato salad, the way Uncle Felix liked it. There were three kinds of salad, two kinds of bean salad, potato salad, rolls and corn bread, chopped fruit and every kind of smoked meat imaginable. The desserts had their own table.

Forrest had never been so painfully aware of Hattie as he was now. A mere glimpse of her had him replaying that kiss again and again. He hung back, trying to tamp down his awareness of every move Hattie made. Not that it worked.

Hattie seemed to be on the same page. Not only did she steer clear of him, she tried to sit two whole tables away. Her mother, of course, had Hattie collecting her plate and steered her to the seat beside him. She sat, giving him a tight smile, but the tension between them was nearly unbearable.

Once they were all seated, Uncle Felix nodded his way. He'd told Forrest a speech needed to be made but he wouldn't make it through one. Forrest was grappling with the same fear when he tapped his plate with his fork and stood.

"I want to thank you all for coming out today. Most of you know me and know I'm not much of a talker but, somehow, I'm still the one making a speech. Bear with me." He smiled at the laughter, sucking in a deep breath for what was to come. "As soon as Webb told us the news, Mabel pulled out her tablet and got right to work to make sure Webb had a proper send-off." He paused, swallowing. "But, even now, I'm having a hard time wrapping my mind around all this. Webb leaving, I mean. Webb is my little brother. Most times, I see him as some knock-kneed boy in a too-big hat getting into all sorts of trouble. Uncle Felix and I have given him a hard time about how many of our gray hairs have his name on them."

There was a low murmur of laughter.

"But the truth of it is, Webb's not a mischief-maker. He's a good man. I never gave Webb credit for how determined he is." He swallowed again. "I remember when Audy and I were headed out with Daddy for something or other and we were going to leave you behind since there wasn't time to mount up another horse. Really, it was because Daddy thought you weren't ready for a day in the saddle." He shook his head, picturing it clearly in his mind. "You were so mad, you were spitting nails. Ten minutes later, here comes Webb, riding bareback, covered in dirt, missing a front tooth if I recall, but happy as a clam." He waited, watching as red crept up Webb's neck and into his face. "I heard later from Old Ike, who loves to tell a good tale, that Webb'd tried a handful of times to get up on his horse—falling off or over or never quite making it up—but Webb didn't give up. He dragged over a stack of mineral blocks, slid onto his horse and got the old horse moving." He smiled at his brother. "Didn't complain once the whole day, either."

There were some cheers and smiles, turning Webb beet red now.

"Most of my memories of Webb are like that. He'd dig in, figure things out and do it right—with a smile. He's always had my back—his brothers and sister and uncle, too. That's who he is. That's why I know he'll be a good soldier." He had to stop then, flexing his fingers—before Hattie took his hand and squeezed it. "Webb doesn't do anything half-hearted. He works hard, tirelessly, and gets the job done. For all the teasing we do—and there's a lot of it—I know I can speak for all of us when I say we are proud of you." He nodded then, his throat so thick he took a sip of his tea. Hattie's hand held tight but he knew better than to look at her. If he did that, he'd never get through the rest of it. "We're all gonna miss you." His voice gave his struggle away, but he lifted his glass anyway. "Here's to you, little brother, and the adventures that are waiting for you. Do your best, give your all and know we support you, one hundred percent."

Webb's face was all squished up then, his lips pressed tight and his jaw rigid. Audy, too. Beau was staring down at his lap, holding on to Tess's hand. He didn't dare look Uncle Felix's way. And Mabel? Well, she was sobbing, Jensen's handkerchief pressed to her face.

"Hear, hear," Bart Carmichael said.

"Cheers." Lena Hall was staring at Webb, blinking rapidly.

Forrest sat, his heart in his throat, to toast and cheer and smile, but he never let go of Hattie's hand. He didn't look at her—that would force his hand and he'd say or do something he'd regret. For now, he'd hold on to her and pretend that everything was fine with them. He needed Hattie more than anything, and he'd take whatever she was willing to give him.

CHAPTER ELEVEN

HATTIE LAY IN her bed with her eyes shut. There was no hint of the sun spilling into her small bedroom but she was awake. Wide-awake. She glanced at the green LED display on her bedside clock. It was a little after five.

It was Monday and Webb was leaving.

Saturday had been the best worst day ever. There'd been no shortage of affection and healing, conversation and laughter—but Hattie had come home unsettled, teary-eyed, with a painful ache in her chest. Things were getting out of hand and someone was going to get hurt. *Someone like me.*

The kiss. The not-real, oh-so-real kiss. Forrest hadn't looked at her once. Not once. From the time she came out of the bathroom with Courtney until she'd climbed into her truck at the end of the night. He'd held her hand through his speech and through the toasts, but after that...

Nothing.

As much as she wanted to clear the air between them, today wasn't the day for it. Forrest, for all his big, gruff exterior, was a bighearted softie. Sending his brother off would be no easy feat. She hated saying goodbye to Billy—and he was only a few hours away. She could only imagine the grief Forrest would feel once Webb was gone.

She kicked off her blankets and tugged on jeans, an old feedstore shirt, pulled on her boots and ran some of Gretta's magic hair stuff through her curls. When that didn't work, she put her straw cowboy hat on her head, grabbed her keys and headed out the door.

The morning was cool, hinting at the coming fall. Not that Texas ever had much fall or winter. If a person was looking for seasons, Texas wasn't for them. But Hattie liked the heat. She liked the sun and floating down the river and drinking sweet tea and riding horses along the paths of erste Baum park. She loved everything about her little town and her state. It was impossible to imagine leaving it or her family. She admired Webb for that, doing something so bold, but her heart also ached for those he was leaving behind. That's why she was driving down the dirt drive of Briscoe Ranch before six in the morning. The Briscoes were her family and, right now, they needed one another.

She slammed her truck door, noting the absence of Uncle Felix's big black truck as she took the steps up and onto the large wraparound porch of the main house. Webb was already gone?

"Saw you coming," Beau said, holding the door wide. His hair was on end, his eyes were puffy and he was in sleep pants and a white undershirt.

"Morning," she said, stepping inside. "Too early?"

"Nah." He yawned, running his hand over his head. "We're all up."

Hattie followed him into the kitchen, where Mabel and Forrest sat at the table. Without saying a word, she poured herself a cup of coffee and made a fresh pot. Once that was done, she opened the refrigerator and pulled out eggs, cheese, bacon and sausage. Mabel joined her, giving her a quick hug, before she pulled out a cast-iron skillet, chopping board and knife. Forrest got up, taking over the bacon and sausage. Beau pulled out the baking mix and started making biscuits.

Not much was said, but soon there were omelets, bacon and sausage patties, and fresh biscuits for all.

"Morning," Hattie said, refilling Mabel and Forrest's mugs.

"Morning." Mabel smiled. "Thanks for this, Hattie."

"I didn't do anything special." She waved Mabel's thanks aside, filled up her own mug and replaced the pot in its cradle. "I was up and out of groceries so I figured I'd mooch off you all." She risked a glance Forrest's way but he was staring into his coffee.

They ate in relative silence.

When Harvey trotted into the kitchen, Hattie mostly talked to him. The big dog seemed like the only one interested in company.

"I gotta get going." Beau stood, stretched. "Practice." He rubbed his stomach. "Probably shouldn't have eaten that much."

"Got lunch money?" Forrest asked.

"Covered." Beau nodded. "I was going to hang out with Tess after school and then I'm helping out with the Junior Rangers." He glanced her way. "Meeting in erste Baum park?"

"Just make sure you've got all your work done," Forrest murmured.

Beau glanced at Mabel, who shrugged. "Yes, sir." He paused, then said, "Y'all have a good day. See you later, Hattie."

"Will do. Thanks for the extra hands." She was still dreading the idea of Levi Williams armed with a spade or hoe but was hoping for the best.

Beau disappeared through the kitchen door.

"I'd offer to come but Jensen and I—"

"No, no, you two go on and have your date." Hattie smiled at her. "Samantha is good as gold. And, I think, I've lassoed her aunt Kitty into lending a helping hand, so I'm hoping things won't get too messy."

"You're braver than me." Mabel chuckled. "Speaking of Kitty, when is your next fitting?"

Hattie sighed. "Thursday morning, I think? Friday is the rehearsal dinner at Hilltop Inn and Saturday is the wedding." Hattie sighed. "Is it wrong that I'm glad I'm working tomorrow and Wednesday?"

"No." Mabel sipped her coffee. "I can't believe how fast it's all come together. It makes me exhausted just thinking about it." She took another sip. "I'm glad Jensen and I are taking the long way around."

Hattie risked another glance at Forrest. His blue eyes were fixed on the window that looked out onto the sprawling lands of Briscoe Ranch. What was he thinking? Maybe she didn't want to know. She stood, carrying plates to the sink, scraping them off and rinsing them.

"I'll get it," Forrest said, suddenly at her side.

"I don't mind." She kept on working.

"You don't need to clean up after us." He sighed, reaching for the plate.

"I ate, too." She leaned away, scrubbing faster.

"Are you really trying to keep me from helping you?" he asked, a small smile on his face when his gaze finally met hers.

No. She offered him the plate. "If you insist."

He took the plate and put it in the dishwasher.

"What's on your agenda today?" she asked him.

"I was going to ride out, try and get a head count on the new calves we have. Afterward, I was supposed to meet Tyson and

Mr. Hillard over at the stockyards to talk to them about some sort of scholarship or sponsorship for the Junior Rodeo program." He took another plate and loaded it. "Why?"

"No reason." She handed him another plate.

"If I hadn't promised Samantha we'd go meet Nana the goat, I'd hang out with you, Hattie, but Samantha is so excited." Mabel always lit up when she talked about her soon-to-be stepdaughter.

"Who wouldn't be?" Hattie grinned. "Nana is quite a character. You and Samantha have fun."

"You know what, *you* could take my place at Junior Rangers tonight, Forrest." Mabel brought the last plate to the counter, pulling out a storage container for the remaining biscuits. "Hattie's got her hands full. Levi Williams, to start. There's Seth Travis who is too cool to take an interest in anything. He's what, seven?" She shook her head. "His little brother, Pete, is adorable. He absolutely worships Seth, poor thing. But he's a bit of a talker."

"A bit?" Hattie laughed. "If that boy has one word to say, he has a hundred."

"Eddie Hillard just breaks my heart. I

don't think I've ever seen a child so shy." Mabel pressed a hand to her heart. "I'm hoping Samantha will pull him out of his shell. She's never met a stranger."

Hattie loved that Mabel was so enamored with her stepdaughter-to-be. Though, to be fair, Samantha Crawley was about as precious a little girl as any Hattie'd met. "I'll keep that in mind. I'll try a buddy system." She frowned. "Who am I supposed to pair Abigail with?" Abigail cried at the drop of a hat. It didn't seem fair to pair her off with another ranger and have their fun ruined.

Mabel laughed then. "Someone with infinite patience?"

"I have to say, as far as sales pitches go, this one stinks." Forrest leaned against the counter, his arms crossed over his chest. "You make this sound about as fun as getting lemon juice in a paper cut over and over for hours."

Mabel shrugged.

"They're not that bad." Hattie was quick to defend her little rangers. "They just need direction is all. And extra hands. I'm hoping that Beau's recruits and the Ladies Guild will be enough so you're off the hook, Forrest." She patted his arm—and regretted it. One touch and she was all off-kilter.

"What about you, Hattie?" Mabel asked, stowing the container of biscuits in the fridge. "Big plans for today?"

"I don't know." She refilled her coffee mug and held it between both hands. "Billy said something about walking through Hilltop Inn and the reception setup, but I'm thinking they can handle it without me. I've been meaning to put up some trim board for ages now, so I might do that."

"You could come ride out, see the new calves, if you want?" Forrest offered, pouring himself more coffee. "After, I can help you with your trim boards, then go see Tyson?"

Hattie was relieved. Going riding with Forrest was something normal they'd do. Before the staring and the touching and the kissing… No thinking about kissing today. Not even for a fraction of a second. "Baby cows and trim boards? Sounds like fun to me."

Forrest smiled, his eyes traveling over her face. "I'll take that as a yes."

She nodded, wishing he'd look at her like he used to—before all of this. Now she realized it wasn't just touch that made things go fuzzy; one long blue-eyed look could do the same. *Take a deep breath, Hattie.*

"Well, then, you two have fun." Mabel waved, smiling as she left them alone in the kitchen.

Hattie decided lingering, alone with Forrest, was a bad idea. "Come on, Harvey, let's get to the barn." She patted her thigh, smiling when the massive dog got up. "You ready?" she asked Forrest.

As soon as they rode out, it was like the last week hadn't happened. Other than the slowly fading bruise covering a good portion of Forrest's face, there seemed to be some sort of silent understanding between them. It was easy again. Hattie had always appreciated how she and Forrest could go for long stretches in comfortable silence. A nod or smile now and then was enough. If Hattie could stop admiring the broad shoulders of the man before her, it would have been a perfectly normal day.

If he hadn't turned to look back, he'd never have caught her staring at him. But he did, and Hattie had to work fast to fill the awkwardness before it ruined the morning.

"I talked to Courtney." As expected, he

drew his horse to a stop until they were side-by-side. “I feel bad for her, Forrest.”

He frowned.

“She apologized,” Hattie went on. “A lot, actually. She said she was horrible and moving here had been hard because her father had just left and her mother is… Well, you’ve met her mother.” She saw his frown soften as she recounted the rest of their conversation. She sighed, glancing his way. “The thing is, I believe she means what she says.”

“Meeting her mother has definitely put a different spin on things,” Forrest admitted. “Not that what she did to you is excusable.” He looked at her. “It isn’t.”

There was a fearsome protectiveness to him that sent Hattie’s heart racing. “No.” Her voice was breathy and soft. “No,” she said again. “She said as much.” She paused. “But there’s more.”

He waited.

“It explains a bit more about the wedding.” She shrugged. “But, it’s a secret.”

He took a deep breath, his frown returning.

“I don’t like keeping secrets from you, Forrest,” she admitted. “I don’t need to. I know, if I tell you something, you'll keep it safe."

He nodded, the muscle in his jaw rippling. "I will."

"Courtney is pregnant." Even though the only thing within earshot were cattle, Hattie whispered.

Forrest's horse came to a stop.

"It tore my heart out, Forrest. I think she's worried Billy's only marrying her because of...of the baby." She rested her hands on the pommel of her saddle. Courtney's grief hadn't been manufactured; it'd been bone-deep and desperate. "She says she's not good enough for him."

"That'd be a hard thing to live with," he murmured. "That sort of doubt."

"Holding on to the past, knowing all this? I can't." She tilted her hat forward, slanting the morning sun from her eyes. "She doesn't have anyone to talk to. I can see how it'd be easier to keep people out instead of letting someone get close enough to hurt you." She looked at him. "Especially after everything she's been through. And having Rebecca as a mother."

Forrest's gaze fixed on her.

Hattie found herself staring right back.

There was nothing easy about this silence. It was alive and crackling between them, chock-full of words she knew better than to say. Things like *Your friendship is the most important in my life* and *I love you* and *No matter what, we have to stay friends*. But all of that could wait a bit. Webb's departure was brand-new—that was more than enough for one day. So, instead of imagining kissing Forrest right here and now, she needed to focus on something else.

"I guess we should get a move on. Those calves aren't going to count themselves." With a light squeeze of her knees, her horse went from a walk to a trot. "Come on, slowpoke." She saw him smile before she nudged the horse from a trot into a gallop.

FORREST WATCHED LEVI WILLIAMS hacking away at what had once been a perfectly good fern with the kid-sized spade the Ladies Guild had provided for the Junior Rangers. After watching Levi in action, he wasn't so sure the spade was a good idea.

"Now," Martha Zeigler was saying, "you'll want to carefully turn the soil."

Hattie, who was sitting between Pete and

Seth Travis, did exactly as Miss Martha—then praised both boys for doing the same.

"What's this turning soil stuff?" Dwight Crawley, who was there with his granddaughter Samantha, sighed. "You dig a hole and put in the plant." He shook his head.

Levi set to work digging a hole, flinging soil over his shoulder and onto Abigail Koch. Forrest winced at the earsplitting wails of the little girl.

"It's okay, Abigail." Gretta Williams soothed the girl, brushing the dirt from her hair and skirt. "Levi." Her tone had little to no effect on her gleeful dirt-throwing son.

"There goes Levi." Little Eddie Hillard's world-weary disappointment almost made Forrest laugh. He'd been assigned to be Eddie's partner and, knowing how shy he was, he'd been doing his best to engage with the boy. This was the most Eddie had said all evening.

"He does seem to be having fun." Forrest leaned aside as more dirt went flying.

"Dwight Crawley." Miss Martha's tone was so sharp, it could have cut glass. "If you insist on being rude, you can go sit under the tree until we are done."

Dwight Crawley's eyebrows shot up.

"And you, Levi Williams," Miss Martha snapped. "Did you hear your mother call you? Stop what you are doing, right this instant."

Levi froze.

Hattie glanced at Forrest, her eyes wide and her smile wider. Forrest had always thought Miss Martha would've been a terrifying drill sergeant. Watching her now, he knew she would have been.

"Now." Miss Martha stood, her silver hair shining in the sun, a force to be reckoned with. She pulled off her gardening gloves and slapped her palm with them. "I won't tolerate this nonsense. Gardening is important work. Gardens give us flowers that are beautiful, yes, but they also give us bees." She slapped her palms again. "Bees give us plants, plants that feed us and plants that let us breathe." Another slap of her gloves. "So, if you're not here to learn how to garden, with respect, you can hand over the tools and go sit on that rock." She held her hand out for their gardening tools.

"Paw Paw," Samantha whispered, "we have to behave. Miss Martha is a super gardener—"

"Master gardener," Miss Martha corrected her gently.

"She knows all about this. And I want to know all about this, so please don't make me go sit on that rock." Samantha turned big blue eyes up at her grandfather.

"Don't you worry, Samantha. I'll only send your Paw Paw to the rock." Miss Martha sighed. "Unless he can behave."

Forrest hadn't figured out if respect or fear was greater when it came to Martha Zeigler. Right about now, it was definitely respect. Not many people would stand up to Dwight Crawley.

"Please," Samantha whispered.

Oddly enough, Dwight Crawley smiled up at Miss Martha. "I'll behave."

"And you?" Miss Martha stared down at Levi Williams. "Are you going to continue to ruin my garden or can you make yourself useful and show Miss Hattie what a good boy you are."

Smart and sassy. Forrest had to grin. There was no denying Levi Williams had a huge crush on Hattie. One Miss Martha had picked up on and was working to her advantage.

"I'm certain Miss Hattie wants you to

learn to help with the garden and the bees, Levi." Miss Martha turned to Hattie.

"I do, Miss Martha. It's an important warden skill, Levi," Hattie added, giving the boy a sweet smile that had Forrest taking a deep, steadying breath.

"I will be the best gardener ever, Miss Martha." Levi smiled up at her. "Just you watch, Miss Hattie."

Hattie gave the little boy a thumbs-up.

"I guess we'll have to see." Miss Martha turned back to the pallet of flowers the Ladies Guild had brought for tonight's adventure. "Now, after you have *turned* the soil—"

"Carefully," Dwight Crawley murmured, chuckling.

"Then you'll sprinkle a light shower of water, like this." Miss Martha used her bluebonnet-painted watering can. "See? Just a little." She held her watering can in front of her. "Let me see you do it."

Hattie cheered on the Travis boys. Abigail managed not to cry. Eddie held his breath, but managed to do it. All that was left?

"Levi?" Miss Martha asked. "Go ahead."

Levi picked up his small watering can and peered inside it. "There's a lot more than a sprinkle of water in here, Miss Martha."

"There is." Miss Martha nodded. "You'll need more after you plant your flower."

"Oh." Levi nodded, being extra careful.

"Very good, Levi." Miss Martha crooned.

Hattie shot Forrest another look. Who knew Miss Martha could be as encouraging as she was intimidating? He winked, the bruises healing enough that winking no longer had him tearing up.

By the time the flowers were distributed and planted, Forrest was sure they'd been there for hours. Hours and hours.

"It's been an hour and a half?" Forrest asked, checking his phone.

"It was fun," Samantha said. "Wasn't it, Uncle Forrest?"

Dwight Crawley glanced Forrest's way. "He's not your uncle yet, Samantha."

"Daddy says it's okay if it's okay with you?" She turned those big blue eyes on Forrest.

He nodded. As if there was any way he was going to tell the little girl no.

"Samantha." Miss Martha waved her over.

"Now what?" Dwight Crawley scowled, leaning forward to see what was happening, then giving up and stomping over to them.

"You survived." Hattie grinned up at Forrest.

"Barely." He shook his head. "How often do you do this?"

"Once a month." She wiped her cheek with the back of her hand. "It's fun. The kids have fun."

"You have something—" He pointed at the smudge of dirt on her cheek. "Dirt."

Hattie swiped at her face, spreading more dirt onto her cheek.

"No." He shook his head, chuckling. "That went from a little to a lot." He pulled his handkerchief from his pocket, used one of the kid-sized watering cans to wet it down, then wiped the dirt from her cheek.

"I guess you can't say you're really enjoying yourself unless you get a little bit dirty?" she asked, tilting her face up.

"Well, then, you must have really enjoyed yourself." Forrest grinned. "A lot." He kept wiping, pretending she had mud on her forehead.

"There, too?" She frowned. "How did I manage that?"

He shrugged and kept on wiping, down the other side of her face.

"Forrest?" Her eyes widened. "I don't have it there? Do I?"

He leaned forward again, to wipe her other cheek, but she leaned back and he cracked up.

"You're terrible, you know that?" she asked, laughing.

"It was kind of funny." And he liked hearing her laugh. "But, yeah, I think I got it all."

She rolled her eyes. "Well, other than *that*, thank you for tonight." But whatever else she was going to say was cut short by the rising voices of Dwight Crawley and Miss Martha.

"I can afford a watering can," Dwight Crawley was saying.

"I didn't say otherwise, did I?" Miss Martha replied. "It's a gift."

"For what?" Dwight asked, crossing his arms over his chest.

"For Samantha. I have to have a reason to give your granddaughter a gift?" Miss Martha sounded as shocked as she looked. "It's a little gift, Dwight Crawley, no strings attached."

Luckily, Samantha had been preoccupied collecting all the empty bean packets to notice the tension between her grandpa and Miss Martha. But, once Miss Martha called to her, the little girl came running,

"This is for you, Samantha." Miss Martha offered Samantha one of the kid-sized watering cans.

"Oh, thank you, Miss Martha." Samantha was all smiles. "I love gardening."

"I can tell." Miss Martha nodded her approval. "And that is why I am giving this to you." She shot Dwight Crawley a narrow-eyed stare. "I hope you will enjoy it."

"That's very kind of you, Miss Martha." Hattie wore a panicked look on her face, turning to Forrest for help to defuse the escalating situation.

"Well, aside from a certain person, I would say tonight was a great success." Miss Martha sent another dagger-filled glance Dwight Crawley's way.

"Am I supposed to infer I'm that person?" Forrest hadn't thought it was possible but Dwight Crawley seemed to puff himself up even bigger as he added, "You are an insufferable woman."

"*I* am insufferable? Me?" Miss Martha stabbed her pointer finger repeatedly at Dwight Crawley's chest. "Talk about the pot calling the kettle black."

"Samantha, how about we go and take a look at erste Baum?" Hattie held out her hand. “I think Miss Martha and your Paw Paw have some things to work out.”

“Okay, Miss Hattie.” Samantha took Hattie’s hand and started skipping toward the large tree. “My Paw Paw can get grumpy sometimes.”

“We can all get grumpy. Can’t we, Forrest?”

Forrest looked at her, his eyebrows high. “I don’t know what you’re talking about. I am never grumpy.” He grinned.

“My daddy said you used to be grumpy with him all the time.” Samantha stared up at him. “But I’m glad you are friends now, Uncle Forrest. I don’t like it when people are grumpy.”

It had taken a long time for the Briscoe and Crawley feud to come to an end, but thanks to Jensen and Mabel it was over. “I don’t like it when people are grumpy, either.” Forrest smiled down at the little girl who would be his niece soon.

The three of them walked across the meadow, hand in hand. The sun was setting and the giant tree cast a long shadow that reached across most of the meadow.

“I remember when I was little, my brothers and I used to chase the shadow and see who could get there first." Forrest crouched and pointed out the outline to Samantha. "See that? Sometimes, on the right day, the shadow seems to run across the meadow."

Samantha stared at the shadow. "It's not moving very quickly now." The little girl looked at him. "I bet I could catch it."

Forrest stood. "I bet you could."

He and Hattie stood, side by side, watching as Samantha raced across the open field. Hearing her giggle made the ongoing argument behind them less important.

"Did you really do that?" Hattie asked.

"Yep. And I always won, too." Forrest smiled. "You can ask Audy if you don't believe me."

Hattie laughed.

Forrest was so caught up in the smile on her face that he almost didn't see Rebecca and Courtney Hall marching toward erste Baum. Rather, Rebecca seemed to be dragging Courtney toward the tree. At first, he considered turning Hattie around and heading back toward the garden, but then they'd have to deal with Dwight Crawley and Miss Martha and whatever that was about. This way, it was only Rebecca.

Samantha was jumping up and down and

waving, her black curls bouncing in the evening breeze. "I did it! I did it!"

Hattie clapped her hands. "You sure did."

"Oh, look, a firefly." Samantha jumped up and down. "Can I chase them?"

"Of course. Don't touch them—they have fragile wings. And stay right close to the tree." That's when Hattie saw Rebecca and Courtney, and grimaced.

"Well, that was certainly a reaction." Forrest chuckled. "We can always get Samantha and head back."

Hattie peered back in the direction they had come. "No. I'm not sure what's going on, but I'm pretty sure Jensen wouldn't want Samantha in the middle of all that." She watched as Samantha ran in a circle. "Besides, look at how much fun she's having."

Forrest didn't argue. While great progress had been made with Dwight Crawley, the man wasn't exactly all warm and jolly. He was just about as gruff and opinionated as the woman he was currently arguing with. Technically, the two of them could go at it for hours. Forrest shuddered at the thought. "So, Rebecca Hall it is." Without thinking, he took her hand.

He probably imagined the catch in Hattie's breath and the slight shiver that seemed to run up her arm. But he hoped he hadn't. He hoped Hattie was just as lost and caught up in all the out-of-control sensations that seemed to bounce back and forth between the two of them. *But hoping something doesn't make anything real.*

"What a surprise." Rebecca Hall turned, giving them both a sullen once-over. "And what brings the two of you out?"

"Is it your Junior Rangers meeting?" Courtney asked. "Billy was telling me all about it. How you two were a part of it when you were little and how you're carrying on the tradition with the kids in Garrison. I think it's wonderful."

Forrest thought that might be the first real smile of Courtney's he'd seen. All because Hattie had listened to her and forgiven her. *All because Hattie has a heart of gold.* He turned his hand, threading their fingers together and fitting her palm against his.

"Yes. That's exactly why we're here." Hattie's voice seemed a little high-pitched, but she smiled at Courtney. "Feel free to join us next time you're in town." She turned, checking on Samantha, before adding, "You're a teacher after all."

Courtney smiled in return. “I’d like that. Thank you, Hattie.”

“And your Junior Ranger meetings always end with a yelling match?” Rebecca Hall pointed across the meadow at Dwight Crawley and Miss Martha.

“No, sometimes there’s a fistfight.” Forrest scratched his jaw, staring up into the branches to hide his smile as he went on. “Once there was a knife fight, wasn’t there, Hattie?”

Rebecca Hall was staring at him in horror. But once Hattie started laughing, the woman’s eyes narrowed to dangerous slits and her tone was razor-sharp. “Oh, how quaint. Small-town humor. That’s why I choose to live in the city.”

“Mom.” The look of horror on Courtney’s face made Forrest feel just the tiniest bit guilty. “Forrest was trying to be funny. You don’t have to be mean.”

“I’m dizzy,” Samantha called out, giggling and falling onto the green grass with a sigh.

“Does she belong to one of you?” Rebecca asked, frowning in Samantha’s direction.

“She’s my niece,” Forrest said, daring Rebecca to say a word about Samantha.

“How nice.” Rebecca waved her hand,

as if dismissing the whole situation. "Let's just get this over with, shall we? There is a perfectly adorable chapel in town. I don't understand why you want to have an outdoor wedding. Especially here. There are bugs. And people. It doesn't make any sense, Courtney."

"Billy said it's good luck." Courtney stared up into the tree, walking close to the massive trunk and resting her hand against the bark. "I like the idea of getting married here. I know, I know it's not in the church but… This place is special to Billy. It means something to his family." Her smile faltered. "And I think Billy and I could use the luck, don't you? I mean, everyone could use good luck."

Now that Forrest knew about the baby, Courtney's comment had more meaning.

"Luck is always a good thing." Hattie nodded. "But, I don't think you and Billy need to worry about that."

Courtney gave Hattie the biggest smile.

"So that's what people do?" Rebecca pointed at the tree. "They get married under a tree and live blissful, happy lives?" She shot a disbelieving look at her daughter. "It's a tree, Courtney."

Samantha ran up just then, grabbing Forrest's hand. "It's erste Baum. Daddy and Mabel say it's a special tree."

Rebecca ignored Samantha.

"Your daddy and Mabel are right." Forrest smiled at Samantha. "So is Billy. A lot of celebrating happens under erste Baum, for good reason. It's been here, stayed here, through storms and droughts and hundreds of years. To me, that's pretty lucky. If getting married here gives a couple just a little bit of that luck, why not?" Forrest liked the way Hattie's hand tightened on his. He liked the way she was looking up at him even more.

"I guess that means you and Hattie will get married here?" Rebecca Hall sneered.

It was all too easy to imagine marrying Hattie here, before their family and friends. "If Hattie said yes, I'd marry her here in a heartbeat." He meant every word he said. But as soon as the words were out of his mouth, he saw the look on Hattie's face. Her smile gave way and in its place was gut-wrenching sadness. He didn't know what that look meant or why she pulled her hand from his, but he was going to find out. The sooner the better.

CHAPTER TWELVE

HATTIE SAT AT her mother's kitchen table, a cup of coffee in her hands. She'd put in extra-long hours Tuesday and Wednesday but, as promised, she'd risen with the sun this morning to have breakfast with her family.

"You made the paper," her father announced, making a sweeping arm motion as he draped it open on the tabletop. "Warden Carmichael, you're a hero."

"Again." Billy yawned, scratching his messy hair. "What did you do now?"

"Was it dangerous?" Her mother glanced at the paper. "I don't want to know if it was dangerous."

"I'm right here." Hattie laughed. "Safe and sound."

"Ahem." He picked up the paper, cleared his throat and read.

> "Local game warden Harriet Carmichael made a visit to the Hill Country

Sleepaway Camp and took several animals with her. Campers got to meet several native species including a tarantula, a horned toad, a rare Texas map turtle and a king snake. Campers were able to handle axis deer antlers, an armadillo shell and the horns of a bighorn sheep."

He cleared his throat and continued.

"Warden Carmichael went on to say that educating the young is one of her favorite things to do. Quote, 'Answering questions and watching the kids get excited ensures the land and wildlife we so enjoy today will be protected and cared for tomorrow.'"

"It was a slow news day." Hattie sighed.

"I think it's because people like you, Hattie." Her mother patted her shoulder. "You put folk at ease, always have. Hasn't she, Billy?"

"Yep, Warden Harriet is a gem." Billy took a sip of coffee, but he was smiling.

Hattie was torn between laughing and sticking her tongue out at her older brother.

"You're interrupting me." Her father peered over the paper at them.

> "One camper said he wanted to be a game warden when he grew up while another said they wanted to be a veterinarian so they could care for all the animals."

"Isn't that nice?" Her mother patted her arm. "That has to make you feel good, Hattie."

"You mean Game Warden Harriet?" Billy winked.

"Okay, Willie, how about we give it a rest?" Hattie pointed at him. "Does Courtney know you used to go by Willie, I wonder?"

Billy scowled.

"Even more interesting," their father went on, "were reports of unusual behavior amongst local wildlife."

Hattie glanced at her father. "What?" She didn't know about this.

"Sightings of Game Warden Carmichael and one Forrest Briscoe exchanging public affections, including one scandalous kiss—"

Hattie threw her napkin at her father,

pleased when it hit the paper and knocked it from his hands. "Ha ha."

But her father, mother and brother were all laughing.

She rolled her eyes, smiling in spite of herself. Yes, it was *sort* of funny. It was. And it wasn't. Not that they knew how all of this was weighing on her. Lying was wrong, no exceptions. Her parents had taught her that. And yet, she and Forrest were doing just that. Not some little white lie, either. The two of them had spun quite a yarn—their actions making the deceit that much worse.

"I didn't mean to upset you." Her father was studying her. "It doesn't say that."

It was a good thing Garrison and the surrounding towns were too small for a gossip column in their paper or she and Forrest might just have wound up there. She shook her head. "I didn't think it did, Dad."

"I don't know." Billy reached for one of the fresh baked biscuits from the basket their mother had placed on the table. "I'd consider it newsworthy."

"Stop picking, you two." Her mother gave them both a stern look. "This is the first minute we've had, just to ourselves, and I'd like to enjoy it."

Hattie took a biscuit and passed the basket to her father. "Where is Courtney?"

"Her mother thought they all needed to go into Austin for a spa day." Billy shrugged. "I guess a trip to Brooke's salon wasn't what she had in mind."

Lucky for Brooke. And yet, Brooke wouldn't let someone like Rebecca Hall get to her—she'd have given back as good as she got. *I wish I could learn how to do that.* Then again, she didn't want to do anything that would rock the boat for Courtney and Billy. Saturday was coming, the wedding would be over and Mrs. Hall would be gone. *Along with the need for me and Forrest to keep up this deception.*

"Pass the jam?" Billy asked.

Hattie reached for the mason jar with their mother's fresh peach preserves and passed it to her brother, and then sliced open the still-warm biscuit on her plate. "Light and fluffy."

"Of course." Her father scooped skillet fries, scrambled eggs and thick, sliced bacon onto his plate. "Your momma's breakfasts are the best."

"Or maybe you're just used to my cooking after thirty-two years." Their mother sat beside their father and put her napkin in her lap. She'd always sat there, not on the opposite end of the table.

"Thirty-two years?" Billy shook his head. "That's a long time."

"Is it?" Her father winked at her mother. "Doesn't feel like it." He patted her hand. "What do you think, Glady?"

"No time at all." She tilted her cheek up for his quick kiss. "Now, eat up before the food gets cold."

It was the best breakfast Hattie had enjoyed in a long time. The food was good, yes, but it was the company that made the difference. When it was the four of them, like this, everything felt right with the world.

"Courtney's really enjoyed being here." Billy was helping himself to seconds. "So much so that she mentioned moving back here."

"Oh, Billy, that would be wonderful." Their mother was beaming with excitement. "To have us all here—I'd never want for more."

"What about work?" Hattie spread jam on her biscuit. "You've worked so hard to become a partner."

"I have." Billy nodded. "But there are more important things than work, aren't there? Family? What is it you always say, Dad?"

"You can get more money—you can't get more time." Their father nodded. "It's true." He nodded, studying his son. "It's a big change, son. Moving back here from Austin."

"It won't happen overnight. You know me—I like to break things down and look at all the outcomes." Billy reached for another biscuit. "I won't rush into anything. I never have."

"Until you met Courtney, that is." Their mother smiled.

Hattie glanced at her brother. Now that she knew the reason for her brother's quick nuptials and Courtney had shared her worries, Hattie found herself looking for any sign of hesitation or uncertainty or regret on Billy's part. All she saw was love. It was written all over her brother's face. From the warmth in his eyes to the broad smile on his face. Her brother was happy. Really, truly happy. "I'm glad you found someone who makes you smile like that."

"I could say the same." Billy pointed at her with his fork. "You're…different now."

Hattie frowned. "What do you mean?"

"I don't know." Billy shrugged. "Different." He glanced at their parents. "Help me out." He paused. "Moony-eyed? Is that the right word?"

"I am not moony-eyed." Hattie rolled her eyes. "That's downright silly."

"Uh-huh." Billy chuckled. "Dad, here, was the one that said it."

Hattie turned to her father.

"Guilty." Her father held up his hands. "But you were."

"I have never been and never will be." Hattie set her knife down on her plate and crossed her arms over her chest. This was getting out of hand. "When and where did this supposedly happen?" If she knew, she could make sure not to react that way again. *As if I've had any control over my reactions to Forrest.*

"First at the dress shop." Her father nodded. "Then, again, after the… Well…at Webb's party." He was grinning.

After Forrest and I kissed. She'd been breathless and stunned and her heart had been doing all sorts of gymnastic-like maneuvers—there was no denying that. Forrest had kissed her, after all. Had she been moony-eyed? What did that even mean?

"It's not a bad thing, Hattie." Her mother smiled. "It's perfectly natural. It's part of falling in love."

Hattie shook her head. Those were the very words she didn't want to connect with Forrest.

"What do you mean no?" Billy put his napkin on his plate and sat back. "If you're trying to say you two aren't in love, don't bother."

Hattie swallowed. They weren't in love. They weren't. And the last thing she wanted to do was spend one more second of her time trying to convince herself of that. "I'm shaking my head because we're having this conversation. Forrest and I...well, we're still just Forrest and I." She shrugged, waving her hand dismissively. "You're the one getting married. Not me."

"True." Billy grinned. "I am."

"Anything still needing to be done?" She stood, gathering up everyone's plates.

Billy paused to think. "I need to head over and pick up all the Christmas lights—"

"Fairy lights," their mother corrected him. "They're fairy lights this time of year. And very romantic."

"Right." Billy winked. "I need to pick

them up and go over the music with Mikey. He's playing guitar for the ceremony."

"I hope Rebecca's made her peace with that." Her mother's smile grew tight.

"Don't you worry yourself over that." Her father caught their mother's hand. "There's just no pleasing some people, Glady."

"He's right, Mom. Besides, it's not up to her. This is what Courtney and I want." Billy stood and looked Hattie's way. "Feel free to tag along, if you want."

"If you promise to stop with all the mushy talk and not mention Forrest, I'll go." She smiled, picking up the stack of dirty dishes. "Oh, and, after you help me with the dishes."

Billy chuckled. "Deal."

She nearly sagged with relief, the knot of tension in her stomach easing. Tagging along with Billy would get her out of her head—which was just what she needed.

"You don't have to clean up." Her mother stood, trying to take the plates out of Hattie's hands.

"You cooked. We clean." Hattie evaded her mother and carried the dishes to the sink. "That's the way it always works." She set the dishes down, tossed a hand towel to Billy and turned on the water.

Conversation wandered from how Mabel and Jensen's romance had brought an end to the Crawley-Briscoe feud, how Hattie wanted to add more pens on her property for those animals that needed rehabilitation before being released into the wild and the recent thwarted attempt to plow down erste Baum for some corporate chain store.

"That reminds me. Your Junior Rangers meeting Monday at erste Baum park. What's this I hear about a dustup between Dwayne Crawley and Martha Zeigler?" Her mother collected her knitting basket from the sideboard and carried it to the table.

"How did you hear about that?" Hattie asked, scrubbing a skillet while Billy finished loading the dishwasher.

"Rebecca." Her father sighed. "She and Dorris Kaye are two peas in a pod."

Except Dorris, for all her gossip, didn't have a mean bone in her body. Hattie couldn't say the same about Mrs. Hall. "They were both riled up about something." Hattie nodded. "And everyone within a mile's radius could likely hear them carrying on."

"Talk about two peas in a pod. Are there two more cantankerous, opinionated, hardheaded people alive?" Billy hung up the kitchen towel he'd thrown over his shoulder and assessed the state of the kitchen. "We good? Pass inspection, Mom?"

"I'm sure it does." Their mother didn't look up from her knitting. "You two go on and have fun. And don't forget to get an extension cord or two. You're going to need them."

Minutes later, Billy and Hattie were climbing into her truck and headed for Old Towne Hardware and Appliance. "I've got a craving for a milkshake," Billy said as she parked the truck.

"You just ate a dozen biscuits." She stared at her brother, wide-eyed.

"Eight." He counted off on his fingers. "We can wait awhile. If you want, you can even call Forrest and see if he wants to join us. You know, give him a second chance to break your record."

Hattie shook her head but decided not to acknowledge his offer. "I see how it is. You know I'll beat you so you're trying to delay the inevitable?"

Billy laughed. "And that would be?"

"Me." She turned off the truck. "Beating you. Again." She climbed down from the truck, hoping her plan had worked and there'd be no further mention of Forrest.

She was sure it would have, until the door of Old Towne Hardware and Appliance opened and Forrest Briscoe walked out.

FORREST SMILED, HIS morning brighter the moment he laid eyes on Hattie climbing down from her black-and-white game warden truck. Billy Carmichael came around from the passenger side, took one look at him and started laughing.

"Do I want to know?" Forrest asked, looking between the two of them. "What did I miss?"

"Were your ears burning?" Billy asked, shaking his hand in greeting.

"Mine?" Forrest grinned, his gaze instantly drawn to Hattie. Seeing her in faded jeans, a too-big Texas Native T-shirt, and her favorite boots kicked his heart rate up. Triple time. "Nope. Should they be?"

Billy shrugged.

"Interesting." Forrest tucked his thumbs into the belt loops of his jeans. "Talking about me?"

Hattie rolled her eyes and tucked a wild copper curl behind her ear. "Oh, for Pete's sake, Billy was trying to get me to invite you for milkshakes just so he wouldn't lose to me. Again." Those mossy green eyes of hers looked everywhere but his way.

She was out of sorts. Because of him? "Not missing me, then?" He couldn't help himself.

She sighed, those hazel eyes narrowed when they finally met his.

"Ouch." Billy laughed. "Pretty sure that's not the look of love, Forrest. Looks to me like you're in trouble. What did you do?"

Forrest had been wondering the same thing. Since the Junior Rangers meeting, he had gotten radio silence from Hattie. He'd thought Monday had been a good day. Breakfast, horseback riding—even the Junior Rangers meeting. Considering Webb had left that morning, that he'd enjoyed himself so much, was saying something. "I'm not sure, but I think you're right."

Hattie was outright scowling now. "He's right about what?"

"I did something wrong." He was probably only making things worse, but her scowl had him grinning ear to ear. "To earn that look, I mean."

"Oh, no." Hattie blinked, her scowl fading and a look of panic crossing her face. "It's Thursday."

Forrest and Billy exchanged a look and nodded.

"Thursday." Hattie squeaked. "My last fitting." She shook her head. "Billy—"

"Go on." Billy nodded. "I'll meet you there when I get things taken care of here." But he leaned close to Forrest to ask, "No hello hug or goodbye kiss?" Billy pretended to whisper, but there was no way Hattie missed the question. "You really *are* in trouble. It's not looking good for you, Forrest."

"Fine," Hattie snapped, spinning on her heel and marching right up to Forrest. She sighed, stood on tiptoe and pressed a kiss to his cheek. "Better?" She was all sass.

"I didn't say a word." Forrest held up his hands—then caught hers in his. "Hold up." He smiled, sliding an arm around her waist and moving closer. "My turn." He bent, running his nose along the curve of her ear, and pressed a kiss to her cheek.

He'd meant to tease her a little but it'd backfired on him. All it took was the feel of her in his arms, the fruity scent of her shampoo and the slight hitch of her breath when his lips made contact to have him reeling. Him. Not her. No, she was hurrying off down the sidewalk without a backward glance. He was the one staring after her with his heart pounding out of his chest.

"You got it bad." Billy clapped him on the back of the shoulder. "If I hadn't seen it with my own eyes, I'm not sure I'd believe it."

Forrest scrambled for a response, but his heart hadn't slowed and his lungs seemed dangerously low on air. All from one kiss. A kiss on the cheek, at that. Kiss or no kiss, chances were he'd still be fumbling and tongue-tied this way. Hattie did that to him.

"I get it." Billy's tone was sympathetic.

Forrest shook his head, finding his voice. "You do?"

"I'm glad it's you." Billy was suddenly serious. "I mean it. Hattie… Well, she's special. I don't want her winding up with some yahoo that doesn't know that. You do."

"She is." Forrest smiled. "There's no one like Hattie."

Billy nodded, giving him a long, hard look. "No one. Don't forget that, either."

"I won't." This, Forrest understood. He'd all but threatened Jensen Crawley when he'd asked Forrest for his blessing. Mabel was his only sister and it was his job to protect her. The same applied to Billy and Hattie.

So far, the idea of losing Hattie's friendship had kept him from telling her how he felt. But now… Well, he was thinking about it. A lot.

"Good." Billy was back to his easygoing self. "I'd better get my to-do list done so I can beat Hattie's milkshake record."

"Good luck with that." Forrest patted his stomach. "You've got a stronger stomach than I do."

They parted ways and Forrest headed home with hardware to fix Uncle Felix's showerhead. Uncle Felix was strong as an ox and tough as leather, but every now and then he'd get a pain in his back. His therapeutic showerhead did wonders. Of course, it'd have to break right when he needed it most, so Forrest had overnighted the part and was determined to have it up and running, quick.

Uncle Felix wasn't one to complain, but he'd been in obvious discomfort the last week or so. Always moving around in his chair. Standing and shifting from foot to foot. Stretching and wincing. If Forrest hadn't heard his uncle talking to baby Joy –

who was pretty good at keeping secrets, seeing as she didn't have all that many words yet—Forrest might never have found out about the broken showerhead. Once he did know, there was no way he was going to sit around and do nothing about it.

Even Audy and Beau can't complain about me doing this.

His brothers kept playing the "you're injured card" to keep him from doing too much, but he was itching to do something. While he appreciated their concern, he was done sitting around while everyone else was working hard. Watching others work while he was sitting idle didn't sit well with him. He was a doer, a fixer, through and through.

"Harvey." He nodded at the massive dog waiting inside the front door. "Someone forget to feed you?" He shifted the paper bag and the beat-up metal toolbox that had been his father's. "Let me put some of this down and we'll get you fed."

Harvey's tail wagged in answer.

"No," Uncle Felix said, pushing out of his leather recliner in the living room. "Someone did not forget to feed him. Harvey, now, quit telling tales."

Harvey's tail kept wagging.

"Shameless." But Uncle Felix gave the dog a pat. "What's in the bag?"

"A few odds and ends. And your showerhead."

"How'd you know about that?" Uncle Felix frowned, his forehead creasing deep.

"Joy told me." Forrest smiled. "It's an easy fix. No point in you hurting."

Uncle Felix bowed up then, his hands on his hips. "Who said I was—"

"I said." He shook his head. "How long has it been broken?"

"I don't need looking after. I was getting around to it," Uncle Felix thundered on. "I can do it myself and don't you think I can't."

"I know you can." Forrest stared into the bag, respecting the older man's drive to be independent. "But here's the thing. If you or Audy or Beau or Mabel tell me to sit and rest one more time, I'm afraid I'll lose my temper. So how about you let me install this showerhead so I feel like I've done something useful."

And just like that, Uncle Felix went from scowling to smiling. "Antsy, aren't you?"

"That's one way of putting it." Forrest shrugged. "We good to go?"

"Go on and fix it. You keep that temper

of yours in check." Uncle Felix nodded and followed along, Harvey bringing up the rear.

As far as Forrest knew, he didn't have much of a temper. It wasn't like he'd start slamming doors and throwing things. But, instead of pointing that out, he headed to his uncle's bathroom to assess the situation.

"I figured as much." Forrest eyed the nozzle. "Easier to replace the whole thing."

Uncle Felix grunted in agreement.

With Harvey sprawled across the tile floor and Uncle Felix leaning against the bathroom counter humming some classic country tune, Forrest got to work.

"How's Hattie?" Uncle Felix asked.

Forrest paused, glancing his uncle's way. "That was out of nowhere." He reached into the toolbox at his feet for a wrench.

"Was it?" Uncle Felix mumbled something under his breath. "I've been meaning to talk to you."

Forrest finished unscrewing the broken showerhead. "I guess now that you've got me pinned in your shower you might as well go for it." He put the old showerhead on the floor and the wrench into the toolbox.

Uncle Felix laughed. "That's what I was thinking."

Forrest shot his uncle another questioning look. "This should be interesting."

He took a deep breath. "I figured I'd speak my peace and let you make what you will from what I've got to say." He paused.

Forrest opened the box of the new showerhead, stopping long enough to look his uncle in the eye. "You've got my attention."

"A long time ago—" Uncle Felix chuckled. "So long ago now, it feels like a different life." He sighed. "When I was about Beau's age, a bit younger maybe, I was sweet on a girl. For years. She was…well, she was my first love. Not that she knew it."

It took everything Forrest had not to stop and stare at his uncle.

"She was the sweetest thing—smarter than me and pretty as a picture. I walked a little straighter with her by my side." There was a smile in his voice. "There wasn't a thing I couldn't tell her—same for her, I like to think. We were friends—like you and Hattie."

Forrest stopped pretending to work and listened to his uncle.

"I wanted to tell her how I felt and marry her, but I didn't want to chase her off or lose her friendship."

Forrest nodded. His uncle's story was sounding a little too familiar. If anyone else had been telling him this, he'd have been more skeptical of their motivation. But not Uncle Felix. He wasn't one for baring his heart, not ever. Telling Forrest this story was important, that much was clear.

"We graduated and her folks wanted her to go off to school and get educated—as folks do. She was excited, too. To get out and see the world and all that." He shrugged. "If that's what she wanted, I wanted her to have it. We were friends—that wasn't going to change."

"You told her?" Forrest asked, his throat tight. "Before she left?"

"Almost. I almost did. But in the end, I let her go without sayin' a word." He shook his head. "After that, no one came close to her. I tried, I did, but it was better to be alone than settling. I had a good life—you know that. I have all of you. I'm a lucky man. But there's not a day that goes by that I don't wonder what would have happened if I had said something. Would she have run for the hills or told me she loved me? Would she have married me instead of Tom Eldridge?" He shrugged. "I'll never know. I've loved

Barbara for the better part of my life, Forrest, and now that I've been given a second chance with her, I'm not going to waste it." He paused, his gaze intense. "But take a lesson from your uncle, here, and don't be a fool. I don't know what's going on with you and Hattie, but you make it right. You tell her the truth and you do whatever needs doing so that you don't spend the next thirty-plus years regretting all the things you didn't say."

When the box with the new showerhead had slipped from his hands, Forrest didn't know. But he wasn't holding it—it was on the floor.

"All right, now that's said and done." Uncle Felix nodded at the box. "I hope you didn't break that one, too."

Forrest continued to stare at his uncle.

"Forrest?" Uncle Felix glared at him.

"Yes, sir." He stooped and picked up the box. "It's fine."

"Good." Uncle Felix pushed off the counter. "I think I'll round up a cup of coffee and read the paper." He grinned. "Hattie's in it, by the way. The paper. Talking about the next generation saving the animals and whatnot. That girl loves her work. She's big-hearted. A lot like Mabel that way."

Forrest nodded. She might be shy when it came to her personal business, but Hattie never tired of talking about her work. She was proud of her job and proud to be a game warden. Anyone who knew Hattie, knew that. It was one of the things he loved most about her—that spark of compassion. She was smart and capable. Firm but gentle. And her laugh? Nothing made him happier than the sound of her laugh.

"You know what needs doing." And with that, Uncle Felix left Forrest to mull over every single thing his uncle had said.

His uncle had loved Barbara Eldridge his whole life. He'd chosen to be alone instead of settling for someone else. To some, it might sound drastic but to Forrest it made sense. How could he ever love anyone the way he loved Hattie? Since he knew the answer to that, there was only one question left. What was he waiting for?

CHAPTER THIRTEEN

Hattie spent the next two days throwing herself into anything and everything—doing her best not to let thoughts of Forrest derail her. If she didn't stay occupied, memories of his smile or hug or the brush of his lips on her cheek or the way her heart nearly leaped out of her chest when she'd seen him at Hardware and Appliance were waiting. She had no choice but to face facts. When the wedding was over, she was in for a world-class heartbreak. But first she had to smile her way through the wedding. She wasn't going to ruin this for her brother, Courtney or her parents. So, until it was absolutely necessary, it made sense to avoid Forrest and any further need to pretend that they were in love.

Due to limited seating at the rehearsal dinner, Hattie didn't have to worry about Forrest. Rebecca Hall was a little too tickled that Forrest wouldn't be able to attend. The woman hadn't bothered to hide her irritation with Forrest and his teasing. Poor Courtney was all apologies but Hattie assured her it was okay. And it *was* okay. The more time she had to mentally prepare for the wedding, the better.

But Saturday morning rolled around and, after a mostly sleepless night, Hattie felt certain she wasn't remotely prepared. Forrest would show up, looking his best, acting like she was his someone special and her fool heart would believe it all.

After taking a look at her rat's nest hair and puffy, red-rimmed eyes, she was grateful Brooke had insisted on doing her hair and makeup.

"What happened to you?" Brooke eyed her as she walked into the salon.

"No sleep." Hattie sat in the chair. "Fix me, will you?" She smothered a yawn. "I don't want to embarrass anyone."

Brooke gave her shoulders a squeeze. "Don't you worry about that, Hattie." She began pulling out tools and sprays and creams and clips. "You'll never guess what I heard this morning."

Hattie blinked.

"Kitty and Twyla Crawley stopped into the coffee shop this morning right about the same time I went in for mine." She stopped, turned, moved a box of foil wraps aside and reached for a cup. "Here." She pressed the cup into Hattie's hands. "Something told me you might need one."

"You are my favorite person in the whole world, Brooke Young—er, Briscoe." She smiled and took a sip. "Go on." While Hattie wasn't one for spreading gossip, she didn't mind listening now and then. As the owner of the only salon and barbershop in town, Brooke always had plenty to tell. Normally, she didn't share with just anyone. But for Mabel and Hattie, there was no holding Brooke back.

"Dwight Crawley is taking a date to the wedding today." Brooke carefully worked the knots from Hattie's hair.

"Oh." Hattie hoped it wasn't Barbara Eldridge. Dwight Crawley and Felix Briscoe had both been courting the woman, but she'd hoped Felix had the edge. "Do we know who?"

Brooke shook her head. "Twyla told Kitty to hush before Kitty could say."

Hattie sipped her coffee, letting Brooke chatter on about how Mr. Green, owner of Garrison Gardens on Main, was redecorating his upstairs loft for his daughter and grandchildren. “And Miss Patsy heard all about what Rebecca Hall said, about her red hair? She is so furious, she told me she wants to go blonde next time she’s here.” Brooke grinned. “Like Marilyn Monroe, she said.” She talked about the big fundraiser the Junior Rodeo Club was working on, the city council opening and how Mabel should run, and a handful of other tidbits that passed the time.

“Almost done. Close your eyes,” Brooke said, sweeping a brush over her eyelids. “This color will make your eyes emerald green.” She blew on Hattie’s eyelid. “Open.”

Hattie opened, then blinked rapidly. “My eyelashes feel heavy.”

“That’s because you have on extra.” Brooke nodded. “And they look amazing.”

Hattie frowned.

“Don’t frown.” Brooke smiled. “No frowning at all today, you hear me?” She waited for Hattie to nod. “Ready?” When Hattie nodded again, Brooke spun the chair around so she could see her reflection.

Hattie was in shock. “I look…so…”

“Beautiful?” Brooke asked. “You are, Hattie. With or without the extra lashes and waves styled into your hair." She glanced at the clock. "You'd better high-tail it over to the bridal shop. Kitty mentioned she and Judy were helping you all get dressed over there. Smart, in case any last-minute pins or fixes are needed." She carefully hugged Hattie and shooed her toward the door. "See you in a bit."

Hattie barely blinked when she was strapped into the corset. She didn't wince when she looked at her own reflection. In fact, she leaned closer for a better look. How had Brooke managed to make her look so… Different?

Courtney was all nervous laughs and giggles. It was easy for Hattie to step in and give her the encouragement she needed—since her mother was incapable of doing it.

All in all, she was surprisingly un-queasy when she, Lena and Courtney arrived at erste Baum park. She and Lena helped Courtney fix her dress and the three of them walked down the path to the tree. Strands of paper lanterns and white flower garlands had been woven through the lower branches of the tree, creating a sort of canopy over the rows of white chairs full of wedding guests.

"Thank you for sharing your father."

Courtney hugged Hattie close. "You're amazing."

Hattie's throat was too tight to answer, so she hugged her back.

When Mikey Woodard started playing the guitar, the ceremony began. Hattie went through it all in a daze. She forgot about how she looked or who was there. Her brother was getting married. Her brother was going to be a father. And he was so happy—it was written all over his face.

When the *I do*'s were said, the bridal party took pictures while the guests rearranged the chairs, added tables and set up a suitable reception space.

"You are one hard woman to get a hold of, Hattie Carmichael." Forrest pulled out her chair for her. "I got the feeling you were giving me the cold shoulder."

It's just Forrest. It's just *Forrest.* No matter how handsome he looked, she wasn't going to get all weak-kneed and tongue-tied. She wouldn't. "Or maybe I was so busy with work and real life that I was too busy?" Her teasing tone fizzled out midway—right about the time his blue gaze locked with hers. Forrest. Her heart did that happy skip thing she was beginning to recognize before launching into orbit.

He sat beside her, his eyes never leaving her face. "Is that so?"

She nodded, taking a much-needed sip of water. Had he always been this gorgeous? How had she never noticed?

"You look..." He shook his head, a long, slow breath slipping between his lips. "You take my breath away, Hattie Carmichael."

Hattie's cheeks were warm, warm enough that she used her linen napkin to fan herself. A quick survey told her what she needed to know. "There's no one around, Forrest. You don't have to say—"

"Hattie, come on." Her mother waved her forward. "I know your daddy is going to want to dance with you."

Great. Wonderful. She hopped up and set her napkin on her plate. "I should go."

Forrest stood, too, hooking her arm through his and leading her around the table to the edge of the parquet floor that had been laid down for dancing.

"I don't think I've ever been as happy as I am today." Her mother slipped between them, resting a hand on both their backs. "Seeing you so happy." She shook her head, staring up at Forrest, then turning to Hattie. "Well, I'm going to stop so I don't start crying and ruin my mascara." She sniffed.

"Come on, Mom." Billy took their mother's hand and led her onto the dance floor. He shot a wink Hattie's way. Hattie blew him a kiss.

When Courtney and her father danced by, Forrest stooped to whisper, "You okay?" His hand rested on her bare shoulder.

She nodded, the tingle of his touch like a bolt of lightning.

"You sure?" he asked.

She glanced up at him. "I am." It would be so easy to believe he cared about her. The way he was looking at her now, with concern and tenderness, was real enough. And Forrest did feel those things for her—but not the way Hattie wanted.

Tomorrow, they'd have to tell everyone the truth, and life would go back to normal. There was nothing wrong with that, nothing at all. Until recently, she'd been perfectly content with her life. But now… It'd be hard to get over him. But that was tomorrow. Why not enjoy today.

"Forrest." She hesitated, ridiculously nervous. "Would you dance with me?"

He grinned. "You read my mind."

Forrest was tall but, since Hattie had never danced with him before, she hadn't realized just how tall he was. "I guess I see why women wear heels now. Other women, that is. Not me."

He chuckled. "Oh?"

"You're way up there, Forrest." She smiled. "If we dance too many times, I could wind up with a neck ache or something."

He kept on chuckling. "Guess we'll have to keep an eye on the situation and make sure it doesn't get to that point."

She rolled her eyes.

"Wearing your boots?" he asked.

"Of course. Can you imagine me in heels?" She was giggling at the thought of it. "I'd never have made it down the hill—let alone the aisle." She giggled some more. "You'd have to carry me by now." She snorted.

Forrest laughed hard then.

Which kept her laughing. Another snort slipped out.

"I ever tell you how partial I am to that sound?" His face seemed closer now. And his eyes? Oh-so blue.

"My…laugh?" She could stare into those blue eyes for hours.

"That." He grinned. "And that other thing, too. That little snort."

"You are not." She sighed. "It's—"

"Contagious?" he finished. "Adorable? One hundred percent Hattie." He brushed the hair from her shoulder, the muscle in his jaw tightening.

It wasn't the corset squeezing the air out of her lungs, it was all Forrest. "Forrest Briscoe." Her voice was shaky. "You say things sometimes and I almost believe them."

A slight frown creased his forehead. "If I say it, I mean it."

She shook her head, the ache in her heart returning. "Maybe last week, before all this, but now?" She didn't want to think about the picture he'd painted. The two of them getting married, right here beneath erste Baum. She pretended to pick lint off his immaculate white shirt. "I know better. You're my best friend, Forrest. You know that, don't you?"

Forrest's jaw muscle leaped. "I do."

"I know you're going to tell me I'm your best friend, too." She waited, staring up at him. "Anytime now."

The corner of his mouth kicked up. "You are and you know it." But the hand on her back pulled her closer. "No matter what else changes, Hattie, that will *never* change."

If her father hadn't tapped her on the shoulder, she'd have pushed until she knew exactly what he meant by that. But her father cut in and her questions would have to wait.

"You look pretty as a picture." Her father sighed. "Nice to see your fella taking notice of that, too."

Hattie glanced Forrest's way. He was talking to Mabel and Jensen, but every now and then he looked her way.

"I want to thank you for all this, Harriet Ann." Her father's voice grew gruff. "I know this hasn't been easy on you. Courtney and Billy had quite a tale to tell us last night and, I have to say, you never fail to amaze me."

"I don't know what you're talking about." Was he talking about her and Courtney's past or the baby or…? No, she didn't want to know. Chances were, she'd wind up crying. "Don't you dare make me cry, Daddy. My eyelashes will fall off and Mrs. Hall will light into me for causing a scene."

He chuckled. "Your eyelashes, huh?" He peered more closely. "Well then, I guess I'd best behave myself." He patted her cheek.

"But you let me take care of Rebecca Hall, you hear me?"

Hattie rarely heard her father use the dad-tone, but there it was. Her father was ready and willing to go all papa-bear on Rebecca Hall, and Hattie couldn't stop smiling. "Behave yourself, Daddy. At least for today."

"Fine." He sighed, nodding. "But tomorrow, the gloves are coming off."

Hattie was so surprised, she started laughing—and snorting. A quick look showed her that Forrest had heard and, yes, he was laughing right along with her.

FORREST COULDN'T DECIDE which was better. Dancing with Hattie meant he got to hold her in his arms. Sitting beside her, wedged close at the near-packed table, had them pressed side by side. Making her laugh until she snorted and laughed all over again would never get old. He didn't mind just watching her, either. He'd never noticed how expressive she was. When she talked, it was a full-body experience. From the fluid shift of her expressions to hand gestures to the slight tilt of her head. When Hattie was engaged in a conversation, all of her was engaged.

Audy nudged him. "You're staring."

"And your point?" Forrest asked, glancing at his brother.

Joy smiled up at him. "Hi," the toddler said, waving up at him.

"If it isn't my favorite Briscoe…" Forrest held out his hands out for the toddler. "Come to the best uncle in the world," he whispered. "I know you like me better than your daddy and I don't blame you."

Joy squealed and clapped her hands as Audy transferred her into Forrest's arms.

"You think you're so funny." Audy sighed, smoothing his daughter's dress into place.

"Unca Fo." Joy kissed his cheek, then rested her head against his chest.

Forrest patted her back, rocking from foot to foot.

"Beau and I have been talking. About the Hattie situation." Audy was all business.

"The Hattie situation?" Forrest echoed, smiling in spite of himself.

"Beau has some ideas—some stuff kids have done for prom proposals and the like." Audy ran a hand along the back of his neck. "Not sure it's really your style, but then I realized you don't have a style."

Forrest smiled and kept on rocking. "Did

you come over here to help me or cut me down?"

"A little of both, I guess."

"I appreciate the thought but I'll figure out the Hattie *situation* on my own." Forrest's gaze shifted toward Hattie, smiling up at her brother, as they moved around the dance floor.

"Let me know how that works for you." Audy chuckled. "I know you've only got eyes for Hattie, so I'm guessing you didn't see who showed up late?" He leaned closer, whispering. "Mrs. Hall can't be happy about it—considering that's all anyone is talking about."

Forrest hadn't heard a thing. "Go on. You've got my attention."

"One Mr. Dwight Crawley and, wait for it—it will blow your mind." Audy paused for effect, grinning.

"My mind is ready to be blown." Forrest arched a brow, then said, "Your daddy is an odd duck, Joy. And don't you forget it."

"Martha Zeigler," Audy announced, proud as a peacock.

Forrest stopped rocking. "Say what now?"

"Yep." Audy pretended to rub his nose, while subtly pointing. "Look for yourself."

Forrest followed Audy's gaze. "You're right." After that yelling match at the Junior Rangers meeting, he'd figured the two were more likely to go for the jugular than say a kind word to one another. And yet, here they were. A surprisingly handsome couple. "My mind is blown."

"I know." Audy nodded. "Just about everyone was slack-jawed and staring when they showed up." He sighed. "Rebecca Hall's tail feathers are all ruffled. I get she wants today to be about her daughter and she's not a Garrisonite so she can't fully appreciate the gossip value behind Miss Zeigler and Mr. Crawley, but it'll be her temper that casts a shadow on her daughter's wedding day."

"I know I don't say this very often so don't let it go to your head but...you are right." Forrest smiled—he couldn't help it.

When Audy stopped laughing, he said, "As long as you and Hattie don't do anything foolish—like another serious lip-lock—there's a chance y'all might get out of here without any more gossip." Audy shrugged. "Maybe."

It was a mighty tempting idea. "No more kissing," Forrest murmured.

"Not ever?" Audy gave him the side-eye.

"You know, that's gonna really slow down the whole courting thing."

Forrest laughed.

"At this rate, you should take a lesson from the older generation." Audy nodded at the dance floor.

Sure enough, Dwight Crawley and Martha Zeigler were dancing. Dancing? Forrest was hardpressed not to stare. Pretty much everyone else was, too. When the couple passed Hattie and Billy, Hattie tripped over her brother's feet and turned to search him out. "What?" she mouthed.

Forrest shrugged in answer, smiling.

"You got Joy?" Audy asked.

Forrest peered down. "I think we're good." Joy's eyes were closed and she was breathing deep and even against his shoulder.

"I don't know how you do it." It bothered Audy something fierce that Joy always fell right to sleep when Forrest was holding her. "But, since you've got things under control here, I'm gonna go ask my wife to dance." Audy was off, weaving through the crowd to extract Brooke from her conversation.

Forrest sat, careful not to jostle Joy, and let his gaze wander. It was hard not seeing Webb. He'd noticed the slightest spark between Lena Hall and his brother. Now the girl stood off to the side, talking with Miss Patsy, her aunt Velma and Dorris Kaye. If she hadn't been laughing, Forrest would have felt sorry for her.

Jensen and Mabel held Samantha, the three of them spinning around the dance floor.

Audy and Brooke didn't seem to realize that the song playing had a quick beat. They were slow dancing, eyes closed and all wrapped up in one another.

"You sitting this one out?" Earl Ellis, owner of the local feedstore, asked as he sat in one of the vacant chairs. "Looks like you plumb wore out your dancing partner."

Forrest nodded.

"I remember when Tyson was that size." He chuckled. "But he was never that still. I don't think he slept for the first two years of his life. Wore me and his momma out." He sighed, leaning back in his chair. "On nights like this, I miss my Joanie awful bad. She loved to dance. Why, she'd have danced until the music stopped."

Forrest smiled. "I see one or two ladies who wouldn't mind a dance, Mr. Ellis." He nodded across the dance floor. "Judy Eldridge would probably love being rescued." Poor woman had been cornered by Rebecca Hall and was getting an earful.

"In need of rescuing?" Mr. Ellis stood up. "I'm on my way." He winked at Forrest and headed straight for Judy.

The look of relief on Judy's face had Forrest chuckling.

"What are you laughing at?" Hattie asked, sitting beside him.

"Nothing." He shifted so he could see her better. "People, I guess."

Hattie leaned closer. "You could have knocked me over with a feather when I saw the two of them dancing."

"Who?" he teased.

"You know who." She rolled her eyes. "How's sweet Joy?"

"Sleeping." Forrest yawned. "You think I'd offend Mrs. Hall if I took a snooze, right here, with Joy?"

"I don't think. I *know*." She rested her hand on Joy's back. "She's getting so big."

"Growing like a weed." With Hattie this close, Forrest could study the curve of her smile and no one would be the wiser. Beneath the lanterns and twinkle lights overhead, there were a million shades of red and gold in her silky-smooth hair. "Brooke do your hair?"

Hattie rolled her eyes. "Forrest, I know you don't like it when she—"

"I like it," Forrest interrupted.

"You do?" She didn't believe him. "Since when?"

"I don't recall ever saying I *didn't* like it, Hattie." He smiled. "I like your hair any way you want to wear it."

She blinked, her expression smoothing. Like she was stepping back—putting distance between them. He didn't like it. Her smile was forced. "I should go see if I can help with the cake."

"Or you could stay here and we could talk." He waited. "I'm pretty sure there are plenty of folk to help with the cake."

"I just…want to," she mumbled, standing. "I can't sit here and pretend…" She stopped, shook her head and walked off.

Forrest wasn't sure what he'd said to send her running, but something had happened. After he returned Joy to Audy, he did his best to stay by her, but she seemed equally determined to dodge him. If he was getting a piece of cake, she was helping serve punch. If he was getting punch, she was cutting cake. He sought her out for a dance, but she was nowhere to be found. For a while, he thought she'd left. But then Billy and Courtney were getting ready to leave and there she was.

Forrest knew that look. It was the same look she'd made before she'd doubled over in the Bluebonnet Ice Cream parking lot… Her nerves were getting the better of her. She handed out sparklers to all the guests before grabbing her own.

"Have one for me?" he asked.

She swallowed, holding out the unlit sparkler for him.

"You good?" He took the sparkler.

She nodded, paused, then shook her head. "I don't know why I'm…feeling so emotional." She shrugged. "It's silly."

He smiled. "I don't think so. Your brother got married."

She took a deep breath and stared up at him, her eyes sparkling with tears.

"Hattie…" He groaned. "It's okay." He shook his head, taking her hand. "It's good."

She nodded, sniffing. "I won't cry."

He stared up into the trees overhead, his heart lodging in his throat. He couldn't bear Hattie's tears.

"Hattie, hurry," Glady called out, waving them down the path. "Get in line."

Forrest led Hattie to the end of the path so they were standing right beside the black limousine waiting to take the newlyweds away. He helped her light her sparkler and slipped his arm around her waist when the crowd erupted in cheers. Billy and Courtney came running down the path, a hundred sparklers lighting their way.

"It's so pretty," Hattie whispered, glancing up at him.

"Beautiful," Forrest answered. But he wasn't talking about the sparklers or the happy couple. He was talking about Hattie.

Billy pulled Hattie in for a long hug. "Thank you for everything, sis," Billy murmured, before letting her go. "You take care of her, Forrest."

"I will." Forrest shook Billy's hand. Even if Hattie never fell in love with him, he'd always be there for her. "Count on it."

Billy nodded and helped Courtney into the limo.

Hattie was gripping his hand as the taillights disappeared, lingering long after most of the guests were headed back to the tree or making their way to their cars.

"I can't believe it's over." Hattie's voice was shaking as she looked down at their joined hands. "Tomorrow, everything goes back to normal." And she didn't sound happy about it.

He squeezed her hand. "Is that a bad thing?"

She shook her head. "No. No. It's good." She glanced at him. "It's just… Well, there are some things we'll need to set right."

Not yet. He pulled her close to him. "Hattie—"

"No." Her eyes went round as she stared up at him. "Whatever you have to say will have to wait. I won't cry. I won't, but don't get serious, okay? Please. Everything else can wait until tomorrow." She swallowed. "But it's not tomorrow yet." She stood on tiptoe. "And since Rebecca Hall is standing right there and who knows who else…" She kissed him.

Forrest didn't give a fig about who might be watching. He had Hattie in his arms. He was kissing her. Soft lips. Warm breath. Fitting against him like she was made for him. He ran his fingers through the wavy fall of her hair before pressing his hand on the bare skin between her shoulders. But Forrest had to pull away. This was too much. He didn't want to share this with anyone. Kissing Hattie was too personal for that.

"Forrest?" she whispered, her arms still around his neck.

"I can't do this here." He cleared his throat. "Not like this. I can't."

Luckily, Mabel called Hattie over or Forrest would have told her he loved her. He watched her go, thinking about tomorrow and how his time was running out. Hattie didn't know it, but none of this was pretend. And when he told Hattie he loved her, the only audience he wanted were the people he loved most.

Before he got down on one knee and poured his heart out, he wanted her parents' blessing. He had no idea what Hattie was going to say, but he was pretty sure he'd get a yes from Bart. *Only one way to find out.* With a deep breath he walked toward Bart Carmichael.

CHAPTER FOURTEEN

HATTIE HAD NEVER been so ready to say goodbye to someone. Then again, she'd never met anyone as exhausting as Rebecca Hall. It probably didn't help that she hadn't slept for more than fifteen minutes straight last night—no more than a couple of hours altogether. She was bleary-eyed and hoping for a nap.

"I really don't know why this had to be such a production," Rebecca Hall said. "It's so kind of you, but there was a perfectly good breakfast at the Hilltop."

"Well, you're family now," her father said, holding open the front door.

"Yes, you've said that." Rebecca slipped on her sunglasses and walked out and onto the front porch. "I do so appreciate the hospitality. You are gracious hosts."

Hattie saw both her parents hesitate. Waiting for the other shoe to drop?

"I appreciate you getting Webb's address

for me." Lena gave Hattie a quick hug. "I don't know if he'll remember me, but maybe he'll want a pen pal?"

"I'm sure he'd like that," Hattie agreed. She could picture the shock—and huge smile—on Webb's face when he received a letter from Lena Hall. "Something tells me, he'll be a very loyal pen pal."

Lena's cheeks went a nice pink. "We'll see."

"I'd planned to take a cowboy home with me, as a keepsake." Aunt Velma peered up at Hattie through her thick, black-framed glasses. "Instead, I'm going home empty-handed."

"Not quite." Hattie handed her the romance book she'd picked up at the resale shop downtown. "I'm not sure he's as handsome as Bernardo but I thought he was a pretty handsome cowboy."

"Well, yee-haw." Aunt Velma's smile was half-hidden behind her glasses. "You're a thoughtful one, Hattie. You make sure and keep that cowboy of yours close by. You never know when I might come swooping in after him."

Hattie stood on the porch with her parents, saying more goodbyes as the three Hall women climbed into their rental car. Lena honked the horn as they pulled away from the curb, and they all waved until the car turned off their street and was out of sight.

"I swear, I'll need to restock on antacid my next trip to the store." Her mother sighed, leaning against the porch railing.

"I know it was a lot, Momma, but there's no doubt in my mind that Billy and Courtney had the wedding they wanted." She hugged her mother. "All thanks to you."

Her mother hugged her back, pressing a kiss to her forehead. "Oh, look, there's Forrest." She patted Hattie on the back and let go. "Morning," she called, waving.

Hattie turned, frozen. "Why is Forrest here?" Her stomach did that awful twist thing and her palms went clammy.

"He said something about getting trim boards?" Her father shrugged.

Right. The long-delayed trim board expedition. Why today, of all days? Hattie had a good idea why he was really here. He was probably just as ready to clear up the whole pretend relationship thing as she was. The churning in her stomach doubled. Her poor heart missed a beat, a razor-sharp pain making her whole chest tighten.

"Morning." Forrest took the porch steps two at a time, a huge bouquet of purple irises in hand. "How are you all?"

Don't look at him. Definitely don't make eye contact. The few dreams she'd had the night before had been full of Forrest and those blue eyes. She swallowed, eyeing the flowers. A peace offering? It made sense. Her parents had been so delighted over the idea of the two of them together. *Mine isn't the only heart getting broken today.*

"Well, I'm not ashamed to say it's nice to have my house back." Bart chuckled, waving Forrest inside. "Might as well go in so we're not air-conditioning the front porch."

"Morning, Hattie." Forrest turned a brilliant smile her way.

She blinked, resisting the pull of his gaze. *It's not working.* "Morning?" *Oh, that smile.* "You're almost back to normal," she mumbled, waving a hand at his face. "Just a little green and yellow." Not that it made him any less handsome.

"Guess I had to work my way through the whole color wheel first." He held the door open for her, pulling it closed behind them.

"It was sweet of you to bring flowers, Forrest," she whispered, painfully aware of how close he was to her. Not as close as he'd been last night, when she kissed him... She shook her head. "I think my folks are going to take this pretty hard." Her stomach made an alarming sound, so Hattie hurried on, "Momma's favorites are daffodils." Why had she said that? Why did that matter? It was a kind gesture.

"I know." He nodded, following her parents into the kitchen.

"Here, Forrest." Her mother pulled out her step stool to reach one of her prized delft pitchers. "I think those will look just lovely in this."

Forrest nodded, handing over the flowers. "Just the thing."

"Aren't they lovely, Hattie?" her mother asked.

"I know they're Hattie's favorite." Forrest reached out, turning one flower forward.

Hattie was frozen. Those were for her? Why had Forrest brought her flowers? She didn't need them. She knew what was coming... But she appreciated the gesture. "They're beautiful. When I'm on patrol, and they're blooming, I always look for them."

"You said it was like they were waving

at you." Forrest nodded, his gaze sweeping over her face.

He might mean well but the flowers, the memories—bringing all that up made things ten times worse.

"There." Her mother stepped back, turning the pitcher.

I'm so sorry. Her poor parents. Her stomach grumbled again but Hattie ignored the looks of all three of them and pretended nothing had happened. "I think I need more coffee." If she was going to make it through the morning, she might need a whole pot of coffee. She stood and poured herself a steaming cup. "Want one?" she asked Forrest.

"Thank you." Forrest nodded. "Something smells good."

"There are cinnamon rolls. Those Hall women eat like birds." Her mother shook her head. "It's no wonder Rebecca is so out of sorts all the time."

"Momma." But Hattie started laughing.

Her father chuckled. "Out of sorts? You're being awful kind, Glady."

Forrest shook his head, but he was smiling. And every time he smiled, Hattie wound up doing the same.

"Well, now." Her mother shrugged. "She didn't strike me as a very…happy person."

For some reason, that had Hattie laughing even harder. So hard, a snort escaped.

That snort was all it took to get Forrest laughing. Once he was, Hattie had a hard time stopping. Every snort seemed to get the other three laughing all over again.

"Woo," her father said. "Nothing like a good laugh to start the day off right."

Forrest stacked several of her mother's cinnamon rolls on a plate and carried the plate and mug to the table. "Anything new?" he asked her father, who was scanning the newspaper.

"Nothing worth mentioning." Her father flipped the page.

"No news is good news," her mother added. "I'd be fine with a few days of peace and quiet."

"I'll drink to that." Forrest raised his coffee.

It was all so familiar. So comfortable. Part of her wanted to rip off the Band-Aid but… Part of her wanted things to stay as they were. No, she didn't want Forrest to pretend he loved her. She wanted him to truly love her. Her heart shuddered and her stomach roiled all at once. "Forrest." Hattie rubbed her eyes, hating the sting of tears in her eyes. "I didn't know you were set on doing the trim work today." She glanced at him.

He studied her long and hard, those blue-blue eyes far too bright and alert. "You look tired. Didn't sleep well?"

"I didn't sleep at all," she admitted. "All the excitement, I guess." *Or the fact that today—right now, apparently—I'm about to have my heart reduced to dust.* She sipped her coffee, wincing when her stomach groaned.

"Hattie, honey, are you all right?" her mother asked, sitting beside her and taking her hand. "Didn't eat enough?"

She did her best to smile. "I'm fine." *As long as I don't cry, I'll be fine.*

"Your stomach is saying otherwise." Her father peered over his newspaper.

Forrest stood, put a cinnamon roll on a plate and carried it to her.

"Thank you," she said, barely glancing up at him. "I ate more than I should have."

"Your stomach disagrees." Her father set his paper aside. "Unless you're having stomach issues again? Forrest, she used to get so stressed, her stomach would make monster-movie noises."

"That's what Bart called them," her mother explained to Forrest, all the while patting her hand. "Is something wrong?"

Hattie glanced at Forrest, her eyes burning.

Forrest was staring at her, puzzled.

"I… I…" Everything was wrong. She knew she had to tell her parents the truth—that this was all a lie—but she couldn't say it. She couldn't. "Maybe I am still a little hungry."

And with that, her father went back to his paper, her mother started knitting and Forrest started eating his mountain of cinnamon rolls—but those blue eyes of his never left her face. Was he waiting on her? If he was, she wasn't sure the truth would ever come out. No, no. Enough. Tears or no tears, she couldn't keep going like this. All she was doing was delaying the inevitable. The sooner her heart was broken, the sooner she'd start to heal. At least, she hoped that's the way it worked.

FORREST WAS WORRIED. He knew coming into it there were no guarantees. He could tell her he loved her and she might look at him like he was growing a second head, then brush the whole thing off. In a way, he hoped that's exactly what she'd do. If, that is, she didn't love him, too. That was his first choice.

In Hattie's eyes, he'd caught a glimpse of the same bone-deep sadness he'd seen the night of the Junior Rangers meeting and last night, at the reception. Like she was expecting the worst. And since this sadness had only cropped up after Rebecca Hall had spouted off about Hattie, he worried that that woman's words had taken root.

He knew it was nonsense. But Hattie… Well, she wasn't used to that sort of nastiness. It made sense she'd take it to heart. That's what she did, listened and absorbed. Even when what was said was nothing more than a pile of hogwash.

"You going to eat?" he asked her.

She'd poked her cinnamon roll and pushed it around on her plate, but she had yet to take a bite. Both her parents stopped what they were doing, waiting, leaving Hattie no choice. She was scowling at him when she took a bite. All he could do was grin.

"Happy?" she asked.

"Almost." He sighed, wishing this was

easier. He had words—a whole lot of them—but thinking them wasn't the same thing as saying them. So far, all he'd managed to do was stare at her and make her scowl at him. *Not off to a good start.*

"Almost?" Her voice wavered and she set her fork down. "Right." She nodded, sitting up straight. "I guess now is as good a time as ever?"

He nodded, noting her frown. She was talking about something else entirely but she was right. "Bart, Glady," he started, watching Hattie nod. "That was some wedding."

Hattie deflated, shooting daggers his way. He shrugged.

Bart nodded. "It was, wasn't it."

"I never imagined it could come together so fast," Glady agreed. "Though I'm plum tuckered out."

"It was a lot of work. Lots of people to sort out and details to plan." Forrest swallowed, his lungs near empty. It was now or never. He'd gone over what to say, but in the end he figured it was best to say what was in his heart, his eyes locked with Hattie's. "When Hattie and I get married, I don't want it thrown together. I want all the bells and whistles. Not city hall or something small. Nope. I want Hattie in a big dress—and in your boots, not heels."

"Forrest." Hattie shook her head. "Stop it. Stop." She was blinking furiously. "This isn't right."

"You're right." He was up and coming around the table, stopping her before she cut short his hopes and dreams. He knelt before her. "I guess I was getting ahead of myself."

"Forrest, what are you doing?" She tore her gaze from his, glancing at her parents.

"I'm trying, poorly, to tell you that I'm not pretending, Harriet Ann Carmichael. I love you." The words had come out all at once and his lungs were aching.

Hattie was staring at him, in shock.

"In the beginning, I was. Maybe. Maybe I've just been too thickheaded to see what was right in front of me. But then I guess I hoped pretending all this would give me a chance to show you how good we could be together. How we're meant to be." He took her hands. "There was a whole lot of ducking and dodging and circling around things. I was too worried I'd lose you. And I didn't think things through. I know that now, but we both know I'm not the best at...talking feelings."

A tear slipped out and ran down Hattie's cheek and his heart fell.

"Bart," Glady whispered, followed by the scrape of chairs as Hattie's parents left the room.

"Even if you don't love me, I want you to know the truth." It was hard to go on. "You're the sort of woman a man wants in his life. I do, more than anything. You're a partner in all things—someone who'd never give up during the hard times, never let me give up. You're the best person I know. The best friend a man, or woman, could want." He swallowed. "You're the only person I could ever give my heart to... If you want it."

"But you..." She shook her head. "You..."

"Have been a fool for waiting so long to tell you I love you?" He nodded, feeling more and more uncertain. "Yes, I was. I am. But I promise I'll love you until the day I die, and I hope, more than anything, you love me, too." He paused. "And if you do, you'll marry me because I can't see a future without you at my side."

She pulled her hands away and wiped the

tears from her face. For a second, Forrest worried he'd break.

But then she cradled his face in her hands and she was searching his eyes like her life depended on it. "I love you, Forrest." She was smiling. "I love you and I'll marry you—at city hall or in a church or under erste Baum." She ran her thumbs along the sides of his face. "Because I'll get you for a husband."

Forrest closed his eyes. "I was scared you were going to say something else."

"Like?" she whispered softly.

He grinned. "I'm your best friend—"

"You are, aren't you? That's not going to change. You said so yourself." She ran her fingers along his jaw. "And if you said it, you meant it."

"I did. I do." He was grinning now; he had to. "I know you, Hattie. I know your heart. And I'm so grateful that it's mine."

Another tear slipped down her cheek, but she was smiling.

"Oh, come on now, Hattie, don't you cry," he pleaded.

"Don't worry, I won't break your face this time." She pulled him in, tilted his head back and pressed a kiss against his lips.

Forrest threaded his fingers through her wild and curly hair and held on, savoring the feel of her mouth against his. "All this time…" he murmured, between kisses. "All this time and you were right here, with me." Her lips were made for kisses—his kisses. "All that time wasted."

"I was no better." She stroked his cheek.

"I guess we'll figure this out, together?" He smoothed her hair back.

"That's what we've always done." She smiled. "One thing I know *now.* Nothing has ever felt so right." Her eyes sparkled, but there were no more tears. "I know where my heart belongs."

"I'll keep it safe." He sat back. "Will you marry me, Hattie Carmichael?"

"I will." Hattie nodded quickly. "Yes."

Forrest stood and pulled her into his arms. "I'd be content to stay like this all day, but your folks might not approve." He loved the way Hattie giggled, burrowing closer to him. "How about, *after* we go get your trim boards, we go pick out a ring."

Hattie laughed. "I can't think of anything better."

"Hold up." Forrest held up one finger, his heart full. "I think I can."

"Oh?" She waited.

"This." He tilted his head, smiling as his lips met hers.

* * * * *

COMING NEXT MONTH FROM

HARLEQUIN

HEARTWARMING

#415 THE COWBOY'S UNLIKELY MATCH

Bachelor Cowboys • by Lisa Childs

Having grown up in foster care, schoolteacher Emily Trent readily moves to Ranch Haven to help three local orphans—just not their playboy uncle, Ben Haven. The charming cowboy mayor didn't get her vote and won't get her heart!

#416 THE PARAMEDIC'S FOREVER FAMILY

Smoky Mountain First Responders • by Tanya Agler

Horticulturist and single mom Lindsay Hudson looks forward to neighborly chats with paramedic Mason Ruddick. He was her late husband's best friend, but he can't be anything more. Unless love can bloom in her own backyard?

#417 THE RANCHER'S WYOMING TWINS

Back to Adelaide Creek • by Virginia McCullough

Heather Stanhope wants to hate the rancher who bought her family's land. Instead, she's falling for sweet Matt Burton and his adorable twin nieces. Could the place she longs to call home be big enough for all of them?

#418 THEIR TOGETHER PROMISE

The Montgomerys of Spirit Lake

by M. K. Stelmack

Mara Montgomery is determined to face her vision loss without any help—particularly from the stubbornly optimistic Connor Flanagan. Can Connor open Mara's eyes to a lifetime of love from one of his service dogs...and him?